THE SPY IN
THE CITY OF BOOKS

Stephen O'Connor

Stephen O'Connor

1 Spy in the City of Books

THE SPY IN THE CITY OF BOOKS
Copyright © 2010 Stephen O'Connor

Cover Art by Jim Higgins
Cover Package by Digital Media Design - www.dmdgo.com

Lili Marlene
Words and Music by Mack David, Hans Leip and Norbert Shultz

For Edwin Poitras, who went where few dared.

My legs are strong no longer, as you say;
I am not fast on my feet; my hands will not
Fly out to punch or throw.
I must yield to slow old age,
Though in my time I shone among heroic men.

The Iliad, Book XXIII

1

At six in the morning, not only his apartment, but the entire Pollard Mansion was quiet. The dim rooms were redolent with the aroma of coffee. It had been brewed by timer – to Martin LeBris' mind one of the greatest practical uses of technology in the modern world. *"As quiet as the turning of pages in the holy books at dawn,"* the poet had written, and there was something sacred in the stillness that pervaded the high-ceilinged rooms of his "City of Books." In the thin light of morning, Martin scanned the well-ordered ranks of titles. His books ascended the walls on long shelves that ran ladder-like from the floor up to the gumwood molding. He had been a bibliophile from the distant days when his mother had brought him to the Andover Book Store, where the little boy watched the fireplace glow among the rows of mute testaments.

With money she'd set aside from her job at Woolworth's, she bought his Christmas presents there, two books he selected called *Corsairs of the Gold Coast* and *Indian Warriors of the East*. The fierce Mohawk, and the grizzled pirate perched with his spyglass in the rigging still peered from the ragged jacket covers among the other volumes ranged about him in leather and gold. He went to a bookcase where he had stored some of those that were in sets, or whose bindings were gilded. Most had been published in the 19th century.

He paused for a moment, watching his reflection in the glass doors of the old bookcase. It was as if his own French-Canadian grandfather were looking back at him. *"Bonjour Maurice,"* he said. The short thick snow-white hair, glasses, the ruddy face and even the flannel lumberjack's shirt. He could almost hear that gruff, familiar voice: *"Viens ici, toi."* Come here, you.

How the years had flown, as he donned this livery of age. He shook his head and smiled at the reflection; he had become his grandfather. Martin turned the key once and opened the glass doors. He inhaled the beloved mustiness of leather and paper. Green, black, and brown were the spines, but the letters were gold. Saintly companions, soft whisperers, undying confidants. They spoke of forgotten sieges, duels, palace intrigues, falconry, conquests; the solitary guard at the king's door, betrayed and bleeding – unwilling to yield. The secrets of the dead, the dreams of the living, and the rhymes of the forlorn poet who put trembling quill to parchment under the myrtle bough and wrote *can love be rich and yet I want?*

There were histories, diaries, epics, romances, speculations, musings, ramblings, essays – there was bilious colic and laudanum; currants in the orchard and tea by the fire. And of course, there was one whole shelf dedicated to the classical Greek and Roman works he collected. Between sips of the hot Colombian coffee, his hand glided over Coleridge's *Table Talk and Omniana*, Stevenson's *Virginibus Puerisque*, Kingsley's *Hypatia,* and settled on a slim blue volume by Lord David Cecil called *The Stricken Deer* because the title struck his fancy.

"*The Stricken Deer* . . . what is this?" he wondered. Something that he'd picked up at the Brattle Bookstore, or some flea market, and forgotten, or had never had a chance to look into. He returned to the kitchen, where Hannibal, his aged cat, raised his head, ears twitching, but did not stir. "Look at me now, Hannibal," he said to the cat curled in its bed of fleece, "an old man in his slippers, rummaging through dusty books older even than himself. *Is this the promised end?"* He sighed and laughed softly.

He sat at the table and opened the book. It was a life of the poet Cowper. The tenor of the morning changed as he read the inscription on the frontispiece:

I was a stricken deer that left the herd
Long since; with many an arrow deep infixt
My panting side was charged, when I withdrew
To seek a tranquil death in distant shade.

Martin put the book down, closed his eyes and saw the face the verse had conjured – Odette. There were so many faces that lived only in memory now, but they were vivid. "I couldn't save you, Odette," he said aloud, "I'm sorry." In the last half century, he had apologized often, through wakeful vigils in the solitary night, to that lingering ghost, which spoke to him from amid the echoes of the guns of 1944 – from beyond the thin veil that separates the living from the dead in time and memory.

He gulped some coffee, and his gaze ran along the rows of books that lined the floor to ceiling shelves, this world he had created for himself – for what? To remember? To forget? To wait in a fortress of tranquility for revelation, or just for death? And waiting, to call back the days of fire-placed, rocking-chaired bookstores, the world of youth, the world of peace, before he had known killing and had to steel his mind against the smell of death, sickening wounds, and all the grim havoc of war.

Yes, he was an old man, tired of the tumult of life. He'd lived much in his mind since 1945 and sought only the companionship of the ages, of blind Homer and Marcus Aurelius. And yet he wondered whether the duty that the philosopher spoke of did not demand that he had now lain sixty years in a damp, unmarked grave near the broken remains of the woman who died for France, and for him, or for the man he was back then: Patrice Quenton, spy, inserted into occupied France to serve as a liaison between London and the French Forces of the Interior for the Office of Strategic Services. That had been his real duty, weightier than anything he owed her for love, or so they told him.

Duty – that was a word that could create moral dilemmas for a man beyond any other in the language. "If I could've saved you, Odette," he murmured, holding her image in his mind like a withering flower. He hadn't even been able to save her body. He would like to have placed it under a stone of black marble inscribed with her name, and the simple epitaph: *Morte Pour la France*. That would have been right for her. But her grave was unknown. He shook his head slowly; his eyes narrowed and his mouth turned down, the morning tinged with gray as in a low voice he spit out the words, "Nazi bastards!" Hannibal's ears twitched as he watched with eyes like yellow marbles the silent old man gazing long through the brightening window, an empty cup hanging from his hand.

The world was on fire.

The pilot, or some crewman forward, was screaming at him to jump. Martin's knees were trembling. He wanted to know if they were over the drop zone, but the Liberator shook so violently that he and the men behind him were knocked to the floor. Flak tore at the fuselage as the rattling shell of the cabin filled with choking acrid smoke.

He heard a desperate shout, "Jump for Chrissake! They got our number!" His static line was hooked. He crawled to the open door, which was not in the side but in the belly of this airplane. The craft lurched and he was thrown out before he could jump. A rush of wind and flapping fabric – then he was jerked up like a puppet on a string as the silk chute billowed.

The deep hum of engines faded from his ears as he fell away from the airplane, but the hiss and glare of anti-aircraft fire still shocked the night, exploding above him with a force that jarred his teeth, and in a matter of seconds Martin heard a roar. A fireball lit the white hemisphere of his chute, searing the dark soffit of the ragged clouds. Flaming wreckage tumbled earthward like defeated angels. He recalled for an instant, vividly, the face of a crewman who just a few minutes before had been telling him that Winston Churchill could drink any man in England under the table and wondering at the reality that the man, and the entire crew of nine, had been incinerated. All dead – only he – falling, falling through the night, young and scared and everything yet to come as the fates unwound the threads. Odette, I'm sorry.

2

The sun dappled the terrace of the Kaisergarten, an upscale café on Kaiserstrasse in Munich. A chalkboard on an easel displayed the day's special: *Schweizer Wurstsalat mit Essigurken, Paprika und Käsesterfen*, eight Euros. Adelbert Lustig, squinting as he read, nodded his gray and well-groomed head approvingly. He picked up the cloth napkin, shook it out, and spread it over his lap as an aproned waiter brought two tall beers and set them down. "*Prost, Herr Hoetger*," he said to the man who sat at the other side of the small table. He tucked his tie into the gap between the buttons of his shirt and raised the tapered glass.

His companion, Karl Hoetger, nodded absently and looked up from the documents he'd been perusing, apparently surprised to find the beer in front of him, his blue-gray Cazal sunglasses reflecting the table, his beer, and the vase of cut flowers, purple and yellow, in their convex lenses. They lent to Hoetger's look, Adelbert thought, a lizard-like aspect, cold and bubble-eyed. He was younger, perhaps in his late thirties; he too was dressed impeccably, but more casually, in an open-collared linen shirt and pressed jeans, his square face framed by shoulder-length hair.

"*Prost*," he said, raising his glass.

The waiter returned for their order. When he had gone, Hoetger leaned over the table and said, "Where did you get it?"

"Ach, these things don't stay hidden forever, my friend. When Bruno Lohse, that great Nazi art thief died, the remaining members of this Schönart Anstalt Trust opened his vault in Switzerland. It was nothing like the collection that Göring had looted from museums and from Jews all over Europe. The Allies uncovered most of those works hidden behind false walls at Berchtesgarten. But Lohse's Swiss vault contained some valuable pieces and over twenty bound diaries full of information, records, Lohse's recollections. One member of the Schönart Anstalt Trust is a personal friend, and he allowed me access to them. While everyone was focused on the works of art, I discreetly paid him a fair price and came into possession of one of the diaries. As soon as I saw the reference to Gestapo Colonel Horst Grahamar and his precious cross, I knew that you would make it worth my trouble."

"Had anyone else seen this notebook before you bought it?"

"No one who knew enough to be able to make anything out of it. Just a pile of dusty notebooks, and I was able to purchase the crucial one quite discreetly. It was illuminating on many counts. All this time I thought that Göring had been so very generous to give his maid that Vermeer, *The Woman Taken in Adultery*. Lohse writes that Göring gave it to her because he knew the painting was a counterfeit."

He chuckled to himself, and while Hoetger examined the documents once more, Adelbert's gaze wandered over to the young women who took their lunches in the shade of the beech trees that rose amid the tables, and came to rest on a pretty blonde waitress who leaned against the wrought iron fence enclosing the wooden benches and picnic tables of the Kaisergarten's terrace. He watched as she exchanged a few words, or perhaps a telephone number, with a man who, Adelbert thought sadly, could be his grandson. His face brightened in contemplation of the long glass of amber liquid that stood in front of him and of the check for forty thousand Euros that had been deposited in his account at the Müncher Hypothekenbank that morning.

"So Grahamar had his own Bruno Lohse? Someone who advised him on looted art?"

"Well, something like that. This fellow seems to have dealt primarily in rare books, prints, letters, that sort of thing. The only problem for Grahamar was that his "adviser" was an agent for the OSS, known then under the identity of Patrice Quenton. I don't know what his real name was, but you can find out."

Hoetger continued to scan the pages, rubbing his smoothly shaven jaw line. "Lohse says here that Quenton was an American agent, from Massachusetts?"

"That's right. How does Lohse put it? That after the liberation, Quenton let his mask slip, and then he disappeared. He also says that it was this agent who stole Grahamar's cross, that "highly valuable artifact from Spanish South America." And Quenton may still have it. Certainly it has never surfaced since the war. Well, you'll see it in there. I marked the pages." He finished his beer and broke into a broad smile, feeling the glow of the alcohol. "You remember the Bee Gees?" He sang in English, "The lights always shine in Massa-chusetts . . . "

"Before my time, Herr Lustig. I know it's a place where they amused themselves by hanging witches."

He drew a laptop from the leather bag that rested against his chair and opened it. Lustig watched the reflection of the screen's light in the sunglasses as Hoetger hunched over it, pushing the hair back behind his ears and tapping the keys rapidly. These young people were always playing with computers. He breathed the warm air and enjoyed the pleasant sense of lightness as he drained his glass. Finally, Hoetger said, "Of course there's not one Patrice Quenton currently listed as living in Massachusetts." He folded the laptop and replaced it in the leather bag.

Lustig shrugged. "Lohse gives the name of the Resistance group he worked with, 'The Heart of the Cross of Lorraine.' The French haven't hidden those names. They've honored them in public ceremonies. Should be possible to find out who this Patrice Quenton was."

"Oh, I will find out." Hoetger smiled for the first time. "You know me. I'll have the cross. God knows I've been looking for it long enough. At the same time, I'll settle an old score with this American, if he's still alive."

Adelbert Lustig's face darkened. "Listen, Hoetger . . . " He paused as the waiter approached and set down their plates. He ordered another Trappist, and continued, "I don't know what you intend to do, but if it gets ugly, I only ask that you forget how you came by the knowledge. I merely provide information. I'm not responsible."

"Of course not, Adelbert. You are only one among a number of people in the art world who have what we might call 'criminally exploitable contacts.' You are insulated. You have only to remember that there are very few mutes in jail. Whatever you say, say nothing."

Adelbert moved as if his chair had suddenly become uncomfortable. "I've never been one who needs that sort of reminding, have I?"

"If you had . . . "

The older man leaned over his plate and said firmly, "I don't need to be threatened either. In my business discretion is an absolute."

"Of course."

"I confess I feel bad for the American agent, Karl. He was only doing his job, too."

"Yes, yes. What did that Irish writer say? 'It seems that history is to blame.'"

"That's true," the older man said, nodding pensively, holding a forkful of *Wurstsalat* before his bemused face, "history is to blame for so much."

But he noticed that Karl Hoetger was not listening, nor was he eating his *Sauerbraten*. He was studying intently the documents before him, his mouth turned downward in grim concentration. And Adelbert repeated, half to himself, "It seems that history is always to blame."

3

Martin drew himself from the reverie, or pulled himself out of it, like a man climbing out of a dark well. That happened sometimes, even after all these years. He set his empty cup in the sink and got dressed. His footsteps echoed from the high ceiling of the stairwell as he descended. He pulled the Buick Le Sabre out of the garage and drove to the Windsor Shop, just to run the engine. He didn't drive much anymore, and never at night.

He returned with *The Boston Globe* and a box of cat food. He always paused on the spacious landing of the old stairway to admire the stained glass window. He knew its history, as he knew the history of all the things that interested him. Joshua Pollard had been the original owner of this grand old residence that had long since been divided into five apartments. Pollard had designed and commissioned the window in the 1840's, when this Colonial Revival home with its grooved Corinthian columns had been his manorial estate, dominating the lands that rolled at a shallow incline down to the Merrimack River. He had been the majority owner of the Dutton Fabric Company, one of the first companies to harness the power of descending water to turn the turbines housed beneath Lowell's "miles of mills."

The symbols of industry were not lacking in the scene depicted in the high arched window. In one corner, a golden beehive sent forth a winged army of workers while a barge laden with bales of cotton wound its way along the blue ribbon of the Middlesex Canal. In the distance, white pillars of smoke rose from the smokestacks of squat brick mill buildings. All these served as a backdrop for the central figure: the mill girl – the worker saint of the Church of Commerce. Her placid, translucent face gazed not toward heaven, but toward the Pawtucket Falls, the source of industrial power, the reason for the house, and for the city. The motto below the scene was the motto of the city itself: *Art is the handmaid of human good.* Art as in *artisan* or *artifice*, Martin thought. Maybe we would say *technology*, but still a damned fine motto.

Martin gazed appreciatively at the inscrutable face framed in dark crescents of hair, and at the slender hands which held a long spindle wound with cotton thread. The silence was broken by the opening of a door to one of the apartments in the hall below. Another dark-haired woman, of some thirty years, emerged and hurried toward the great old staircase. It was Luz Morales, an immigrant from Colombia who lived below him with her young daughter. She was a hair stylist at Ronda's Top Cut, where she trimmed Martin's hair once a month.

"Good morning, Luz," the old man said. She stopped, with fingers spread over her heart, an engaging feminine gesture that made Martin smile.

"I did not see you there," she said.

"Well, as the poet said, *An aged man is but a paltry thing, A tattered coat upon a stick...* I'm sorry if I startled you, dear," and he meant it, for in the three years since the Colombian woman had moved in, he had become quite fond of her, even to the sad extent of sometimes wishing that he were a younger man, though the memories he had of his life as a lover were distant. Fondly, but rather coldly recalled. It was a peace that made true friendship with a woman more welcome.

"You have a poem for everything," she said, smiling.

"Yes, strange, isn't it?" It had always been the way his mind worked. He could recite lines of poetry, or lines from some old film, or something someone had said fifty years ago. He still remembered codes from his OSS days. How clearly, standing there on the landing, he could hear the BBC voice, through the static of the radio, and time: *And we have a message for Trevor. We will meet you at Apple.*

"Martin, I wonder could you do me a favor today." For some reason, Martin's heart always welled with tenderness toward this young single mother and her six-year-old child. The colored light that filtered through the stained glass and fell on her hair and face suggested those immortal visitors who came to men in days when the oak was sacred and heroes strove with gods. His still revered the faith of his youth in many ways, but Martin's true religion was the Church of the Imagination. Art is the handmaid. Thou art the handmaid. She had told him that Ana's father was still alive, an American, but that he had left them after two years of marriage. What could he love more in life than Luz and their little girl, the old man wondered. The fool.

"Certainly, dear, do you need me to watch the child?"

"Well, I have to get her a birthday present, and I can't let her see...if you're not busy. I won't be long."

"Take your time, Luz. I enjoy her company. I may take her for a walk in the park. And I'll keep her close by."

"I trust you, Martin."

He turned his head and began to ascend the stairs, for those simple words had stirred emotions whose depths he could not explain to himself and that he wished to hide from her. It was strange, but her trust was something of great value to him, a precious gift, and he knew that he would do anything in the world to guard it. "An aged man is but a paltry thing indeed," he thought, "and I'm becoming damned emotional in my dotage," but he knew that this need to have and guard the trust of this woman was derived in part from his failure to be able to save the woman who would never be far from his thoughts. He smiled and called down the stairs, "You know where I'll be, Luz."

"*En su ciudad de los libros,*" she called up and heard him laughing as he opened his door.

"Yes, yes, in my City of Books." He sat at his desk and opened a drawer, from which he drew out a box of stationery and a pen. He pulled from his pocket a letter he'd received a few days earlier from his old Resistance friend, Jean Michel Courvoisier. He unfolded the letter and read it over.

Dear dear dear friend,

I was just reading a new edition of Horace's Odes and Epodes. It gives at least five alternative readings for the fifth line of Ode 38, each one supported by a mass of textual evidence (the recent discovery of a new manuscript of Epode 6 however couldn't be included). And all of this reminds us (once again!) what a powerful classicist Hölderlin was and how he anticipated the Zimmergelehrte by several decades. And at the same time I am listening to the new Von Karajan directed Wiener Symphoniker; they have a new cellist and three very young recorder players which gives the orchestra just the right amount of je ne sais quoi to keep up with the tremendous efforts always demanded by Von K. Mahler's Sixth Symphony is rather disappointing, losing too much of the poignancy of the second part by playing down the allegro just that little bit too much, and the choir in the finale is just too mediocre for Karajanian

standards anyway. Spring has hardly arrived, I am already anxiously awaiting the Beaujolais Nouveau of the autumn, but waiting makes it all the more exciting and so on. So that's what I'm doing. What are you doing?
Marius

Marius. Jean Michel was still fond of his old CCL *nom de guerre*. He had been a scholar, book dealer, and aspiring linguist when the Second Republic crumbled. The shelves of his little bookstore in Lyon had been filled by the Nazis with the works of second-rate German propagandists. Jean Michel, enraged, had taken to printing anti-Hitler, anti-Petain tracts on a mimeograph machine in his basement which he signed "Marius," after the revolutionary leader in Hugo's *Les Miserables*. He left his broadsides on street corners and in the stations of the SNCF until he was driven to give up the mimeograph machine, pick up a gun, and fight for the Resistance in and around Lyon. He had saved Martin's life within five minutes of meeting him. Martin put down the letter and wrote:

Old Friend:

I've just finished Coleridge's Biographia Literaria, in a very fine early edition, and am meditating on The Iliad once again, because, as Gladstone said, 'The Iliad teaches us how to die.' It seems that's one thing we never learned to do, mon vieux copain, though there were many who tried to teach us."

4

Martin heard footsteps on the stairs, and Luz's voice *"Si, mi amor*, I think the cat loves you, but..." He couldn't catch the rest of the sentence.

He slid the letter into a drawer. "The door is open," he called, and smiled as mother and daughter came in. Ana carried a doll, a folded checkerboard, and a box of checkers. A pink purse hung from a strap over her arm. The child nodded sagely as the mother gave her instructions regarding her demeanor, for which she had the highest expectations. When Luz had gone, Ana picked up the cat and carried it into the library.

Martin called to her. "Ana, come here, sweetheart."

"Why?" she asked, poking her head around the corner of a winged chair where she sat with the cat in her lap.

"I need you," he said.

She ran to his side and looked up expectantly. He put a hand on her shoulder and asked with judicial gravity, "Do you know how to peel an egg?"

Her eyes widened, and she nodded her head vigorously, pushing the strands of brown hair from her face, eager to prove herself. "Yes. Because I do know how, and I've done it before."

He told her to wash her hands and gave her the egg, which occupied her for several minutes.

"Well I wouldn't have believed it," he said, when she presented the peeled egg in her little fingers.

"Was that really going to be a chicken?" she asked.

"Well, yes, it could have been."

"Oh, the poor mother chicken. I feel bad for her." She paused and added, "I'd better stay here in case you need me to peel that other egg."

He gave her the other egg, and soon they were having egg and toast and talking. The form of conversation was really more of an interrogation. "Why did God make bad people?" she wanted to know.

"Well, God didn't make them bad, they just went wrong somewhere and became bad."

"Didn't God know they were going to be bad? He knows everything."

"Well, that's a big question. You ask big questions, Ana." Acting in *loco parentis*, he was afraid of saying something with which her mother would disagree and didn't really know what to say, or how to try to explain free will or God, to her or to himself. "You're an awfully deep thinker for a six- year-old," he said.

"That's because I'll be seven on Monday," she said. "Did you know, Martin, that no one can really do magic? Only God. God's the only person who could do magic. Really, he's not a person, he's a saint. The biggest saint there is. And a long time ago, before even you were born, the bad people chopped the heads off the people who believe in God."

He smiled and said, "Yes, leave it to those bad people to think up bad things to do." The kettle whistled and he went to the stove to pour a cup of tea.

"And they chop their heads off. Would you be sad if I died? I would be very sad if you died. I would be crying. Martin, I have one question for you. If I died would I be still six, or seven years old in heaven forever, or would I grow up in heaven?"

Feeling a bit of a philistine, he murmured that it was all a mystery which was beyond them, and that it was too sad to talk about little girls dying, especially her. But she was not ready to leave divine mysteries, and asked him, "Is Eve and Adam real, or just a fairy tale?"

"Why don't you ask the sister at your school? Or your mother. I haven't . . . I haven't studied those questions. Why don't we play checkers?" he asked, rising to get the board and box of checkers she'd left on a coffee table. He put a CD of *Bach's Musical Offering* in the Sony player while he was up.

"Oh, there's some pretty music for you," he said.

"Do you want to be black or red?" she asked.

"I'll be black."

"Then I'll be red. But can I go first?"

"Yes, you can go first."

As she frowned over the game, he felt relieved that her questions had ceased, but the worst was to come. "I think my dad is bad," she said. "He gets drunk."

Martin surveyed the board casually, thinking very carefully about what he was going to say. "I got drunk years ago, Ana. Probably made a spectacle of myself a couple of times too, but it doesn't mean I'm a bad person, does it?"

"I know that," Ana said. "My friend Casey's mother even said that she got drunk when she was in college." And she added in a sort of mumble, "An' she probably made a speckle of herself too."

She looked at him as if she were weighing something in her mind. She pulled a strand of brown hair across her bottom lip and said, "Your move."

"Oh yes, I'm sorry, let me see..." He slid his checker into the gap between two of hers. "Always move into the gap. Good rule of thumb," he said.

She leaned over the board, pushing air around in her mouth, puffing out one cheek, then the other. She exhaled, moved a checker into his path, a one for one sacrifice, and said, "My father is bad because when he got drunk he hit my mom, and she was bleening, I mean bleeding and the police had to come, and he did some other bad things and I was only like four or five, but I know he's not nice like you are. That means he's bad."

Martin felt that there was something wrong with hearing about Luz's personal life this way, through her child. He felt as if he were reading her mail; on the other hand, he wanted to know, because he was concerned. The thought of anyone hitting Luz stirred an anger in him that he had not felt in many years. And Ana must need to talk about these things and was probably waiting for some words of reassurance – some wisdom from the old man. What could he say that she would understand?

"Ana, I wouldn't be surprised if with that bad there is some good somewhere, and maybe it will come out. But if he was hurting your mother, well, he has to learn that a man doesn't, shouldn't, hurt a woman, ever, and maybe he will learn that lesson, and the good will come out."

"I don't think he will learn that lesson, and that's why my mom gets worried sometimes. I heard her tell my Tia Liliana on the telephone *estoy preocupada con el*, and that means, 'I'm worried about him.'"

"I think the police will make him behave. He won't be allowed to hurt your mother, or he'll have to go to jail." He had tried to choose his words carefully, but the little girl seemed to sense that he was just mumbling platitudes, and she had ceased to pay attention. She slid a checker along the board.

"You don't want to move there, do you Ana? I'll double jump you."

She frowned. "Do you still have the book about the frog and the toad?" she asked.

"I brought it back to the library, but I got a Tim and Ginger book."

"You went to the library?"

"That's right. I don't have any books you would like."

"Were you quiet? You're supposed to be quiet in the library. You have to whisper."

"Yes, I was very quiet."

"You are right, Martin, because this music is very pretty. Do you mind if we don't play checkers anymore? Let's read the book."

They read *Tim and Ginger: To The Lighthouse*, and then Ana read *Clifford the Big Red Dog* while Hannibal, the big yellow and white cat, sat in her lap, purring in languid semi- consciousness.

When she had finished her book, Martin could see that the little girl looked restless, and he suggested they take a walk over to the park. The retreating winter had abandoned its rearguard; shrunken, dirt-covered snow drifts huddled in the shade of great bushes and in cool corners hidden from the sun. Ana climbed on the massive gray boulder that stood like a stone ship sailing across the park. She had been castigating the old man thoroughly because he had admitted that he didn't know who the Jonas Brothers were. "You really need a TV, Martin," she said.

"Oh, I entertain myself with my books."

"But then there's nothing in your books about the Jonas Brothers."

Martin laughed. She swung her small pink purse and jumped off the rock, landing beside him. "Sister Carmen said that you have to forgive all the bad things people did, especially if they are sorry, and you have to let go of the past."

Let go of the past. Would that I could. His smile faded as he watched a silver Toyota glide around the park for the second time. "Excuse me, angel, what kind of a car does your father drive?"

"He drives a truck. Do you like broccoli?"

"Yes, I like it very much."

"I don't like it. Why do you want to know what kind of a car my father drives?"

"Just thinking about cars."

The habit of mistrust, once learned, once internalized, was hard to lose. Martin watched the car, which had pulled over alongside the park, idling just beyond a row of shrubs while the child skipped across the rock. No one emerged from the car, but he saw a figure in the driver's seat. And then he saw something that made his old heart pick up its pace. The face in the car had turned toward him, and something rose before it for a few seconds. Martin was sure it had been a camera.

"Walk this way with me a bit, Ana."

The car pulled out, and Martin walked toward the corner, hoping to get the license plate as it passed, but he couldn't make out the number clearly as it turned away from him and drove off toward Pine Street, where he watched as it turned right. If the car turned right again, at the light at Westford Street, it would pass by again at the bottom of the park.

"Walk with me to the other end of the park. Let me see how fast I can move," he said. The pain and stiffness in his left knee told him not to try to move too fast.

The little girl danced along beside him, singing snatches of songs to herself, and jumping occasionally, attempting pirouettes that never amounted to more than a half turn and a giddying loss of balance.

"Hide here from the monster!" he said to the little girl, leaning against an oak tree, where she joined him shuddering and asking in mock terror, "Does the monster see us?"

Peering around the tree, he saw the silver car moving toward them along Westford, and he whispered, "No, but I see him." He stepped out and stood on the sidewalk as the car came toward them, and the driver, seeing him so close, pulled a sharp left away onto Rutland Street. He could see the plate, but the letters or numbers blurred and merged as he tried to focus on them. His eyes were not so sharp as they had been even ten years ago.

"Is the monster still there?" Ana called out from behind the tree.

"No," Martin said, "he's a very timid monster after all. He ran away."

"What color was he, Martin?"

"Green."

"Like a green snake?"

"Exactly."

"We'd better watch out for him."

5

Martin was reading *The Iliad*, thinking, and dreaming. One volume was open before him. He held it over the cat, which slept in his lap. Another was spread face down on the side table, where a single ice cube melted into a tumbler of scotch. He liked to compare the Lattimore and Fitzgerald translations. Strangely enough, he had first read Homer in French, with Brother Beaulieu at St. Louis de France School.

Dis-moi Muse, de cet homme subtil qui erra si longtemps
Après qu'il eut renversé la citadelle sacrèe de Troiè

Though Maura Halpin, his mother, had been Irish, his father was Quebecois, and for his sake, she had agreed to send Martin to St. Louis de France School. From such a simple decision, what a turn his life was later to take.

Now, he found he wanted to reread the books that had inspired him in a past so distant it seemed another life – the days of football practice and Latin verbs, of humid summer nights when leaves began to murmur outside his screen, presaging the sudden blast of thunder that rattled the windows and roused his poor mother, sending her into her closet with the heavy black rosary entangled in her trembling fingers.

Martin reveled in the thunder's roar, imagining King Lear on the heath bellowing "Blow you winds! Crack you heavens! Smite flat the thick rotundity o' the world!" or something like that, while he sank deeper into *Bleak House*, *Walden*, *War and*

Peace, *The Hound of the Baskervilles*, *Père Goriot*, or Chapman's translation of *The Iliad*. Late, late into the rain-soaked night he read, until he dropped the book on his chest and fell into the book's world in dreams, swinging a heavy sword at bronze-clad Trojans or running from some dark entity across the trackless English moors.

At the age that he had attained, he had begun to acquire a new and odd feeling – that of a person with a history so long that it seemed to him that he had led several different lives, and he turned back on his past and was beginning to recall friends who had lain forgotten in his memory for years. After rummaging through the contents of long undisturbed boxes in a closet in the back room, he had drawn out old photos, letters, *cartes postales*, and maps of France, which he pored over, retracing the lost paths of the war, and admitting to himself sadly that he had forgotten where certain events had occurred, though he could recall them in detail. The internet had opened a door to the cloistered world of the City of Books. Working from scraps of information, he had reconnected with old friends, rediscovered the settings of fragmented memories, and had even found a photo of the *Nathan Hale*, the transport ship that had carried him to England.

He had never spoken much about the war years, even to his veteran friends in Lowell. The spy game was difficult to communicate. Only those who'd lived through it could understand the panic willed into mere anxiety, the thin line called discipline that held back the rush of fear in a man who knows he is being hunted by an efficient killer, a killer who will try to make him talk before he's buried moaning in a barracks yard or tossed in a nameless ravine. The old images came back to him in the quiet hours of night – the charred black remains of the aristocrat who had sheltered a band of *maquisards*. He'd been suspended from a tripod and burned alive.

You couldn't explain the thoughts that ran through the mind as one fingered the cyanide capsule in its tiny packet and almost longed for the peace it would bring, wondering at the same time, "If I don't swallow it when the time comes, can I survive? Will I talk?" The L pill: L for lethal.

He recalled the beautiful windows of the church where the Resistance had met, where Père LeBrun had whispered to him, "You must come and go carefully. If the Germans find out, I will pay dearly." And he did. Blind Homer had said it well.

Remember every valor of yours,
For now the need comes
Hardest upon you
To be a spearman and a bold warrior
There shall be no more escape for you . . .

LeBrun was no soldier, but he had the right stuff. *Remember every valor of yours . . .* a stocky, bespectacled priest with the airs of silent chapels and solitary devotions about him. "By God," Martin said to himself, "it was a man's heart that beat under the simple *croix de bois* that hung on his black cassock." *He took his way among the champions helmed in bronze.*

He heard a vehicle pull into the U-shaped driveway that led up to the curving semicircle of granite stairs and Corinthian columns that graced the portico of the old Pollard Mansion. He took off his reading glasses and looked at the digital clock on the bookcase: 12:17. He rubbed his eyes and reached for the small glass of scotch on the table. Twelve-year-old Glenlivit, a birthday present from his sister Edith. She never forgot his birthday, which had been in September. An octogenarian. He reminded himself to call her.

He put the book down quickly. Someone had flung the front door open so that it slammed against the wall of the entry. He tossed the cat on the couch and moved to his own door, Hannibal trailing behind him, tail twitching. The low drawling voice of a man in the hall downstairs became clearer as he opened his own door. He walked quickly to the bookcase, and stretching to reach the top shelf, pulled back two of the eight blue volumes of *Clarendon's Rebellion*. He withdrew a pistol and stuck it in the waistband behind his back. A little health insurance. He pulled a suit coat from a hook inside the closet door and put it on as he walked out the door.

"Luz . . . Luz . . . open 'a door. *Abra la fuckin' puerta!* I just wanna talk."

There was silence for a moment; without breaking it, Martin descended to the landing.

As he peered into the foyer below, he heard her open the door. That was a mistake, Luz, he thought. She should have called the police, and her neighbor across the hall was away. "Al! Go home! Call me when you're sober if you want to talk! Leave, or I'll call the police!"

Martin moved down the stairs, watching the man push the door wider and wriggle unsteadily past Luz as she tried to block him. By the time the old man walked through the door, Al was holding Luz against the refrigerator, one hand at her throat. "Give your husband a lil' kiss. *Un besito?*" he said.

"My friend," Martin said in a clear voice, "let her go. You're going to wake up the child. Come on. Go home. You're drunk."

The young man turned, releasing Luz, a clenched fist still held in the air where her throat had been. He reeled slightly, squinting at the figure of Martin outlined in the light from the hallway. He took a few steps toward him. He stood about six feet. Brown shaggy hair fell onto the leather collar of a denim jacket. He wore a mustache, and a few days worth of rough stubble darkened his jaw.

"Why donchoo . . ." His mouth twisted, as he attempted to conjure up the appropriate curse. The lamp of his brain flickered behind dull eyes.

"Go home," Martin repeated. "I'm not going to let you hurt Luz or disturb the child."

"Fuck you . . . ol' man. Mind ya business. You tryna . . . you tryna tell me? Who the fuck ah you anyway?" The young man's lips curled in disdain.

"I'm nobody," Martin said.

"Nobody, eh? Ha! Huh! Yer fuckin' right there. You know who I am, Nobody?"

A feeling like spite for the ignorant creature was kindling in him. "Yes," he said slowly, "I know who you are. Better than you know yourself. You're a man who wants a woman's love, and you're too damned stupid to realize that you had it and that you threw it away and pissed on it because you loved getting drunk more than you loved her.

It was too good – maybe you didn't think you deserved it – and you had to ruin it. And now you come back here to her – a drooling drunk disgusting pig trying to scare her into loving you, like she owes you love? You know what she owes you, *boy*? She owes you shit. Now haul your sorry ass out of here, and when you want to know what went wrong with your love life take a look in the mirror. A long fucking look."

A low growl rose from behind the twisted face as he lurched toward Martin, but he stopped short, recoiling as he found the barrel of a gun in his face.

"Martin, no!"

He heard the desperation in Luz's voice.

The old man took two steps back, and said, "Whoa boy! Walk on out of here, or you'll find a hole where your knee used to be."

Al's eyes widened. A momentary sobriety straightened his back. He paused, like a wind-up toy whose spring was losing its torque. He looked once more at Luz, who seemed to be holding her breath, her terry cloth housecoat clutched at her breast, and then at the old man who was glaring hard at him. "I'm leaving," he said, moving toward the door as Martin stepped aside to let him pass.

The younger man stopped with his hand on the door knob. "Hey, Nobody, you know what Luz Morales, you know what that means in English? Loose Morals. That's her real fuckin' name. Bitch."

He flung the door open and turned, searching for some departing insult to hurl, but only succeeded in mumbling, "I'll see you again, when I ain't drinkin'. You ain't the only one got a gun."

Martin stepped out onto the portico, wanting to see if he was driving the silver Toyota, but the pickup Ana had mentioned was parked on the gravel driveway, almost blocking the stairs. There were ladders tied down on a rack and a few bundles of shingles in the back.

"You'd better pray you *never* see me again. Was a time I wouldn't need a gun to put you in the hospital. I'm old, but I'll tell you this. If you hurt Luz, I'll be looking for you with the equalizer. I have a license to carry, and I will be carrying. You come for me with a firearm, you'd better be a good shot. When I shoot, I hit my target."

The man opened his side door and leaned his forearms against the door frame of the cab. Shaking his head, he said, "You watch too many movies, old man."

"I don't watch any movies, Al. I'm just telling you exactly how it is."

Luz came out on the porch, a coat thrown over her shoulders. "Let me call a cab! You'll kill someone!" she said, but the truck door closed and they heard the engine turn over. The headlights lit the graveled walk. An unsteady hand ground the gears, and the ladders, tied too loosely, clattered on their racks as the truck rolled out between the stone pillars at the entrance and turned onto Venice Ave. Martin shoved the pistol into the belt beneath his suit coat. Strands of dark hair had fallen over Luz's pallid face, which was lined with worry and apprehension.

"I'm so sorry, Martin. Is that pistol loaded?"

"Nah," he lied. "Just wanted to scare him."

He followed her back into her apartment, where she sat on the couch under the picture of the Sacred Heart, her bowed head in her hands. Martin studied this image of Jesus: one hand raised in a gesture of benediction, the other, nail-wounded, drawing back the red robe from his breast to reveal the flaming heart entwined in a crown of thorns, a single drop of precious redemptive blood falling. A rosary was draped around the corner of the frame. He felt as if blood were wrung from his own heart as he watched her. So strangely like the other in her devotion to her child, in her love, and in her pain. *Corazon, coeur*: the heart. *The heart of the cross.*

She raised her head and said, "Oh my God, I'd never forgive myself if he hurt you."

She was trembling. Martin wanted to put his arms around her, but that was in another life. He said, "I was thinking the same thing. About you. Next time just call the cops."

"I should have. You can't reason with him when he's drunk." She pulled a Kleenex from the pocket of her house coat and wiped her eyes. "It's not true what he said, I swear by *El Sagrado Corazon*." Her voice broke, and she reached behind her to touch the frame of the holy image.

"I know that, Luz."

"He was always accusing me of things. He threatened men that I worked with. He made up things. But all I care about is raising my daughter. I've dedicated my life to her. I don't need any man."

"You're a wonderful mother, Luz."

"I thought he might be coming to bring her a birthday present." She shook her bowed head and the hair fell in a dark curtain before her face, reminding Martin of the old Greek women he'd seen at the wake of a friend, rocking in grief with their black lace shawls pulled over their heads. "He doesn't even remember."

He wanted to ask her how she had come to be involved with such a sad specimen of a man, but he thought that story might be for another time. In any case, he'd seen it before. They're on their best behavior until the woman is in too deep, and then they start to tighten the grip, let the beast out of its cage.

"Where does he live?" Martin asked.

"I don't know anymore. He talks crazy. He says he stays in different places. That no one ever knows where he is. He was always a suspicious man. When he lived with me, he had another room somewhere. Everything is a lie. Everything is a secret. He thinks someone is always out to get him."

"Sounds like he's into something illegal. Does he ever mention getting rich?"

"Oh yes, he's got big plans. Talks about buying a house in Jamaica. He's not just doing roofing. He's involved in something. I don't want to know what."

6

Like his friend, Martin LeBris, Jean Michel Courvoisier, scholar and *Chevalier de la Legion d'Honneur*, led a life as tranquil in his old age as it had been tumultuous in his youth. His wife, Linde, was from Antwerp, where she had first admired him playing chess against a grave African gentleman at a table on the terrace of Oud Arsenaal, where she served draught De Konincks and sandwiches to a varied clientele in the evenings. During the day, she was completing her science degree. Jean Michel, in those post-war years, was a young professor at the Universiteit Antwerpen, teaching Linguistics and Literature.

In the early eighties, they'd bought and restored an 18th century stone farmhouse in a small village called Panissières, west of Lyon. There was a great raised fireplace and five and a half hectares of land, including a landscaped garden where Linde cultivated herbs and vegetables. The outhouse had been leveled, and replaced with a modern W.C. in a room that was attached to the house; where, Jean Michel used to tell his cringing guests, he always brought his carbine, due to the size of the spiders that congregated in the vicinity of the toilet. Their two children were gone, young Geert to Canada and Nicola to Brussels, but they both came home at Christmas, and sometimes visited in the summer with their own spouses and children.

Jean Michel would never have believed that one day he would retire to a life of such peace, spending the mornings in study, overlooking green fields and the red tiled roof of a distant home where a column of smoke rose a like silent prayer from the hearth of old Guillon, the sheep farmer, and where now, a man with a walking staff and backpack hiked the trail at the edge of the wood. Every day he thanked the unseen power that seemed to have guided his life.

Such a thin line, the elevation of a gun, the path of a bullet, the timing of a patrol. I should have been killed a hundred times with that crazy American, LeBris. I knew he was American from the beginning, though I never let on. He might have fooled the Germans, and the other FFI, but not me. He hid it well, generally, but I caught a hint of that joual basilectal Quebec French underpinning. The dipthongs instead of long vowels, and all the little occasional slips: toé instead of toi; pis instead of puis; y instead of il; and sometimes even icitte instead of ici, or pantoute instead of pas du tout. St. Brieuc in Brittany, he told us. I don't think so, my friend. I used to curse America just to watch his reaction. He'd seem to agree. He never said a damned thing, but I could see him getting pissed off.

Martin LeBris. I have to invite him to visit us here. He hasn't been back in twenty years.

He shook himself and refocused his attention on the screen of the laptop that sat on the desk in front of him. Page thirteen. He needed to finish this last part of his essay for the *Journal of French Language Studies*: "Nouvelles Elements Syntactiques de la Langue d'Oïl." He read what he had written the previous day, and went back to his outline and his notes. He had been writing for some time when he heard a noise in the kitchen. It sounded as if Linde had dropped a glass on the tile floor. He walked to the top of the stairs and called out, "Are you all right, dear?"

When he heard nothing, he began to descend the stairs. He stopped suddenly. Something that had slept in his heart these many years awakened and told him to beware, and at the same time he remembered that two former members of the CCL had recently met untimely deaths. An agent from GIGN had come by to tell him to be vigilant. He mounted the stairs to the second floor again, and took the Berthier 8mm carbine from his closet, and a box of ammunition from the shelf. He snapped the five-round magazine clip in below the stock, drew back the bolt, and slammed it home.

When he emerged from his study with the weapon he saw a man standing at the foot of the stairs with a pistol to Linde's head. He recognized him: it was the man he'd seen walking the trail at the edge of the field. The man said nothing, but shook his head, *No*. Jean Michel knew he had to put down the carbine, yet he paused. He suspected very strongly that he and Linde would both be dead shortly and that it would be better to take this man with them. When he raised the rifle, the man ducked farther behind her, daring him to fire. He would have to shoot through his wife, who stood sobbing, eyes asking him . . . what? He didn't know, but he could not bring himself to pull the trigger, and while he hesitated, the man fired. The bullet struck him in the leg, just above the knee. He dropped the carbine and tumbled down the stairs.

He regained consciousness in a gasping rush and saw the man standing above him with an empty pot dripping water. Opening his eyes, he felt a biting pain in his leg and heard his wife speaking through rapid breaths, "Let me put a tourniquet on his leg, please. He's an old man. Take whatever you want."

"You," the intruder said to the woman, "shut your mouth." He addressed them in German, and Jean Michel couldn't help but remark on the accent. Bavaria, he thought. He pulled Jean Michel up to a sitting position, his back against the wall. "And you, tell me all you know about Patrice Quenton, and do it fast."

"If you wanted to be a Gestapo," the old Frenchman said, "you're too late by sixty years."

The intruder smiled, pressed the gun against Linde's shin, and fired. She screamed and Jean Michel lunged forward, grimacing in pain, clutching at the gun, and pulling the long hair that hung about the man's shoulders. But Jean Michel was old, and had spent the last half century in the library. The German twisted from his enfeebled hands and hit him hard in the jaw. His head jerked back and slammed into the wall. He was dizzy. The visitor continued calmly. "Once again, tell me all you know about Patrice Quenton."

"He was a member of the Resistance, I think. It was a long time ago."

"What was his real name?"

"You mean Patrice was not his real name?"

He pressed the gun against Linde's leg again.

"Wait, you bastard!"

"Name?"

Jean Michel knew that this man was an assassin. Assassins don't leave victims or witnesses alive. It would be better for Linde to die quickly than to die slowly, but it went against every fiber in his body to give in to this killer. He could never do it. "Paul Rainville. I believe his real name was Paul Rainville."

"You're lying and your wife must keep paying."

"Wait, wait," Linde cried, "His name is Martin LeBris. He lives in America. In Massachusetts. You can find the address on the letters in his desk. I'm sorry, Jean Michel. I'm sorry."

"It's all right my dear. I'm sorry I've led you to this. *Ik zie oe geerne.* I love you."

The intruder lifted the gun from her leg, put it to her head, and fired. Jean Michel was glad that it was over for her, but sad that the course of his life had run back to the days of the rat hunt, as if some Nazi out of 1944 had materialized to complete the job they had never managed. He sensed the shadow of the gun in front of his face. He remembered how he had been wondering at his good fortune only that morning, and he had lived to see his wife tortured before his eyes. He recalled the Greek philosopher who had written, "Call no man happy until he is dead."

"I'll say this for you old *maquisards,*" the German said, "you die like men." He smiled approvingly. "Good for you."

Jean Michel Courvoisier did not respond. He was sure that Martin LeBris had been warned, as he had, and he prayed that he would be ready for this bastard. *Martin was always ready, and please, God, let him be so now. He was the best of us. Avenge us, Martin, one more time.* He reached for Linde's hand. "I love you," he whispered again, and he pictured her smiling on the terrace of Oud Arsenaal when the shot struck his skull so that he fell across her body.

7

Detective Gerry O'Neil was on unofficial business when he stepped up on the front porch of Frank McGuin's neat white colonial. Before he could ring the doorbell, he heard Frank call him from inside a fenced-in pool area at the side of the house.

McGuin was a former rock n' roller who had gained local celebrity with a song he wrote and recorded in the seventies called "You Don't Know It's Over." He was now a heavyset, middle-aged music teacher who had every reason to be cynical but was always trying to be optimistic, which was one reason Gerry admired him. If it was over, he didn't seem to know.

He was not wearing a bathing suit, but tattered jeans and a Patriots T-shirt. The tarp was still over the pool. It was April, and the sun had only just begun to recall the earth to life.

The two shook hands, and Frank gestured toward a white plastic table and chairs on the concrete apron near the diving board. "I just cleaned them," he said, and glanced at his watch. "The sun is over the yardarm. You want a beer? There are still a few Amstels in the cooler by the grill."

"Still a bit early for me, Frank. You have coffee?"

"I just made some a half hour ago." He ambled into the house while Gerry sat taking the sun for the first time since winter had retreated. A pleasant daydream flitted across his mind. The scene he revisited had occurred when he was in the army, stationed in Fort Hood, Texas, before he went to Nam. When his "colleagues," as he used to refer to the men in his unit, would go to the whore house, he would go to the library and study Spanish.

And after he met the Mexican beauty perusing a volume of Octavio Paz, he learned the language in three months. Total physical response.

Marina Martinez was her name. The one that got away. He could see her now, turning toward him on the chaise lounge beside her father's pool. In the shimmering light reflected from the water she lifted her sunglasses and smiled at him.

"*Que bonitos ojos negros tienes,*" he said. What beautiful dark eyes you have.

Her smile broadened, her teeth so white against her olive skin. Stretching languidly, catlike, she said, "What a delicious heat. I'm sleepy." She reached out and stroked his forearm while the whole scene burned into his memory, forever filed under passion, cross reference: youth. How many times in memory had she turned to him and smiled once more, and softly spoken those words.

He often wondered what became of her when the letters stopped arriving at his base in Da Nang. It hurt, so far from home, to remember her dark hair and gypsy eyes. "What a delicious heat. I'm sleepy." When he was off duty, he was often angry, and seldom sober, and others paid for the sense of loss that twisted his heart. He tried not to think of that. He thought of Gina, the woman that now meant home, and yes, love, after years of a downwardly spiraling marriage. Gina had not gotten away. Or maybe it was he who was in her snare, but he rejoiced in his captivity. "POL," as his pal old Private First Class Duggan used to say: "Prisoner of Love."

McGuin came out with a tray on which were neatly arranged two coffee mugs, a creamer, and a bowl of sugar. Gerry got up to open the gate, and took the tray, which he set down on the plastic table. The detective sipped his coffee and grimaced. "Oh, I'm sorry, but this is wretched stuff, McGuin . . . "

"I don't know. Cheryl used to make the coffee."

"It tastes like you dropped a condom full of coffee in boiling water. It's just . . . brown water." He shivered in disgust and pushed the coffee away across the plastic table.

"It's good Lowell water," McGuin said. "Try some sugar in it."

"How long has your wife been gone, Frank?"

"About three months. And it's been tough on the kids," he said. "You know I was looking at some pictures the other night. We were out on Martha's Vineyard when Eddie and Ashley were small. They have the oldest merry-go-round in the country there."

"The Flying Horse Carousel of Oak Bluffs," Gerry said.

"Is that what they call it? Anyway, there was a picture of Cheryl with the kids on the bobby horses, smiling and waving . . . so happy. And then it's fifteen years later, and she's snorting coke with some bum at Powers' Bar and wants nothing to do with us."

Gerry was leaning back in his chair, his sunglasses two green patches over his eyes. "When did you suspect that she was seeing this guy?" he asked.

"I don't know, but I remember one Sunday, when the kids were over their aunt's house, I put on some James Taylor. She loves James Taylor, and I made her breakfast."

"Hope you didn't make her coffee," Gerry mumbled.

"You know, I tried to resurrect a little of the old romance." Gerry thought for a moment that McGuin said the word romance with, what was the word? *Contumely.* "So," McGuin said, "she says to me, 'If we're going to do it, hurry up. I have things to do.'"

"Ouch." Gerry winced.

"I told her, 'Forget it. I'm going to read the funny papers.' And that's pretty much the way it went for a while. Of course, I found out later, she wasn't interested in romance with me because of the extra-curricular activities. She'd tell me she was going shopping, and she was going down to Powers' to meet this guy."

Gerry shook his head, quiet and considering for a moment. Then he said, "Did you confront her with the cheating?"

"Hell no. I didn't know a goddamn thing. Maybe I suspected, but I didn't find that all out until later. You just don't want to think about your wife screwing somebody else. Even though, looking back, there were signs. Anyway, one morning we were having coffee, her coffee, and she says to me, 'I can't do this.'"

"Can't do what?" Gerry asked.

"That's exactly what I said, and she says, 'This.'" McGuin waved a hand in an arc in front of him. "The house, the kids, me – *this*!"

"Ah, for Christ's sake," Gerry muttered. "Was she going through menopause by any chance? I read an article the other day about some of the insane things they do when they go through the menopause."

"Menopause? I don't know. Mental pause. Anyway, she's only forty-two. But it gets better. The guy she took off with is dealin' coke. In fact, I think that's why she went for him."

"Name?"

"Al Lekakis."

"Jesus Christ. I know him. Slapped his ex-wife around pretty good not too long ago. She lives in the Pollard Mansion right down the street. We also had a case against him for ripping off old ladies with his roofing business. He's dealing coke now? Not surprising, I suppose."

"What a piece of work, right? And before I knew what was happening, she had maxed out the credit cards, and emptied the kids' college funds. I had to change the locks. She was pawning family heirlooms, for Chrissakes."

"That's unbelievable."

"Oh, yeah. Beyond unbelievable. It's horrible and sad, and I don't know . . . Jerry Springer type evil."

The front door flew open with a bang, and a young girl with chopped and spiky blonde hair and an Ozzy Osborne T-shirt was leaning over the porch railing. "Dad, did you disconnect the internet?"

"You know Mr. O'Neil, sweetie."

"Nice to see you, Ashley."

She exhaled impatiently and fixed her father with a cold stare, ignoring the company. "Did you disconnect the internet?"

"Yes, I did. I told you you're grounded today with no phone and no internet. I'm sorry, but you broke the house rules."

She turned and reentered the house, slamming the door shut.

"Don't slam the door!" he shouted, shaking his head as if in recognition of the futility of his orders. "Anyway, my daughter is out of her mind. Anger control problems. Drugs. I had to change the locks a second time, because she had friends over who were stealing stuff from me. One stole my digital camera. Thank God they didn't steal my guitar. I've had that Martin Rosewood since I was twenty. She's grounded right now for smoking weed in the basement. I had to call the cops on her one night. She was assaulting me, and I didn't want to punch her lights out, you know, she's my daughter, for Chrissakes. I didn't know what to do. She's on probation for that. She used to be in the drama club, played Cleopatra in some play called 'The Greatest Love.' She was wonderful, with the makeup and the black wig. That's all done. Her grades went to hell. She's out of her mind. And I talked to a professional, you know the workplace counselors, and she says, 'Well, can you blame her?' Hell no, I can't blame her.'"

"No," Gerry said. "It had to kill them when Cheryl took off like that."

"You don't know. My son Eddie was hanging onto her leg when she left." The corners of McGuin's mouth turned down as he said, "She shook him right off and walked out the door. He cried for days, but Ashley kept it all in, until lately."

"A bad business," Gerry said.

"And Ashley knows her mother left us for a criminal dirt bag. How's that gonna make a kid . . . "

A window flew open on the second floor, and the young girl could be seen leaning out of it. "Frank McGuin is a homo!" she shouted. "He takes it up the ass and in his mouth at the same time! He's a child molester pervert faggot drug addict!"

"Close the window, sweetheart," McGuin called up.

"No wonder his wife left him! He's a loser guitar-playing homo pervert fat pig bastard!" The window slammed shut.

The two men sat in silence for a moment, and Frank rose, saying, "If you don't mind, I think I will have one of those Amstels."

"Hell, get me one too." Gerry said, "This is what an old buddy of mine in Nam used to call 'a moribund situation.'"

Frank set an Amstel in front of Gerry and flopped back into his chair. "Beautiful, eh?" He twisted the cap off, took a long drink, and exhaled deeply, shaking his head, "And what do I say to my neighbors? 'By the way, I'm not really a child molesting pervert, that's just my daughter . . . '" He made quotation marks in the air with his fingers. "Venting." He gulped at his beer and then sat up, looking directly at Gerry. "I hope *you* don't think I might be some kind of . . . "

"No, I don't Frank. Not at all."

"But here's the problem. How would you really know? You think, why would someone say that crazy stuff?"

"Aside from the fact that I've known you since we used to go up in your attic and smoke pot and listen to Hendrix? Would you invite me over here to talk about it if you had something to hide? I am a detective, you know."

The old rock and roller smiled weakly, and Gerry slapped him on the arm and said, "Remember, Watson. It's my business to know what other people don't know."

"Like the name of that carousel."

"Well, everyone knows that but you."

"Probably. Anyway, I don't want to fuck with this Lekakis guy. I never pretended to be a macho man, but you know I still worry about Cheryl."

"Enough said, pal. I'm on it."

8

The incident with Al left Luz shaken for several days. Ana had never woken up; the deep slumber of children must often have saved them from scenes to which they had better remain insensible. Al had not returned, nor left any of his rants on her answering machine, and she wondered what he would recall of the night.

It troubled her to have brought these problems on the old man she had always thought of as gentle and unassuming. She knew that he was a veteran, but she had been shocked at the sudden apparition of this other Martin; the cold command, and easy confidence with the pistol. She was naïve to have accepted his reassurance that it was not loaded. It had been loaded, and she did not doubt that he would have put a hole in Al's kneecap.

After Ana had brushed her teeth and put on her penguin pajamas, Luz read a chapter of *The Tale of Despèreaux* to her, and talked to her about school. Luz turned off the lamp on the little girl's night table, and switched on the night light on her bureau, an illuminated half moon from which a smiling mouse hung by his tail. She leaned over the child's bed to kiss her goodnight. This was always the time when Ana wanted to ask her mother impossible questions about life and death and heaven. But tonight, she held Luz's hand and said, "You know what I realized today? God is not a wish maker."

"A wish maker?"

"No, he's not. God is God. So you shouldn't be mad if God doesn't give you what you want because he already gave us life and the whole world and the people we love and we should be thankful."

"You're such a good girl, Ana. *Te amo muchìsimo. Buenas noches.*" She kissed her daughter again, and as she walked softly out of the room, the little girl called, "Mama?"

"Go to sleep, Ana. What is it?"

"I hope Martin lives a long, long time."

"I do too, dear. Now go to sleep."

"Martin is too old to be my father, right? I mean he's too old that you couldn't get married."

"Oh, I'm afraid so, *mi preciosa.* But you're right, he is a good man, a gentleman. There aren't many like him anymore. Now *duermete m'ija! Buenas noches!*"

Luz went into her room and ironed Ana's blue plaid uniform for the next day. No, she thought, God is not a wish maker, or things would have worked out so differently. For the better, if His power could have directed her to a man who knew how to love her and to care for her and for the precious girl who was already asleep in the next room.

For the worse, too, as she recalled the candles she'd lit before the Virgin at the grotto maintained by the French nuns. There was a book before the trays of silently blazing votives in which people wrote their intentions. So sad. Help daddy get better. *Ayudame María.* Give me your strength. Help me find a job. And she had drawn a pen from her pocketbook and written. "Please, don't let me be pregnant!" God is not a wish maker. Thank God he's not.

After she had showered, she poured a glass of Pinot Grigio, and passing Ana's bedroom, looked in at the sleeping girl. That was when she heard what she did not immediately recognize as a shot, and a brief cry like a bird's call, and a confusion of sounds, a clanging, and something falling heavily on the floor upstairs. She ran into her bedroom, the wine spilling out over her hand and onto her terry cloth robe. As she called 911, she tried to drive the image out of her head, but she couldn't. It was the image of her ex-husband, Al Lekakis, standing over the fallen body of Martin LeBris.

9

Gerry O'Neil caught up with Larry Vega outside The Savoy Lounge. Vega wasn't looking very happy that he had. "Why do you always seem to want to avoid me, Larry?" Gerry asked. "You're gonna give me a complex."

Vega sniffed and spat on the sidewalk. He peered at Gerry suspiciously out of sunken eyes. His dark hair was peppered with gray above the ears, but the Fu Man Chu mustache had gone entirely white. He wore a World Wrestling T-shirt, and a silver bracelet, and as he folded his arms across his chest, Gerry noticed the skull and crossbones on his forearm above the name 'Alice.' He had more ticks and quirks than any five men. He shrugged like a boxer warming up in his corner, stretching his neck one way and then the other. "Last time I saw you, Officer O'Neil, I ended up with my head in a fuckin' bloody turban."

Gerry looked away for a moment, doing his best not to laugh. "All right, so we had a scuffle. That doesn't mean I'm out to get you. You were drunk and disorderly and then you tried to choke an officer. What did you think was going to happen?"

"So that's all you wanted to tell me?" He shrugged and sucked air between his front teeth, making a little squeaky sound.

"I also wanted to give you a chance to do something positive."

"Jesus Christ," Larry said. "I don't know nothin' about anybody else's business." He shrugged and stretched his neck out as if he were wearing a tie that was too tight.

"Larry, you know everyone else's business. You could write a fuckin' book. *Crooked Lowell*, how's that for a title? You know a guy named Al Lekakis?"

Gerry watched his eyes narrow. He shook his head. "No," he said.

"You lying bastard. I've seen you standing outside the Highland Tap talking to him."

"All right, so I know him. I know lots of people."

"How much is he dealing? Who does he work for? Hey, I'm just trying to help this woman, the wife of a friend, whose life he is fucking up big time."

"I shoot the shit with him a little bit. I don't know what he's into. What the hell is this? Trying to help some fucked-up woman? Who do I look like, Dr. Phil?"

"I mean, how would you feel if your mother left you to run off with some scumbag loser drug- dealing wife beater?"

"Not good," Larry admitted, "but I ain't a snitch. I helped you with one thing, and what'd I
get? A crack on the fuckin' noggin."

"You got paid, Larry. It's not my fault you got drunk and crazy and assaulted an officer. Give me a break." He paused and looked away when the door of The Savoy flew open and a bleached blonde in hot pants came out leaning on the arm of a skinny drunk in a leather vest. She was barefoot, carrying her high heels in her hand, stepping gingerly along the sidewalk.

"Listen, I'm tired of this," he continued. "Find out what's up with this guy within two days, or I'm gonna make your life plain miserable. I'll tow your car. I'll follow you around . . . you're on probation for a B and E, right?"

"Yeah, into my own garage! It's a bad divorce, what can I say? This is illegal," Larry said. "In fact, according to my knowledgement of the law, this is harassment."

"Your knowledgement of the law, eh? Then you know it's not only B and E, but violating a restraining order. Won't take much . . ."

"All right, all right. I see what I can find out. Jesus, I didn't know this was such a big deal. I mean, I don't think it's gonna help this woman."

"What, according to your knowledgement of psychology?"

"I mean she made her bed, right?"

"Hey, you may be right, Larry. Just get me up on the low-down," Gerry said.

10

The old man didn't seem to sleep much, but he must have been asleep when he woke to a sound like mice scratching inside the wall, *or something else*. Hannibal raised his head; his ears twitched, and he leaped to the floor and vanished. Martin rose quietly and walked to his dresser, choosing the spots in the floor that did not squeak. He picked up the Llama pistol and moving again to the bed, threw back the covers, arranged the two pillows lengthwise over the mattress, and recovered them. Oldest ruse in the book. He stepped backward, pulled his closet door open, and stood behind it, watching the doorway to the room in the mirror diagonally across the room.

The scratching stopped and he heard a click and the apartment door opening slowly. There was little sound, but he heard the stealthy visitor moving from the kitchen, through the living room library, and toward his room. Carefully, he released the safety on the pistol. In the mirror, he saw a figure appear, and stand there quietly for some time, like some dark statue. Come in, Martin thought, and he did.

He moved as lightly as he could toward the bed, pausing when the old hardwood floor creaked, and shifting his weight slowly. He wore a studded leather jacket. A blond pony tail hung over his back. Martin saw that he was carrying in his gloved hand a foot length of heavy metal pipe which he raised slightly as he approached the bed, and that he was smiling. "*Réveillez-vous, gens qui dormez, Et priez pour les trépassés,*" he said, in a voice that was just above a whisper. In the silence that followed, he seemed to sense that something was amiss; he tore back the covers, and froze for an instant when he saw the pillows.

"Drop the pipe on the bed. Don't turn around," Martin said. He spoke in French.

Karl Hoetger froze for a moment, then turned his head toward Martin, who was moving out from behind the door. He answered in English. "I was just . . . "

"I said don't turn around. Start listening, or I'll drop you cold. Toss the pipe on the bed now, and hold your hands away from your body. Well away."

The other man laughed nervously, the smile now forced, his eyes searching, and his mind calculating the odds. "Of course I will do so. Come on, you are going to hurt someone with that antique." Martin noted the accent. He was German.

He paused then, and Martin knew he would try something stupid. He could hear his breath coming faster. He was too close. There would be no time to give him another warning. "I am dropping it on the..." But Martin sensed the sudden tension of his body, the beginning of a twisting movement, the pipe coming up in his hand. The old man leaned backward, and lost his balance as the muzzle of the old pistol flashed and roared in the dark room. He heard the pipe slam into the wall beside him, and clatter on the wood floor. He found himself sitting between the night table and the closet door, his reading lamp in his lap, and the smoking pistol held out in two hands before him. And while the report of that shot still seemed to reverberate in his ears, he heard his visitor retreating rapidly down the stairs.

He pulled himself to his feet and walked to the kitchen to call the police. The dispatcher said they were already on their way. Luz must have heard. He'd thought that the days of killing were over, and maybe that was why he had hesitated that tenth of a second that had been no doubt the difference between life and death for this intruder. The years had robbed him of his reflexes and maybe of the killer instinct. He remembered once again the wiry Englishman in the OSS armory.

"Oi've tie-ken the sayf-tees owt a' the pistows. Wheah yoh gowin', ye wown nayd 'em. When in dowt, shoot." For years after the war, he'd slept with the Llama under his pillow, still expecting someone to come, but no one ever had come, and now he'd lost the habit of killing, and his hands trembled as he realized that the time had now arrived to reawaken the instinct and to shoot without hesitation.

He went back to the bedroom and looked around quickly. He pulled the pillows out from under the blankets and replaced them at the head of the bed. No sense in letting the cops think that he had been waiting for the bastard.

When Gerry O'Neil arrived, a patrol car was already on the scene as well as Ray Cox's unmarked Crown Vic with the hula dancer on the dashboard. A rookie cop was standing outside the bedroom, putting on the John Wayne swagger. "I've secured the scene, Detective O'Neil," he said.

"Very good, Tom."

"Didn't touch a thing."

"Well done. Is the weapon that was used impounded?"

"I put it in an evidence bag, Sir. He has another pistol."

"We'll need that too. How'd the intruder gain entry?"

"Unlocked window in an apartment downstairs. The tenant is away. Picked the lock to the victim's apartment."

"Hmm. A talented B&E artist."

Gerry gazed quickly at the floor to ceiling bookshelves that lined the walls, and at the piles of folios and magazines stacked in front of them, until his gaze settled on Martin, who rose from the couch as the young officer moved out of the way and pointed in his direction.

"There's Mister LeBris, the inhabitant of the domicile, who fired the shot at the intruder."

"Jesus, Tom, you're even starting to talk like a police report."

"Sorry, Sir. I've written so many lately . . . "

"I know. Thanks, Tom."

Gerry eyed the elderly gentleman, surprised somewhat by his calm demeanor, until he placed his face. They shook hands and the detective said, "I'll be right with you, sir." He stepped into the bedroom, where Ray Cox was already examining the bullet hole high in the wall opposite the bed. Gerry could still taste the gunpowder in the air, the trace of sweetness that hung over many a stiffening corpse.

Ray nodded toward the living room. "Sitting out there drinking coffee like nothing happened."

"He's cool all right," Gerry said in a low voice. "I know who he is – Martin LeBris. Bob Page, the veteran's affairs guy, introduced him to me at the V.F.W. He was OSS. Office of Strategic Services. Parachuted into France in World War II as a spy, served as a liaison between London and the French Resistance."

"Did the French resist?" Ray asked, his eyebrows arched sarcastically.

"Oh yeah, don't let the popular prejudice fool you. There was no shortage of French who stood up. Patton said the Allies couldn't have won the war without them. The Nazis wanted this guy bad. He ran with some group of fighters around Lyon, as I recall. They thought he was French. He was hunted by the Gestapo. You bet he's cool. This burglar had no idea who he was fucking with, old man or not."

"Maybe he did have an idea. Why sneak in at night, with a pipe? Why not wait and burglarize the place when the old man was out?"

"Good point, Ray, but you never know. Crack makes people do funny things." He thought of Cheryl McGuin.

"Crack-heads smash windows," Ray said. "They don't usually pick locks."

"Another good point, Detective. An excellent point, in fact."

"We've met, at the VFW?" Martin asked. They were sitting at Martin's kitchen table. Gerry hadn't thought it necessary to bring him downtown for the interview.

"That's right. Bob Page introduced us."

Martin extended a hand across the table and they shook hands for the second time, "Glad to see you again, brother, especially in this mess. You're a Viet Nam vet, as I recall, Officer O'Neil."

Gerry smiled and said, "Yeah, you want to talk about messes. Call me Gerry, by the way. I won't keep you long. Someone comes in your bedroom in the middle of the night carrying a metal pipe, you'd best take a shot at him, that's the way I look at it. The magic words we have to put in the report, which I think are true by the way, are: 'I was cornered, and in fear of losing my life.'"

The old man nodded, his gray eyes magnified behind his glasses. Looking at him, Gerry thought, you'd never guess what the guy has been through. Just an old French Canadian in a pale blue denim shirt, a former mill worker perhaps. He thought he recalled Bob Page saying that LeBris had retired from the telephone company—worked as a lineman after the war. The old man, his hands folded patiently on the table like a parochial school boy, continued. "I told him to drop the pipe on the bed," he said. "It was in my mind to try not to disturb the young woman downstairs."

"And she says she's sure she heard the pipe slam against the wall and hit the floor, which corroborates your statement that he swung, or threw it at you." He opened a small notebook and pulled a pen from his shirt pocket. "I need to ask you a few questions just because when you shoot at someone in your home, we have to investigate. First of all, where did you get the gun you fired? I know it's registered, but I've never seen one quite like it."

Martin said, "That gun has been with me for a long time, along with the Colt .45, since the war. The day before I parachuted into France, I was taken into the armory with a guy named Perrault, if that was his real name. You never knew, unless someone was introduced as 'Porcupine,' or something."

"This was in the OSS? The forerunner of the CIA?"

He nodded. "Anyway, I selected those two guns."

"They're going to have to test both of them."

"Why, if you don't mind me asking?"

"They have to test them to make sure that the pistol you said you fired was the one you fired."

"Why would I lie about it?" His voice betrayed no emotion or annoyance. Gerry was reminded of Oscar Wilde. *I ask merely for information.*

"You wouldn't. Just regulations. You know some of them don't make sense; it should be fairly obvious which gun you fired from the carbon residue on the barrel, but they always have to double check. I fired my weapon once last year, and they even took mine for a few days." He shook his head and sighed. "Too many lawyers, that's the problem. Anyway, you say this fellow spoke to you? What exactly did he say?"

"He quoted something in French. It's something that used to be said, I don't know if it was on particular nights, like All Saints' Night, or every night, sometimes from the bell tower of a church. Back in medieval times: *"Réveillez-vous, gens qui dormez, Et priez pour les trépassés."*

"Let me see if I can get that," Gerry said, "I had French in high school and college. Wake up, you people who sleep, and pray for . . . trespassers?"

Martin nodded. "Almost. And pray for the dead."

Gerry's brow furrowed. *"Wake up, you who sleep, And pray for the dead.* Who the hell says such a thing? You don't need a crystal ball to see it's not a random break in, Martin. You know that."

"He spoke English too. Told me to calm down, that I'd hurt someone with the gun, 'with that antique,' he said. He had an accent. Sounded German, possibly Dutch or Flemish. I would certainly have liked to hear what else he had to say, but he thought he could knock me down or maybe knock the gun out of my hand before I could kill him. He decided to gamble."

"Smart, but a little reckless?"

"Overconfident, but maybe not. He did survive. He decided I was too old to react, and he was right."

"You keep the gun handy for any reason?"

"To be honest with you, Gerry, I slept with the Llama under my pillow for years after the war. Maybe it was battle fatigue or what they call post traumatic stress these days, but they train you to be, you know, paranoid. And when you live like a hunted rat for a while, it gets in the blood. You can't just turn it off."

"Could you put a name to your fear? I mean when you returned. A specific person or persons? Who were you afraid of, Nazis?"

"Vendettas live a long time in Europe. There are things I did, that I had to do." He paused and Gerry could sense those things rising in the other man's imagination. The younger man knew the feeling, and he recalled the unforgiving ghost that visited him at times, a burning hole in his chest, screaming at him from some hell that he sometimes feared awaited him for what he'd done. Martin continued, "As I get older, I start to be afraid that maybe there is a God, and I wonder will he forgive me, and I know there may be others who won't."

"If we hadn't had men like you, Martin, the death camps might have rolled on for who knows how much longer."

"Don't you ever wonder what your life would have been like if they hadn't sent you . . . if you didn't have to go to war?"

Gerry nodded gravely, but did not reply, feeling Martin would continue, and he did. "It was a different world. Things that don't make sense now, or that seem incomprehensible, were commonplace then. You see, when you joined the Resistance, you knew that there was one very simple rule. If you betrayed the cause, you were dead. That was an absolute. No exceptions. That's the way it was, and that's the way it had to be because it was tough enough fighting the Germans without fighting saboteurs or collaborators within the group."

Martin remembered Daniel DuRivage and his twin brother Roget, the two of them on their knees in the woods, begging for forgiveness. They had stolen a crate of counterfeit money and been caught. Martin could not pass the order off to anyone else.

He executed them. They were buried in the thin swaths of light that shone from the two dark lanterns; only the scraping of shovels in the earth broke the silence of the wood – spectral figures lowering the limp bodies of their friends to those dark, narrow cells. They had now lain there for over half a century, and their imploring voices were as clear in his ears as ever they had been.

"Do you have any reason to think that these people could have followed you after the war, or known who you were?"

"The truth is, I doubt it. My records are sealed at Quantico. If you were to request them, you'd get a date of entry and a date of discharge, and a lot of blank paper. So the sleeping with guns and looking over my shoulder all the time probably was paranoia, but paranoia became a habit over there, reinforced every day because it helped you stay alive."

"I'd very much like to know what the hell he wanted. But my instincts tell me that you're telling the truth and that you did the right thing. We're going to put you up at a hotel for a few days until we find out if anyone else wants to wake you up with a weapon, and why."

"One other thing, Gerry. I haven't aimed a pistol at anyone since 1945. I'm afraid I've done so recently, once before tonight. A few weeks ago, a drunken lout, estranged husband of the young woman who lives downstairs came by. He had his hands on her throat, and I used the gun to get him to leave."

"Yeah, Luz Morales," Gerry said. "I've already taken her statement. She's very worried that this guy was sent by her ex, Al Lekakis, an idiot with whom I'm well acquainted. But, I don't think your visitor is connected with Al. The medieval French thing . . . "

"No, this is something else."

"But you have no specific idea what?"

"None."

There was no hesitation. Gerry looked into his eyes, but could see no guile. He liked Martin, and wanted to believe everything he said, but he reminded himself that a professional spy, a guy who had fooled the French and the Nazis, would hardly find it difficult to fool a detective from the Lowell Police Department.

"Let me get you over to the hotel, just for a few days. We'll get some new locks on your doors, and deadbolts."

"Fine with me. I don't want to be here while my guns are impounded. But I have a cat."

"I'll feed him for a couple of days, if it's OK with you. Even change his litter box if I have to." As he rose, he added, "After the war, you were a lineman for the telephone company?"

"Please, Gerry. The power company. We called the telephone guys 'ladder linemen' or 'clothes linemen,' you know, anything to put them down. They were below us on the pole, literally and figuratively."

"You like the dangerous jobs, eh Martin?"

"Well, they had the safety regulations. But if you wanted to get home, you had to pay attention, be cognizant of what was going on around you."

"Well, then they hired the right guy."

11

Gerry's girlfriend, Gina Santtuchio, was one of the first to buy an "artist's loft" condo in the old mill buildings along the Merrimack River, just behind the downtown. At first, it struck Gerry as too spacious, like living with furniture set up on a basketball court, but after moving in with her, he'd gradually grown accustomed to, and even fond of the high space, and of the long windows that overlooked the river as it broke over a sunken spine of rocks. In the winter, as the snow slanted across their glass lengths, he felt as if he were inside one of those glass balls that when shaken, creates a tiny blizzard in a self-contained world. As the seasons wheeled along, the walls of the loft were hung with new images of light and color, which were refracted and reflected in his own soul as he watched: *that time of year thou mayest in me behold.*

Gina was a freelance writer with a steady column for *Metro Magazine* on the music scene called *City Vibes.* They'd met at The Lowell Folk Festival after Gerry's divorce. He was on detail, wearing his uniform, when she'd run up to him, concerned about an older man she feared was suffering from sun stroke. After the paramedics had arrived, they began to converse, and by the weekend he had fallen like a schoolboy. Though she was close to his age, she retained a youthful energy which together with her intelligence made her an ideal companion.

She was fun; unlike his ex-wife, who had somehow moved from moderately religious to Holy Roller over the years. She had begun to take the Bible so seriously that she seemed to feel the safest path to heaven was through perpetual suffering, manifested by perpetual complaining. It became increasingly difficult for him to compete with her real love, God. When their son, Hugh, went off to college, Gerry formalized the separation that had effectively begun years earlier. Gina had also had an unsuccessful marriage, briefer than his; her nine-year-old son Matt was with his father this weekend.

Gerry put down the paper and hooked his reading glasses over the collar of his Red Sox T- shirt. He picked up his glass of wine and walked toward the island, where Gina was sautéing vegetables over a blue flame. "Smells great," he said.

"You're so easy to please. Do you like this music?"

"You know I do. Alison Krauss. She played the Folk Festival the year we met there."

"Yeah. I could listen to her for hours. She has such a lovely voice."

"Hell of a fiddler, too."

She laid the wooden spoon on the counter and picked up her wine. "You know, I couldn't believe you were a cop when we first met."

"Why? Wait, I know. You never thought a cop would hit on an attractive woman."

"I mean, you were rereading Shakespeare's history plays in your spare time. You were quoting Keats to me."

"*A thing of beauty is a joy forever*. And you expected a cop to be telling you what a great sport wrestling really is."

"Something like that." She lowered the flame, then bent to peer through the glass into the lit oven. "The fish will be done in a minute."

"Not your typical cop. Not your typical soldier. The story of my life. I remember in the Army, I was reading George Santayana on the flight from Boston to South Carolina, heading to basic training at Fort Jackson. So this ugly bastard gung-ho D.I. bellowed at us to empty the bags we had brought with us from "the world" onto the dirt road in front of the barracks. He gave a cursory glance at each pile and kicked it, probably looking for dope. All the time he was yelling at us dumbstruck draftees, 'You are here for one reason and for one reason only! To replace the soldiers who are coming back from Nam in body bags!'"

Gina grimaced and inhaled sharply. "How awful," she said.

He continued, warming to his story. "Our diligent host, from some obscure corner of the military collective unconscious, paused at the pile I displayed. His cretin mind . . . "

Gina sensed that Gerry was on a roll, and she slapped the counter, her shoulders shaking with laughter, trying not to spit out her wine.

"His cretin mind sensed a threat to its cosmology as he looked from the pile to his long- haired, mustached inductee, and said, 'Wass this, you Yankee puke? A book? Are you bringin' a godamn book to basic training?' 'Yes, Sir,' stammered the Yankee puke. 'I thought . . . ' 'You thought? You *thought*? You don't *thought* in the U.S. Army, boy! Pick up that book! Give it here!'"

"Oh, no! What was the name of the book?"

"The work in question, by George Santayana, was called *The Sense of Beauty*."

"Oh, you poor guy!"

"What the living fuck is this piece of shit? *The Sense of Beauty*? I'll show you a fucking sense of beauty, you Yankee faggot!' He proceeded to dance on the tome of aesthetics, and to kick it through the dirt and dry dust the length of Bravo 22's parade and formation area."

When she had stopped laughing, Gina said, "You don't talk that way at the station, do you? 'His cretin mind sensed a threat to its cosmology?'"

"No, I do not."

"Do you get tired of hiding who you are?"

"I don't think of it that way. Some people communicate on one level, some people on another. You have to communicate with people at the level at which they feel comfortable. But it is great being with a woman who's even smarter than I am."

"Flattery will get you everywhere."

"Oscar Wilde. One of my favorites."

"But why a cop?"

"Was Oscar Wilde a cop?"

"Seriously."

"I like it. I mean, can you picture me as a teacher? Selling insurance?"

"No. Nor a lawyer like my ex."

"Hey, it's only ninety-nine percent of lawyers who give the rest a bad name. My job is varied. Sometimes I actually help people. We, modern people, have this idea that the man of ideas and the man of action are distinct and separate. That there's something feminine about the intellect."

"Thus the Yankee faggot."

"Precisely. But Ophelia said that Hamlet was a soldier and a scholar, which seems a natural combination in him. The warriors of the ancient Irish Fianna were all expected to be able to recite the twelve books of poetry."

"What twelve books of poetry?"

"I don't know, but I know they had to be able to recite them. I'm working on a case now; I have to tell you about it. This guy, Martin LeBris. He parachuted into occupied France for the Office of Strategic Services, tangled with the Nazis, lived on the run over there, a legitimate hero, and his apartment looks like the city library. A soldier and a scholar. OSS was full of them. I mean you had to have language skills and a pretty high I.Q. to get in."

"This is the guy who fired at the intruder?"

"The *armed* intruder."

"How dreadful. What did that guy want?"

"Not sure yet."

She opened the oven while Gerry took out two plates from the cupboard and set them on the counter. "Well you two are birds of a feather. I just hope you don't end up like poor Hamlet."

"Ah, well. The readiness is all." He winked at her. "And you know I'm always ready."

He raised his glass. A flight of sparrows cast fleeting shadows as they passed the great window. She set the tray of fish on the stove, raised her own, and tapped his with a soft clink.

"Here's lookin' at you, kid," he said.

12

Outside of Lyon, France, March 1944

Martin consulted the map and in the daylight realized where he was in relation to what had been the proposed drop zone. He had memorized a telephone number in the event that he missed the DZ and the *maquisards*, or Resistance fighters, who were to have met him. He still had his identity papers, but they were a wreck, damp and wrinkled, since he had landed in the Rhône and almost drowned in the bilious folds of his own chute. The papers, the carefully reproduced French civilian clothes, the two pistols strapped inside the realistically tattered short coat were all he carried. But more important was what he carried in his head – guerilla warfare tactics, escape and evasion techniques, spycraft, radio operation, number stations, transposition cyphers, a new identity and a meticulously constructed and carefully memorized back story.

He threw his sack over his shoulder and left the shelter of the hills. He passed along a narrow path cut into the hill that led down to a winding road where an old man trundled toward him pushing a two-wheeled cart, the contents covered with a piece of filthy burlap.

"Bonjour Monsieur. Fait beau, eh?"

"C'est vrai, M'sieur."

He turned and watched the man, bent over his load, moving up the road. What was he transporting in the cart? Thirty pounds of potatoes . . . or a two- way radio? Collaborators, communists, Gaulists, spies, counterspies and those who only wanted to survive. They were all here, and it was impossible to know who was who. On the road, he headed west, toward St. Luc, if he were correct. An old woman in a flowered dress, peddling a bicycle came into view. *"Bonjour, Madame!"* he called as she approached.

She stopped and seemed to want to pass a few moments in conversation. She explained that for many years she had delivered mail on her bicycle to the inhabitants of the three villages along this mountain road. "What three villages?" Martin asked.

"Burzet, St. Luc, Giron." She waved an arm in the air, indicating the road that snaked through the mountains. "I knew you were not from these parts," she said. "I've never seen you. But of course with the war, there are strangers everywhere, running here and there. Where are you from, *Monsieur*?" Her old eyes were warm and open, but of course her heart was hidden.

"From Bretagne, originally," he said.

"All the way from Bretagne? Imagine that! Well, to each one his destiny. I've never been beyond these mountains, but my brother, oh, he has traveled. He's been to Paris!"

"Paris! Well, he is a traveler, that's certain. My automobile broke down on me. I wish I had a bicycle like you. I'm just headed into the village to use a telephone. St. Luc, is it?"

"Oui, Monsieur. It's not far for a strong man like you, just a couple of kilometers. There's a phone in the post office. Tell them you're a friend of Mathilde's."

"Merci, Mathilde," And to tie up loose ends he called out, "Can you recommend a good mechanic?"

"I've never had an automobile, *Monsieur*, but I think LeFevre is the only one."

When the town came into view, he stepped off the road, and ate the rest of what he'd bought from a peasant for a few francs. He tossed the empty sack and bottle into the bushes. Not long after, he was in a telephone booth at the post office. He dialed the number. "*Allo bonjour*," said a woman's voice.

He recited the sentence he had memorized several weeks before. "It's Claude. I'm very sorry to tell you that my mother has died," Martin said.

"I'm very sorry, Claude. I will say a prayer for her soul to *Notre Dame de Neiges* on the mountain this very evening."

Martin ambled through the narrow streets, feeling the scrutiny of a few of the inhabitants. He spotted the elongated red diamond of a tobacconist shop, the word TABAC written vertically down its face. He entered and asked the elderly woman in a drab gray dress for a pack of Galloises, and a box of matches. A group of men were playing *boules* in a small square under a chestnut tree, laughing, and talking loudly as the large steel balls rolled toward the small wooden jack, which they called the "cochonnet," or "little pig."

A picture of peace. He walked slowly up and joined the onlookers, thinking he might pick up some intelligence or even deduce a contact. He was soon gesticulating and laughing with them, assuming their attitudes. When the local priest passed by in his black soutane, the men paused in their game, and Martin took off his hat along with the others, wishing him a good afternoon.

He noticed that someone had left a newspaper on a bench nearby. *La Voix du Midi*. He lit a cigarette and picked up the paper. A quick look through it showed it to be not the voice of the South, but the voice of collaboration. Laval vows to hunt down troublemakers. Jewish instigators in the pay of Moscow disrupt telephone communications in the Rhône Valley. Germans offer assistance in hunting down terrorists. One of the players approached him. He had the look of the young intellectual; his slim physique lost in loose trousers and suit coat, battered shoes, black wavy hair, and spectacles that suggested the scholar. For all that, he struck Martin as the sort of fellow who might be ready for a fight.

"I'm sorry, *Monsieur*, am I reading your paper?" Martin asked.

He snorted. "Do you think I would read that trash?"

"I beg your pardon, *Monsieur*, I didn't mean to offend you."

"Give me a cigarette?"

"Certainly." Martin shook a cigarette from the pack and held it out to the Frenchman. He pulled it out and flipped it into his mouth. Martin struck a match.

"*Merci, Monsieur.*" He inclined his head to the flame.

"I'm just going over to the café to kill some time. Will you join me for a *pastis*?" Martin asked.

The young man was looking past Martin as a vehicle roared into the square. Then he melted into the crowd without a word, one hand buried in his pocket, the other cupping the cigarette to his lips. Martin's heart picked up its pace as he turned and saw the black cross on a German reconnaissance vehicle. A long antenna curved upward behind the turret on which a 20 mm gun was mounted. A DF, Direction Finder, prowling the area in search of unauthorized radio transmissions. The vehicle paused in the town center, its occupants no doubt watching the men at their game. Martin picked up the newspaper. It was too late to move.

He heard the hatches opening and men clambering on its body. The sound of the German language filled him with a vague dread. The engine idled in the street behind him; he turned the pages of the paper slowly. They must be scouring the area within range of the shoot down, and he cursed himself for not having hidden until evening. A couple of Germans were making their way toward the crowd of men, while another went into the tobacco shop. Martin watched the villagers. Some were trying to continue the game as if nothing was happening. Others stood and smiled innocently, and a few eyed the approaching soldiers with ill-disguised malice.

Martin's mind turned back to the books he had read in his youth. *The Indian Wars.* Unbidden, the words that Crazy Horse was said to have spoken before Little Big Horn rose to his mind. *It is a good day to die.* He laid the newspaper down against his chest and slid his hand inside his oversized suit coat, his fingers just touching the Llama's grip. He cast a casual glance about for an escape route. Mountains, steep, but only three or four hundred feet, rose directly behind the row of businesses that lined the market square. Near the summit of one, Martin saw a gleam of white. The statue of the Virgin.

His papers, still damp, would arouse suspicion. They would know that a plane was shot down over the river. No, if they asked for his papers, they would get lead. If he could kill them both before they shot him, he would be running across the square, up the shallow steps, through the alley and into the hills beyond, or perhaps into a dead end, where – he decided not to think of that yet. There would be time. And he knew what had to be done; spies could not fall into Gestapo hands. He cursed himself, thinking that his mission might end here before it had begun. He remembered Perrault's last words as he boarded the Liberator: "If you see a shell casing over there, pick it up. It's worth two cents. Your life ain't worth nothin'."

He looked past the newspaper he held folded over one hand, seeing the gray uniforms, the red stripes, the cold blue-black steel of gun barrels. With cold curiosity, he read the silver thread on the coat cuff *Gross Deutchland*. Greater Germany. "Vous!" one of the Germans called out.

Martin's finger slid onto the trigger. *Where yor gowin' you wown need a sayfety*. True enough. He looked up, slowing his breathing, expecting to see the soldier pointing at him, and settling his mind on slaughter. But a Frenchman had already come forward and in apologetic tones began telling the men, very slowly, that the *eau de vie* was all gone, but that his cousin would have some more soon. The soldiers spoke to each other in German, and then the smaller of the two, in halting French, told the Frenchman to save them a case, and that they would pay him for it.

The quiet German was scanning the crowd. He spoke to the other, and the smaller man said, "A plane was shot down last night and we believe there were survivors. Has anyone seen a stranger in the area who may say that his car broke down?"

The old woman on the road had informed. Perhaps involuntarily, the Frenchman who had sold the *eau de vie* shot a glance at Martin. The Germans followed his gaze and took a step toward him. He began to calculate the odds rapidly. He saw the taller of the two men tug on his gun strap and begin to lower the Schmeisser MP40 submachine gun off his shoulder. They were accurate to about 400 yards, which was four times the distance across the open square to the row of houses and the mountains beyond. He hoped that the third soldier, who had gone into the store and had not yet emerged, was the one who would have manned the turret gun and that there was not a fourth sitting inside the vehicle watching. The shorter of the two men had a normal five shot bolt action Mauser, still slung over his shoulder.

"*Monsieur!*" he said.

The American raised his eyes innocently. "*C'est moi qu'on appelle?*" Are you talking to me?

The calm of the afternoon was shattered as Martin's newspaper seemed to explode; bits of paper flew about like confetti whipped from his hands by a sudden gust, revealing the naked pistol that continued to flash. The soldier who had just been leveling the submachine gun fired as he fell, an arc of shots that dropped a man in the crowd and tore into the leaves of the branches overhead. Martin drew the .45 and kept firing out of both guns. He shot the other German who was desperately shouting something as he threw back the bolt on the Mauser. A Frenchman who had been hit was writhing on the ground nearby and howling, "*Putain de merde!*"

More shots rang out, so close to him that he thought he must be hit, or about to die, but as the second German fell, Martin saw the slim Frenchman who had asked him for a cigarette down on one knee, firing the submachine gun he'd taken from the dead man in the direction of the vehicle. Across the square, the machine gunner, already lowering his legs into the turret, fell backward as red holes exploded across his back and convulsed his body, which now hung upside down from the turret, arms stretched toward the earth, blood already running in thin streams from the fingertips.

The gunfire ceased, and the only sound that broke the stillness was the helmet of the dead gunner bouncing on the running board and clattering onto the paving stones, and then the afternoon held its breath, save for a barking dog in a nearby yard. The wounded Frenchman who had been shouting imprecations at Martin, or at the Germans, or at heaven, was silent now, while the others lay trembling on the ground or crouched behind the chestnut trees about the square, their arms covering their heads, as if that would stop the bullets. They heard the dog barking and then the staccato of boots resounding through the cobbled square, and when they raised their eyes slowly, or peeked from behind the trunks, they saw dead Germans, and two men sprinting hard for the mountains.

13

Gerry O'Neil walked toward the courthouse, coffee in one hand and a notebook in the other. The trees that lined the sidewalk whispered among themselves under a pale sky. Dickie Albert on Channel Five had warned of sudden showers, but so far the sky only threatened. The usual array of losers, alleged perps, haunted-looking victims, heavily tattooed gangsters, and probation violators who appeared terminally hung over, loitered about the stone steps and leaned on the iron railings, smoking cigarettes or talking on cell phones.

He winked at the security guard, whose light blue shirt stretched over a considerable paunch. "Morning, Gerry," he said, and signaled him to go around the metal detector.

"Are you wearing your parachute in front now, Teddy?"

The guard smiled to reveal smoke-stained teeth. He rubbed his belly and said, "That's good livin', O'Neil."

"I gotta sign you up at the Y," he said. "How you gonna chase down Al Qaeda suspects with that bread basket?"

The guard laughed good-naturedly and repeated, "Good livin'."

He went downstairs and through the glass doors that led to the Probation Department, addressing himself to the secretary who sat at a metal desk under pictures of two smiling plump-faced children. "Lieutenant O'Neil to see Mr. Trivedi." The secretary, a young Asian woman with an efficient and professional air, said, "He's in his office, Lieutenant. Just go on in."

"Thank you," he said, as she smiled pertly and turned back to her computer screen.

Dom Trivedi stretched out a chubby hand, which Gerry took. "Have a seat, detective. You need a refill on the coffee?"

"No, I just got it. By the way, thanks for giving me the heads up on the McCormack case."

"No problem. You hear a lot on this job. All right, then." Gerry noticed that the crossword puzzle in *The Herald* was half filled out on Trivedi's desk. Seeing him looking at it, the heavy man asked, "A lover's quarrel-four letters?"

"Spat."

The other man slapped his forehead and said, "Of course. I was drawing a blank. So anyway, I ran that offer by Hector Tamayo. I told him we'd bring his case forward and get the judge to terminate his probation if he came up with some information on Lekakis."

"Some good information."

"Naturally. He bit on that deal right away. He fuckin' hates comin' in here to see me. I can't imagine why. Plus, I used to check on him where he lives. Christ what a dump. I was afraid of bringing cockroaches home."

Gerry nodded. "So what'd he come up with?"

"He says Lekakis is doing some coke dealing and that he carries shit into Boston for the Colombians. He didn't have any names, but he says they hang out at The Tic Toc Club. Lekakis carries it, and they throw him a half ounce, or a big wad of cash. Easier than roofing."

"He carries cocaine?"

"And sometimes cash, probably some weed, whatever."

Gerry was writing in his notepad. He stopped and looked at Dom. "Lekakis is Greek, right? I've never even heard of a Greek drug dealer. What's his connection with the Colombians? I don't get it."

"I asked Tamayo the same thing. Said he grew up on Salem Street in the Acre and learned Spanish on the street. His parents are old school, hard-working, run a tailor shop on Broadway. He just went bad. You get bad apples among the Greeks, the Irish, . . ."

"Go on, Dominic, the Italians . . . "

Dom grinned and shrugged, raising his plump hands. "The Italians, Gerry? The best and the worst of the human race."

Gerry thought for a moment, his pen tapping the armrest of the chair. He sipped his coffee and looked at his notebook, which was still blank, except for the words 'Tic Toc Club,' and 'runner.' "Did Tamayo say where he deals out of?"

"Oh yeah. He mentioned that he used to go to Powers' Bar, The Rainbow, but he got barred from there, and he's been doing business at the Tap Room in Cupples Square. But he ain't stupid. He hides his stash, and he can spot a tail."

Gerry clicked the pen shut and put it in his shirt pocket. He closed the notebook. "A Greek drug dealer," he said. "Strange."

"Gerry, like Jim Morrison said, people are strange."

14

Gerry was having lunch at the station and reading Alex Beam's column in *The Globe* when he got a call from Ray Cox. "That guy you're lookin' for – I spotted him heading east on Westford. I just followed him to the Tap Room in Cupples Square. He's inside now."

"Thanks, Ray. Keep an eye on his truck. I'll be there in five minutes."

He hopped into the Crown Vic, shot up Broadway to Wilder with the lights flashing and pulled up in front of The Kampong Cham Market in Cupples Square. There was the roofing truck in front of the Tap Room. He saw Ray, who got out of his car to join him.

Gerry took off his sunglasses as his eyes adjusted to the dim light inside, a big room with a bar in the center and a pool table on one side, presided over by a framed poster of Irish Micky Ward, the Pride of Lowell, fists raised, wearing his Light Welterweight Champion's belt. A few city workers he knew sat at the bar having a "liquid lunch" and watching the Keno screen, while a drunk played pool with a woman in a tube top who showed off a tattoo of a unicorn on her back above the top of the thong she exposed as she leaned over the table. The city workers nodded and nudged each other; something was up. They were quicker on the uptake than the bartender, a tall skinny guy with sideburns and thin wisps of hair floating over his cranium.

"We're looking for Al Lekakis." Ray Cox was peering around and opening the men's room door.

"Who are you?"

Gerry flashed the badge. "Lowell police."

"What do you want Al for?"

The detective stared at the bartender coldly for a few seconds and leaned over the bar. "Don't fuck with me. Where's Al?"

"Well, he was here."

"I'm losing patience with this guy, Ray."

"Let's arrest him for obstructing an investigation."

"Wait a minute. Wait a minute," the bartender said, raising his palms in a gesture that was meant to convey innocence. "He's in the cellar. I don't know why." He pointed to a door in the back.

"Everybody stay where you are," Ray said to the men who had begun to rise and follow them toward the door. Only the drunk leaning crookedly over the pool table seemed oblivious to the tension, and kept up his monologue, "I'll clear the table like fuckin' Allison Fisher! That babe can shoot pool! Eight ball or nine ball! Run the fuckin' table! Thass what I'm talking about!" The cue slid sideways off the ball as he struck it weakly; he uttered a hoarse laugh and cried "Ah shit!" The girl in the tube top nudged him and directed his wavering gaze toward the cellar door where Ray Cox stood with his right hand inside his jacket.

Gerry walked down the stairs quietly and looked across the cellar. The light from a high window fell on a shaggy-haired man who was leaning over a pile of boxes. He was wearing a Patriots T-shirt and there was an empty hammer holster on his belt. A blonde woman in white jeans was standing beside him with her back to the detective. The spaghetti straps of a powder blue camisole exposed the frailty of her shoulders. Al Lekakis was snorting lines of coke off a piece of paper unfolded on the top box. He rose, sniffing and pinching his nose, and handed a rolled bill to the woman.

"When they said you were a fuckin' loser, Al, they weren't kidding."

The woman jumped backward against the pile of boxes, crying, "What the fuck!" Her face fell when she saw him, because it was Cheryl McGuin. Gerry saw that Lekakis was leaning over, stuffing paper into his mouth. By the time he had his hands on him, he had raised a bottle of Budweiser and was washing the evidence down his gullet.

A search warrant produced nothing at the Tap Room, so if Al was dealing out of that hole, he wasn't stupid enough to stash his supply there. Gerry brought him and Cheryl down to the station, but eventually had to let them go, so as not to waste the department's time trying to prosecute a guy on coke dust. Before he released them, he spoke to them separately. Cheryl, if she was ashamed, did a good job of hiding it, though she may have still been a bit amped up on the nose candy. She reverted to the old "It's my life," routine, and intimated that he didn't understand her background, the difficulties she faced, or the challenges of her marriage, all of which was true.

"I understand one thing." He handed her two three by five photos of her children, Ashley and Eddie grinning on a beach with the ocean, a finger of blue behind them. Maybe that had been the trip to Martha's Vineyard that McGuin remembered. "Your kids love you. Maybe you had a hard life. Don't you want to make theirs better?"

Tears gathered in her eyes, but she wiped them quickly with trembling fingers and said, "Am I free to go now, officer?" She clutched a packet of Marlborough Lights in her trembling hand and Gerry sensed that she was dying to get outside and suck one down.

"Let me tell you one thing, as a friend, Cheryl. A couple of months ago, I got a call that a body had been discovered leaning against a rock at the top of Fort Hill. I went up there and, well there he was, thirty-five years old. The needle was still hanging out of his arm, and in his hands he held a photo of his kids. His dead eyes were still looking at them. There was a rosary entwined in his cold fingers. It didn't take a detective to see he loved those kids, but the dope was too strong for him. He couldn't do it alone."

She snatched the photos out of his hand and crammed them into her bag. "Look, O'Neil, I really really have to go."

He heaved a sigh and said, "Yeah, get out of here. I'm wasting my breath. I'm not talking to a person, much less a mother. I'm talking to an addict. I'm only telling you this for your own good, Cheryl. You don't look good."

"Whatever. Let me worry about me."

She picked up her Diet Coke and the leather bag stuffed, as his search had revealed, with hair brushes, hand cream, lip glosses, a compact, cigarettes, and the two photos, and was gone.

Al Lekakis got a different warning. "Number one: we know you're dealing. Number two: you're messing with dangerous people. Number three: you're fucking up the lives of your ex-wife and of Cheryl McGuin."

"Because I have some Colombian friends I'm a drug dealer? That's racist, officer."

"You're a drug dealer because you sell drugs to people, not because your friends are Colombian."

Gerry turned off the tape recorder. He signaled for him to get up, and opened the door. He followed him out onto the JFK Plaza, out of view of the two-way mirror and out of range of other ears. "One more thing, *Lick-kakas*, if you ever call me a racist again, I'll bang your head on the floor until we have to mop up what little brains spill out."

"I can sue you for threatening me, officer."

"Yeah well, you know what they say, *one witness, no witness.* When I tell you you're fucking with the wrong people, it's not just the Colombians I'm talking about. I'll be watching you, asshole."

Al smiled and said, "Can I have a nice day, officer?" He turned, and Gerry watched him until he crossed the street and disappeared into the Old Worthen.

"Punk," Gerry said.

15

The stranger led the way, and Martin followed. They ran for one hour on mountain paths where they had to pass single file between enormous boulders. They hopped from rock to rock across a rushing mountain stream and gaining the opposite bank, stood on an outcropping of granite, watching *les bergers,* the shepherds, in the valley below leading a flock to some mountain pasture.

"*Elle est jolie, non, La France?*" the Frenchman asked. *Isn't France beautiful?* Martin nodded, smiling for the first time, and mopping his brow with the suit coat he carried in his hand, revealing the two pistols strapped to his chest nearly under his arms.

They paused there to rest, and Martin said, "Thank you for your help, which was very timely. Who are you?"

"They call me Marius. And I suppose you are one of those who fell from the sky?" He made a whistling noise like an incoming missile, and a vertical motion with his hand to indicate something falling.

"Yes. Patrice Quenton. Thank you, Marius. I have some business near here tonight, but I suppose we should put some more distance between us and *les Boches.*"

He pursed his lips and blew out his cheeks in that peculiarly Gallic expression. "*Bon, bah* . . . it doesn't matter. They won't waste their time chasing us here. They thought they might catch you if you were foolish enough to have a radio transmitting for some time, or if they could locate a house where someone in one of the villages was trying to contact you."

Marius unslung the machine gun and laid it on the ground. He walked toward a tree, and standing with his back to Martin, spoke over his shoulder. "But to chase us through the mountains? It's not the way they operate. I regret to say that it is more likely that they will go back to the town and shoot some of the civilians there or that Klaus Barbie or Horst Grahamar of the Gestapo may just choose twenty prisoners in Montluc Prison and have them shot in the courtyard. That's the way they do it."

He shrugged, his back still toward Martin, looking over the valley. "Well, the hour has arrived to purchase liberty with blood, and there's no room for anyone in France who's not willing to pay the price." He turned, buttoning his fly, and picked up the machine gun, looking along its barrel with an appreciative eye. "I think we have ammo for this, too." Then, turning to Martin, he asked, "Who will you contact?"

"I missed the *rendez-vous*. Eventually, with CCL."

He stretched out a hand and said, "Then we'll see each other again, in Lyon, I'm sure." They shook hands, and Martin embraced him warmly. "Damned fine shooting, Marius," he said.

"Always happy to kill *les Boches*. You know how to find your way?"

Martin looked at the sun, and the surrounding hills broken by gray outcroppings and tumbling into green fields dotted with blue cornflowers, all spread before him like a Cézanne landscape. "The village we've come from is that way, *non*?"

"Exactly."

"*Au revoir*."

"*Au revoir, Patrice.*" A moment later, Martin was alone with the sound of rushing water and the "Tchet! Tchet!" of a yellow venturon that watched him from a thorny branch. He pried the cap from a button on his coat. It opened to reveal a tiny compass, which he consulted, fixing his position. The sudden departure of Marius had left him with a deep feeling of loneliness, but he shook it off and rushed again into the woods, where light spilled through the shifting branches of oak and maple. He moved warily toward the rendez-vous.

A stone stairway led up the mountain to a towering figure of the Virgin, which stood on a raised pedestal. The mother of Christ, all white, loomed above him, spectral against the firmament, her face uplifted, her hands outstretched to her people. The moonlit clouds surging along in the mistral gave him the impression that the ghostly figure was moving, or that he was moving. Both, he thought, were true. There was a small plaque below the statue.

As the moon emerged from the racing clouds, Martin read, "*Notre Dame des Neiges, priez pour nous.*" Our Lady of the Snows, pray for us. Martin recalled the nuns of his childhood at St. Louis de France School, their devotion to the Virgin, and the prayers they taught the bright-faced students: "*O Marie, tabernacle et ciboire de Jesus, donnez-moi la force.*" O Mary, tabernacle and chalice of Jesus, give me strength. The words were no longer a rote recitation, but his own prayer for courage.

Somewhere below the sweeping wind, he heard a soft footfall on the stone stairs, and he slid into shadows, his hand gliding reflexively onto the cool grip of the Llama. A young woman stepped into the mountain grotto, carrying something wrapped in cloth. She blessed herself and bowed her head in prayer before the ghostly Mother of God. Could she be a *maquisard*, his contact, or just a woman from the village offering her petition to *Notre Dame des Neiges*? A vehicle wound along the road below, two lights tracing a serpentine route through the black mountains.

After a moment, she raised her head. He heard her whisper to the ghostly image above them, "*Notre Dame des Neiges, mon coeur est à vous.*" My heart is yours. He stepped into the grotto as if he were stepping onto a moonlit stage. Sensing his presence, she blessed herself again and turned to face him. They looked at each other in silence for several seconds, during which it occurred to Martin that this woman standing motionless in the shifting shadows cast as the clouds raced past the moon, with her dark hair pulled back tightly, her large and solemn eyes and her aquiline nose, was Maríanne – the image of *La France Libre*. Her light shawl moved in the wind.

"*Conaissez-vous l'aurore?*" he asked. Do you know the dawn?

She nodded slowly. "*Doux rayon, triste et rechauffant.*" Gentle ray, sad and warming.

At last. He hadn't expected a woman, but hearing the response he'd memorized at Lockwood Hall was gratifying. Her name was Odette, or at least that was the name she gave him; she was a member of the *maquis* group know as CCL: *Le Coeur de la Croix de Lorraine*. Special Operations Executive in London had been in contact principally with an operative known only by the name BEC 22, but the group was large enough to have transmitted information from patrols in several vital sectors of France.

Before they spoke more, she bent and opened the cloth sack. Martin watched carefully, his hand moving to his pistol once again. Bread, *saucisson*, a piece of cheese, and a half-bottle of wine. "God bless you, Odette," he said, as he knelt to eat.

Martin spent the night with Odette in a barn belonging to a man called Roland, a friend of hers, and a supporter of the local *maquisards*. The barn, like the farm itself, was cut into the base of a terraced mountain. Odette said that the barn was occasionally used as a safe house, and that they would take to the mountains again in the morning.

During the night, he was awakened by the squeal of a door moving stiffly on rusted hinges. The corner where Odette had lain was empty. The pistol by his head was quickly in his hand; he slid through the dark toward an aperture where a thin shaft of moonlight flowed into the barn.

He waited, entirely awake as he heard footsteps approach. She hardly seemed surprised to see him standing, gun in hand, by the door, but she looked up at him and whispered, "I had to pee." As she settled in her corner, she added, "Pardon me if I worried you, Patrice."

"Everything worries me, Odette. Everything." He remembered his encounter with the Germans in the square. Stupid. He must never be in such a position until he could acquire new papers.

"That's good. It's the ones who are not worried who are picked up."

Martin seemed hardly to have slept when he heard a deep voice rasping out *La Marseillaise*, and saw Roland's figure outlined in the brightening doorway, a cigarette dropping ash over the tray he carried. He brought some insipid coffee, a couple of slices of bread, and some cheese. "Hard to get real coffee," Roland explained. "This is Hitlerian coffee, fifteen ounces of tree bark, one ounce of coffee." After they had eaten, he returned and put a bottle of wine and a half baguette and a map in Odette's pack, which Martin slung over his shoulder.

They thanked him and climbed back into the mountains. The farm seemed remote enough from the center of the village, but they walked for hours on narrow paths and finally through trackless woods and hillsides. As they hiked along, Martin reviewed carefully and in detail various stories of his identity and tried to recall the lectures he'd heard on the organizational structure of resistance, but he found himself concentrating instead on the feminine shape before him and, as the sun rose higher and she shed her shawl, on the gentle curves of her hips and the body that moved beneath the dress.

When they stopped to eat, Martin checked his compass and examined the map that Roland had thrown in the sack. He asked Odette to point out their current position and the route they would take. She looked over the map for a few seconds, and when Martin saw a perplexed expression cross her face, he said, "Odette, don't tell me you're lost."

"I know exactly where I'm going," she said. "I'm just getting my bearings."

"I don't mean this as an insult, and I hope you don't take it that way, but why send a woman . . . "

"To do a man's job?" It was clear to Martin that he had insulted her.

He remembered the young woman he had trained with in OSS camp in Scotland. She was known to them as China, and weighed all of ninety-eight pounds. She always landed about six miles past a drop zone, carried in the wind like a discarded newspaper, but as tough as any Marine. "No, I have no doubt about your capacity to do the job." He paused. "I'm sorry. I confess, it's my problem. You make me take my mind off of my job. It's unprofessional of me, but there it is."

"Yes," she said, "life goes on, feelings go on, even in the middle of this."

"Are you married, Odette? You can tell me it's not my business."

She traced the course of the Rhône from the Swiss Alps to where it turned northwest toward Lac Léman, through Geneva and into France, joining the Saône in Lyon. Having found their position on the map, she said, "We are east of Hauteville. There is where we are going, Lagnieu." She ran her finger along the route. "From there we will get a ride on the back road to Cheruy and from there to Lyon." She continued to look at the map, and added in a low voice, "My husband was taken east on a cattle car to Maly Trostenets in Belarus." She swallowed, and he noticed that she seemed to be looking through the map.

"Did he die there?"

"Everyone died there," she said, turning away from him. "We had just been celebrating. We were happy because the RAF had carried out successful raids on dams in Germany. Serge, my husband, went to meet a woman who was supposed to have a message for him from a leader of the *Francs Tireurs*. He sat with the woman in a cafe. She got up to go to the lady's room. The men at the next table stood and surrounded him. He was arrested."

"I'm sorry."

"I joined as soon as I could find a place for my daughter. She's seven."

"Where is she?"

She hesitated and said simply, "She's safe, at a children's home in Chambrel."

It was as if she feared that the mention of her daughter would weaken her, and she quickly stood and folded the map. They moved on.

He would always recall those days in the mountains and on the back roads, the two of them moving between safe houses, stopping to pray at a worn stone cross by the roadside and recounting the strange dreams they'd each had during the night. He listened to the simple stories of her rustic girlhood, and saw the bright sorrow in her eyes whenever she spoke of her daughter. Through everything she said, in every action she undertook, he felt the quiet determination of her will to redress the wrongs done to her family, her people, her country. He could never be thankful for the war, yet he felt that some sort of Providence had placed her in his path, that he was meant to be with her, to fight beside her, and perhaps to die with her. And he was trying very hard not to fall in love with her.

16

One night in OSS training, Martin had been hauled suddenly and forcibly out of his bed as he slept. Flashlights blinded his eyes as he was thrown against a wall, held fast by a man on each arm, and slapped in the face. "Jesus Christ!" he had cried. "What the hell?" The flashlights clicked off. The room light came on. And Martin realized what he had done. He had spoken in English. He was never to use English in his training. Never. Captain Perrault scowled as he drew a hand over the bristle of his his buzz cut. The two other men left the room, and Perrault handed his flashlight to one of them as he passed. Arms akimbo, he faced Martin with a disgust he did not attempt to conceal.

"Why are we here?" he asked. "I mean, why are we here?"

"Sir, I'm sorry, I . . . ."

"*En français*, goddamit!"

"*Je suis desolé, mon capitaine.*"

"If I hear one more godamned word of English under any circumstances out of your cake hole before your training is completed, I'll have you reassigned to a PT boat in the Solomon Islands, *candy ass!*" By "candy ass," Perrault meant a slacker, someone who was not pulling his weight, who was not up for the job, and who was a danger to himself, to others, and to the service. The Captain's eyes, dark and intense, searched his face for something: weakness, doubt, or fear, and Martin stared past him at the map of France on the wall, freezing his face into inscrutability.

He never uttered an English expression after that, though Perrault had tried again to startle one out of him on several occasions. There were socials during which stout and scotch whiskies flowed freely, but during which the trainees were taped for Anglo-Saxonisms that might escape their inebriated lips. It was a habit that would endure for many years after the guns were silenced, that Martin, when taken by surprise, would cry out "*Mon Dieu!*" or when cut off in traffic, "*Espèce de crapaud!*" or "*Oh, la vache!*"

Yet there was an incident that he could never explain or account for. One drowsy afternoon while he was traveling with Odette toward Lyon, he came dangerously close to forgetting the war. They had stopped on a hill overlooking a village of red-tiled roofs to eat the lunch that they'd purchased at a roadside café before returning to the fields and lonely back roads where old women in dark blue aprons and muddy boots drove cattle along wheel- rutted roads. She said the place reminded her of the days of her girlhood when she gathered chestnuts in the fall in the hills of Ardèche, chestnuts that her father roasted over the open hearth in a long-handled skillet. "Sometimes I wheeled a cartful in to the town center to sell on a Saturday." Martin imagined her there, a slim girl in a cotton dress and apron standing beside a cart with a hand-painted sign: *Marrons á vendre*. Chestnuts for sale. He smiled at the thought.

As they lay in the grass, chewing the bit of bread and cheese and sausage he'd bought, Martin lost himself in the sunlit branches for a moment. He squinted in the light, and everything seemed to fall away, leaving only calm, gently stirring leaves, and distant memories. The dark veil lifted for a moment from his mind, and he said, "This is a beautiful spot." He wasn't aware that he had spoken in English until he turned and saw Odette's face. "*Qu'est ce que vous avez dit? Vous m'avez parlé en Anglais!*"

He said nothing, but felt a moment of confusion and fear. How had that happened? Odette must have known that he was not French from that moment on. He affirmed that truth with his eyes, and also that she must ask nothing more, and she understood. They could not share particular things; they could only share universal things. Love is a universal thing, and as the light breeze carried the secret he'd let slip into the dim recesses of nearby groves, he took Odette in his arms and felt the power greater than nations, the important beyond all missions, the weakness of the greatest heroes – the soft embrace of a woman.

Later, they indulged in forgetfulness for a while as they lay under knotted oaken boughs and spoke of love. Odette told him of Jean-Joseph, the first boy to love her when she was a young girl in a little village west of Aubenas. He would sit on the wall of the cemetery, watching her walk to the bakery, or loiter at the edge of her father's fields. When she smiled at him, he sent her poems and a lock of his hair and called her his queen and wrote much of his heart and of the pain she was causing him, of how he had to speak to her.

"Well, we did speak, on Christmas Eve, after Midnight Mass in the village. There was a dinner at the little school hall, and there were shooting stars in the cold sky as we walked from the chapel to the hall together. It was beautiful, and he said many endearing things to me." She laughed as she recalled those words, and Martin realized it was the first time he had heard that rich womanly laugh, and he understood the feelings the young man had expressed so long ago.

"It seems at that time that what he wanted most was to prove his love by dying for me."

"I believe I know what he wanted most," Martin said, sliding his hand over the small of her back and inclining his head to nuzzle her breasts.

"You may think so, and so did I. We were both seventeen, and I had resolved to lose my virginity after I read Balzac, you see. We went to a spare room in his house when the rest of his family had gone to Aubenas for the day. We took off our clothes and lay there on the bed. He was trembling, of course. We both were."

Her smile faded and her eyes searched the branches above as if she saw the scene in the little farmhouse room again there. "When it was done, Jean-Joseph began to cry. I didn't know why. I thought that he must be so full of emotion, so full of love, for me, and that was why he was crying. I put my arm around him, and I asked him, 'What's wrong, my love?'

He shook my arm off and got up. He put his clothes on quickly, and just before he ran from the room, he said, I will never forget those words, '*C'est comme les animaux! C'est comme les animaux!*'"

It's like the animals. It was Martin's turn to laugh, and he said, "That's the problem with being a romantic and living on a farm." Then, seriously, his hands buried in her dark hair, he said, "If we survive all this . . . ."

"No, don't say it, Patrice. We can't afford to dream now. Too many have died and still must die."

He had forgotten everything he'd been taught, lost in a pair of brown eyes like a schoolboy, like Jean-Joseph, the romantic farmboy. Perrault would be disgusted with him if he knew. His mission was only to organize and strengthen the structure of resistance, to gather and communicate intelligence, and to sabotage the enemy. But he loved her. *What he wanted most was to prove his love by dying for me.*

"If we have to die, we will die, but if we don't, you and your daughter and I . . . "

She kissed his lips in silent affirmation of this vow. Then, her gaze on the clouds that cast moving shadows over the fields below, she repeated, "If we don't die . . . *if.*" She smiled sadly and shrugged, as if to say that she had little faith in that *if.* "The hours are flying," she said. "We have to get to Cheruy."

Sorrow wrenched his chest, and he remembered, in English, the phrase the poet had used: *unendurably circumstanced*, but watching the face of the woman as she gathered the scattered remnants of their food into the sack, suddenly full of quiet purpose, he recalled his own, and tried to banish those feelings that made him fear for her, for them. He looked west, toward Lyon, and he set his face to the road before him.

17

Gerry, off duty, had gone for a jog. He brought the key to Martin's apartment, because he'd promised him to stop in each day until he returned, to feed the cat and even change the litter box if need be. Martin was sure he'd have a look around, too, but he didn't mind.

Gerry paused to admire the stained glass window at the landing and continued up the stairs. He turned the key and entered the apartment quietly. He examined the old prints in ornamented frames, the postcards and small art photos that nearly papered the kitchen and, through the archway, the bookcases that lined the living room walls, and the stacks of books at their base. "My God, he does have quite a library."

The cat was hiding somewhere, and though he roamed around the apartment calling, "Kitty, kitty, kitty," there was no sign of him.

Gerry wandered into the living room, or perhaps he should call it 'library,' where, with curious eyes he began to scan the titles that lined the walls in floor-to-ceiling bookcases. He was struck immediately by all the sets: *Clarenden's Rebellion*, eight volumes; *Robert E. Lee*, four volumes; *Complete Works of Emerson*, six volumes; *Wits and Beaux of Society*, two volumes; and four volumes of Oliver Wendell Holmes: *The Professor at the Breakfast Table, Over Tea-Cups, The Poet at the Breakfast Table*, and *The Autocrat at the Breakfast Table*. Gerry plucked out the blue volume of *The Poet at the Breakfast Table* and opened it at random:

-Sir, said he, I take stock in everything that concerns anybody. Humani nihil – you know the rest. But if you ask me what is my speciality, I should say, I applied myself more particularly to the contemplation of the Order of Things.

-A pretty wide subject, I ventured to suggest.

-Not wide enough, sir, not wide enough to satisfy the desire of a mind which wants to get at the absolute truth, without reference to the empirical arrangements of our particular planet and its environments. I want to subject the formal conditions of space and time to a new analysis, and project a possible universe outside of the Order of Things.

Gerry flicked back to the frontispiece and checked the date of publication. Incredible, 1872, and the character sounded like Einstein fifty years later. The sun had begun to warm the spring air, and suffuse the library with light, and the moving shadows of the oak boughs outside the second floor windows took on a sudden being in the room. That was what an investigator always wanted to see: The Order of Things.

Gerry thought of the great wheels spinning in the clockwork universe of the Ptolemaic system with the earth at the center of an infinite centrifuge. A system not designed for absolute truth, but only for truth with reference to our particular planet and its mechanics. And it explained everything neatly, except retrograde planets, the parallax view, and so more wheels were added – wheels within wheels turning to the celestial music of the spheres under the guidance of some Master's hand.

There was a whole section of classical works and another of works in French.

He turned on a CD player that sat on a low table in front of a window set between two bookshelves. He pressed play. The room was suddenly filled with the rich music of voices in a counterpoint mathematical and yet...what was the word, he wondered . . . spiritual? Poetic? He picked up the empty CD case that lay in front of the player. *Motets and Madrigals of Orlando Gibbons*, a sixteenth century composer. Late sixteenth, early seventeenth. "The last great English polyphonic composer, and the greatest of his generation." Number one was called, "Farewell to All Joys," which Gerry thought was ironic since it sounded joyful to him.

Gerry saw two dark green volumes of *The Conquest of Mexico*, on a table beside an armchair, and lifted the top one. Several pages had been marked in a peculiar way. The corners of envelopes had been cut off and slid over the corners of certain pages. The book was heavily footnoted, replete with maps. He opened to one of the marked pages.

"Alas!" he read, in the book before him, "the subject of this auspicious invocation lived to see his empire melt away like the winter's wreath; to see a strange race drop, as it were, from the clouds on his land; to find himself a prisoner in the palace of his fathers, the companions of those who were the enemies of his gods and his people; to be insulted, reviled, trodden in the dust, by the meanest of his subjects, by those who, a few months previous, had trembled at his glance; drawing his last breath in the halls of the stranger – a lonely outcast in the heart of his own capital."

"A lonely outcast in the heart of his own capital." Gerry was not surprised that the description had caught Martin's attention, since it might describe the psychology of the resistance fighter in his occupied land. Putting the book down, he saw a large white and gold cat sitting looking at him with a tail twitching like a snake behind him. A spy, like his master.

Gerry walked into a small front room whose single window overlooked Sanders Avenue, casting light across a desk on which sat a laptop computer, and on a shelf above it, a wooden cigar box and what looked like a scrapbook. The cat followed him now, squawking, inquisitive.

He lifted the lid on the box and saw a packet which, as he picked it up, felt surprisingly heavy for its size. Gerry opened it and slid the contents into his palm. It was a heavy silver medal on a light blue ribbon, edged in dark blue. He held it up and examined it. It bore a profile of a crowned monarch on one side, a wreath of laurel surmounted by a crown on the reverse. Without reading glasses, he held it at arm's length to examine the raised letters on its edge: "Martin P. LeBris."

A paper slid out of the packet with the medal, on which he saw the three lions of England. He read aloud the citation: "For conspicuous gallantry and intrepidity at the risk of life."

There were two other medals, each in a blue box. Gerry opened the first box and examined the dull bronze cross, a sailing vessel in its center; the reverse of the medal bore crossed anchors attached to their winding cables. It hung from a dark blue ribbon with a single white stripe down its center. The Navy Cross.

The second was the most beautiful of the medals; "Republique Française." The head of the woman who represented France – what did they call her? Marianne. From her image radiated five white double-pointed rays, encircled by a green wreath of oak leaves and laurel. The medal hung from a red ribbon with a rosette at its center. On the reverse, the words *Honneur et Patrie* were inscribed. Gerry remembered where he had seen it before; pinned to the breast of Napoléon Bonaparte in every likeness he'd ever seen of him. *La Légion d'Honneur.*

He set the box down on the desk and opened the scrapbook, stopping at an old newspaper clipping of a white-haired officer pinning a medal on a young man standing at attention in dress blues. The headline read, "Admiral Nimitz Awards Navy Cross to Local Hero."

There was a German Deutschmark on one page. Looking more closely, he saw the stained edges of the paper. He was sure it was blood. It struck Gerry as somehow incongruous to think of a man who enjoyed listening to polyphonic composers of the sixteenth century plundering the body of a German he'd just shot. But wasn't that what he'd been trying to explain to Gina – what Ophelia had said of Hamlet: *a soldier and scholar.*

Continuing through the scrapbook, he saw an envelope bearing the name Martin P. LeBris and inside it, on a card engraved with the Windsor Arms, an invitation to dine with the king. Impressive.

Here was a photo of a young woman standing before a fountain, squinting in the sun, smiling flirtatiously, one hand on her hip, the other raising the hem of her skirt above her knee. Dark hair, proud eyes, chin raised and turned slightly in a teasing challenge. She was a beauty. Below was written a name: Odette.

There was another box of letters, some in English, others in French. Most were decades old. There was a black and white photo of a smiling girl, five or six years old, dark-haired, in a wool coat, standing at a stone outcropping with a tiny hand pointing toward the valley below. In the distance, snow-capped mountains barbed the line of the horizon. "Amelie, Haute Savoie, 1942," was written on the white margin of the photo. Gerry smiled at the sweetness of the image. There was a yellowing note with the letter, but it was in a densely packed script; again in French. He looked through other photos and letters, getting a sense of a man whose past was in some ways more real than his present. But of course, if he used the computer to communicate with old friends, there would be few letters that were not old. He walked back and pressed the stop button on the CD player; the English Renaissance music concluded abruptly and silence pervaded the library.

The cat had disappeared again. He heard the door open downstairs. He looked out the back kitchen window at the small parking lot behind the old manor. Gerry caught sight of the lion rampant on the grill. Peugeot. A French car. He suddenly felt slightly naked in his sneakers, shorts, and T-shirt; not exactly following the very sensible old Boy Scout motto.

The footsteps indicated that the man had paused on the landing, as he had, and then continued up the stairs. He was speaking to someone. He thought he made out two words: "*Bon, d'accord.*" Was that what he had heard? Was he speaking French? There was no peep hole. Opening the door, he saw a man of below average height, clean-shaven, in his thirties, balding. He wore sunglasses and a light suit jacket, his dress shirt open at the collar. He snapped a cell phone shut and clipped it onto his belt. He approached, smiling. "I'm looking for the man call Martin Le Bris. Do you know him?"

Do you know eem? He spoke English with a distinctly French accent. "Who are you, sir?"

"I'm a friend," he said quickly.

"Is that right?" Gerry asked. The man's suit coat was a size or more too large, perhaps to hide the pistol that Gerry could imagine under the vertical line that broke the smooth flow of the fabric near his left armpit. "Well, someone has recently tried to kill your friend, and now you come here looking for him." An assassin, right out of the movies, with impeccable clothes and a French accent. "Would you open your jacket for a moment, slowly?" Gerry asked.

The Frenchman was still smiling, "And you are?"

"I'm a policeman. You'll have to take my word on that until I can verify it. I'd like to make sure you're not carrying a gun. It's just a custom we have here."

"If I am carrying a gun, per-aps I can explain." He was suddenly serious.

Gerry sensed that something was not right. *Don't think anymore.* He threw a sudden forearm with his weight behind it at the smaller man, hurling him back against the wall. He was on the Frenchman fast, his hand sliding under his arm and turning him in one rapid motion. While his right hand locked in a half nelson over his neck, his left hand closed on the handle of a pistol through the jacket. He tried to shove forward, pivoting, using his legs to throw his weight, to jam the smaller man's face into the corner, so that he could reach under the coat and lift the gun. Welcome to America, Frenchie.

That was how he imagined doing it, in that instant, and he imagined also how he would step back with Frenchie's gun in his hand and take his cell phone to call the station and maybe begin to get to the bottom of what the intruder wanted with Martin LeBris.

That was what he imagined, but none of that happened. As quickly as he had turned the Frenchman into the corner, he felt his own body twisting, pain in his arm, and the man was behind him. His own nose was now in the corner, while hard arms held him in a straightjacket of his own limbs, criss-crossed over his chest and gripped at his sides. He had taken a lifetime of gambles and always come up aces, but he'd lost this one, and now he was afraid because he had felt the gun, and he waited for a sudden movement and a point of pain where the gun barrel would press against his skull.

That didn't happen either. Instead, he felt the grip slowly release, and when he turned, he saw not the flash of a muzzle, but the Frenchman standing with an identification card in his hand. "I tell you please to let me explain you crazy man! My name is Alain Honein, GIGN; in France is like your F.B.I. You can please to just ask me for identification, because you going to get yourself hurt."

"I'm Gerry O'Neil, Lowell Police, but I'm afraid I have no ID to prove it right now. I've been . . . "

"Ah, they say me that you are involved."

"Involved in what?"

"That is really what I'm try to find out. But, *enfin*, the case of Martin LeBris. We can talk somewhere?"

"Thank God you didn't shoot me," Gerry said.

Alain Honein smirked and said, "I'm not going to shoot the gun to someone over leetle misunderstanding." He put his wallet away and bent to brush his clothes.

"Holy crap," Gerry said, stretching his neck. "Are all the French cops as tough as you?" He was happy, in a way, to see that the Frenchman was rubbing his chest where Gerry had nailed him with the forearm.

"I was raised in Lebanon," the smaller man said. "I was under-21 champion of national in the, you know what is the Kenpo?"

"I do now," he said.

"Yes, I study too much the martial art, Kung-Fu, Kenpo. I am a *tough leetle bastard*," he said, smiling again, as if someone had called him that in English, and he was proud to have remembered it. Gerry couldn't help liking this tough little French Arab. He picked up the Meow Mix on the counter and poured it into one of the cat's bowls and filled the other with fresh water. He locked Martin's door and, as they walked out together, began to explain the events which had brought him into Martin's life as an investigator. Alain listened intently, nodding and looking, Gerry thought, as if some terrible suspicion had been confirmed.

18

In Le Café du Petit Coin, Martin listened idly as a Frenchman at the bar in a slouch cap held forth to his companion about the damned Zazous, youths who had been corrupted by listening to American swing music. "Communists, Jews, homosexuals, that's what they are! With their long hair and their big coats. They carry umbrellas for style, but they're too stupid to open them when it rains!"

He was listening to the Frenchman, but he was watching, in the mirror behind the bar, Colonel Horst Grahamar, who was sitting at a small table on the terrace reading *Fleurs du Mal*, as he had the afternoon before. A sleepy German trooper on the sidewalk beyond the terrace kept watch over the colonel and his car. A rifle idled at his shoulder. The proprietor of the café had served him a glass of Cotes du Rhône, which he sipped while he read.

Martin ordered a pastis and carried it out to the terrace, taking a table near the German colonel, who looked over his book pointedly at the intruder, fixing him with a cold stare for a few seconds. It was a warm and sunny September day-the kind of day on which Martin could almost forget about the war, were it not for the fact that his life might depend on the words he chose with this man. He began with the lines he had memorized the night before:

Sois sage, o ma Douleur, et tiens-toi plus tranquille.
Tu reclamais le Soir; il descend; le voici:

Une atmosphère obscure enveloppe la ville,
Aux uns portant la paix, aux autres le souci.

"Forgive me for intruding upon your solitude, sir," he continued in a low voice, "but I would always prefer the company of a man who reads Baudelaire to men who can only talk politics and the war."

The colonel nodded his head, and laying the book face down on the table, drew a silver cigarette case from inside the coat that lay draped over a chair. He tapped the end of the cigarette against the case and said, "*Guten Tag, freut mich.*"

"*Ich spreche kein Deutsch,*" Martin responded.

The colonel laughed and said in French, "So, the only thing you can say in German is that you don't know German."

"Yes, but how is my accent?"

"You sound like a Frenchman speaking German. How is my French?"

"Honestly, sir, and it's not just because I'm afraid you'll shoot me if I say otherwise, you sound like a veritable Frenchman." He pursed his lips, narrowed his eyes, and pushed his fingertips into his thumb. One of his French teachers in the OSS had taught an entire five-week course on Gallic gestures and facial expressions. "Pure French, I assure you."

"From what region?"

"*Eh bien,* Berlin."

The colonel laughed, showing white teeth, as he leaned forward to light his cigarette. He sat back, blowing smoke through his nose. "Prost," he said, as he lifted his glass, and Martin lifted his own. The German seemed to regard him as if he were a bit of a curiosity – an amiable specimen of a conquered race. A race whose culture he admired, and whose people he could have befriended, were it not for the war and his duty. But war was horror, and duty, of course, implacable.

As his thoughts returned to duty, Colonel Grahamar's eyes seemed to twitch, or perhaps he winced for a moment as he looked across the table at Martin, and past him to the German soldiers entertaining a couple of pretty *Lyonnaises* at the bar. "Did I see you in here yesterday?" he asked, "Monsieur..."

"Quenton," Martin said. "Well, Captain..."

"Colonel. Colonel Grahamar."

"Gah-mahhah?"

"Gra-hamar."

"Gra-am-mair. Oh, that's hard, that. Let me see, yesterday was Monday. It wasn't Lent; it wasn't Easter Sunday, so yes. The answer is yes, I had a drink yesterday, Colonel Gra-amaire." He smiled and shrugged, "Maybe two." The colonel was also smiling when he asked, "May I see your identification, please?"

"Yes, of course, of course. I hope I have it. Ah, here it is. Germans always want to see papers. I think that's why you're here, really, to check everybody's papers; then when you see they're all in order, you'll go home." He pretended not to notice that the soldier leaning against the colonel's car, just on the other side of the open terrace a few feet away, had aimed his rifle at him as he reached into his shirt pocket, though a bored-looking soldier at the door had already patted him down when he entered. Slowly, he drew out his identity card and tossed it on the table.

The colonel eyed him narrowly as he picked it up. "Patrice Quenton. St. Brieuc. That's where, in Normandy?"

"Britanny, Colonel, if you please. We Bretons are Celts. We don't like to be confused with those Calvados-guzzling Northmen."

"Please accept my apologies. So why are you here quoting Baudelaire to me in Lyon?"

Martin laughed aloud, and said, "Colonel. You don't think I came to Lyon just to quote poetry to a German colonel? I quote poetry to everyone. Most people stare at me as if I were a damned Bolshevik. That's what I get for displaying my education."

"So why are you in Lyon? And why do you choose a café frequented by the Führer's troops?"

"As for the café, it's close to the Hotel Napoléon, where I'm staying. If the Germans like the wine or the pastis here, that's no business of mine. As for why I'm in Lyon – books, Colonel, books. You see, I am a collector." He said the word with all the pride of one who claims an illustrious rank. "It may sound unpatriotic, but the war is the best thing to happen for me in France. Whole libraries have been emptied in the turmoil. Junk dealers, and bric-a-brac men, who know nothing, are ready to part with wagon loads of rare old books as if they were worth no more than yesterday's newspapers. I have just bought a lot of 2500 books, to start, and I am going through them all. I had to rent a second room at the hotel just to store them. I could be here for some time."

"Have you found anything of interest?"

"You can have no idea. And one book in particular that, well, my heart nearly stopped when I found it at a . . . "

"What is the one book?"

"Oh, and if I tell you, you would steal it and bring it back to the Rhineland, no?" With the little finger of his right hand, he pulled down the corner of his eye. "Eh? Come on, tell the truth."

The colonel smiled and flipped his identity card back to him. "Listen, Monsieur..."

"Call me Patrice, if you like, sir."

"Patrice. I think you're probably a decent fellow – maybe even a good fellow, but if you speak in this careless way to other German officers, they may beat you severely, who knows, even shoot you. Now, I appreciate books also – I'm not a collector like you, but tell me what rare book it is you've found here, and I give you my word as a gentleman I will not try to take it, no matter what it's worth."

Martin eyed him suspiciously. "A man that looks like such a gentleman, sir, should have the integrity of a gentleman. Why do you want to know?"

The German shrugged and drew on his cigarette. "Intellectual curiosity," he said, the words mingling with smoke as he exhaled. "The same reason I read Baudelaire. I can't say that I quite enjoy all of it, mute violins, and poets with enormous wings. I much prefer Hölderlin, of course. But it's our duty to try to understand the French people and their culture. And some of it is quite beautiful."

"Intellectual curiosity in the middle of a war. Well, Victor Hugo said that if he had not been a poet, he would have been a soldier."

"*Voilà*," replied the colonel, amused.

The soldier standing at the colonel's car eyed Martin as he drew his chair closer to the table. "The volume in question is a historical work. *L 'Histoire de l'Abbaye-aux-Bois*, with the amours of the infamous swordsman Beaurivage. He was a sort of Casanova. Let's be honest, Colonel, eh? Germany has not produced men like that."

"There you go again. And are you such a romantic, Monsieur?" the colonel asked as he tucked the volume of Baudelaire into his briefcase.

"Quite the contrary, Colonel. Women love heroes, and to be a hero under occupation – that is a brief career."

"Brief and tragic," the colonel concurred, "ideal for a romantic."

"No, I thank you. Unlike Victor Hugo, I never dream of military glory. It is not for the vows of Beaurivage, or the sighs of his ladies I sought this volume. You can look it up in Hervé's catalogue; it contains original color plates by Vignon."

The colonel sat impassively gazing at Martin, who appeared to be awaiting his reaction with anticipation. Finally, he said, "I am afraid my own education has been neglected, my friend. I confess this means little to me. So it is the plates that give the volume its value?"

The Frenchwomen at the bar burst into sudden laughter, and one of them pushed the German soldier playfully, saying, "You're a devil, you!"

The soldier smiled and said, in a heavily accented French, "Yes, but it's true, isn't it?"

Martin nodded and continued. "I have a buyer who thinks so. The work is beautiful, and very rare. I am tempted to keep it for myself, if you want to know the truth." Martin sensed that the German officer, who listened attentively, holding his cigarette loosely as he ran a thumb along his jaw line, was feeling at ease. He began to relax and an inner voice whispered to him that he would survive the encounter, and that it was time to throw his final card.

"Herr Colonel, I have not been entirely truthful with you."

"You disappoint me, Monsieur."

"Well, what do I know about you Germans? I said to myself, if the man is a fool, or if he is not a gentleman, I will say nothing. But you strike me as a gentleman and as a man one can talk to."

"How kind of you to say so."

"I did not just come here because it's close to my hotel."

"Ah." He brushed a bit of ash that had fallen on his black uniform, picking at a piece of lint on the golden eagle that clutched an encircled swastika above his right breast pocket. "Proceed, if you please."

Martin looked around and drew his seat a little closer, leaning over the table in a confidential manner, his hands drawn up before his chin. "I have access to other things. A letter written to Napoléon by his brother the Duke of Naples, another from Victor Hugo to the English poet Swinburne, a letter from Louis XVIII to the Comte de La Châtre. These things are quite valuable."

"Very interesting, and what do you need from me?"

"Protection, of course. We can both become wealthy. I know what is valuable and can advise you on what you need to buy, or take, eh? In return, you give me a letter that I can show to nosey functionaries, railroad officials, cargo inspectors, stating that whatever I am carrying back to Brittany is not to be delayed or impounded."

"So you would work for me as a procurer of valuables. Göring has his Gustav Rochlitz, and Bruno Lohse, and I would have you. Interesting. But I don't know you, do I?"

"I'm just like all businessmen everywhere, Colonel."

"Practical?"

"I'll accept that. I was going to say greedy."

The colonel looked at his watch, drank off the last of his wine, ground his cigarette butt into the ash tray, and inclined his head to Martin. He reached into his pocket and drew out five francs.

"Please, have a drink on me. Here is my card. Call on me when you have a chance. I should like to see this valuable book. And bring anything else that is of interest. We may be able to work together. *Es var nett, sie kennenzulernen, Herr Quenton.*" As he slung his coat over his arm, he added, "You really should learn German."

"Colonel, did you know that Baudelaire's stepfather was a soldier? General Aupick."

"Most interesting. I hope to see you again, Monsieur." He pulled on his cap, threw his coat over his arm, and walked purposefully out the door, responding to the sentry's salute with a cursory wave. The trooper hurriedly opened the back door for the Colonel, then jumped in front next to the driver. The engine turned over, and the black car disappeared along the Rue des Colombes, its small swastika flag fluttering in the breeze.

Martin tucked the colonel's card into his pocket and added to himself, "General Aupick. Baudelaire hated that bastard."

He finished his pastis and had another, his body finally relaxing back into his chair. He would not go home until much later, when, he knew, they would already have come to inquire about him with the hotel manager, and would have examined his room and the extra room that Marius had filled with old books, some of which were indeed valuable.

Two German soldiers at the bar, their arms around each other's shoulders, a glass of lager in their free hands, waving their beers in march time, crooned the song that the Germans and the Allies both loved: Lili Marlene. The girl who waits in the lamplight outside the barracks. The love every soldier dreams of, the love that waits in a pool of light when the darkness has eaten enough of the innocent.

Vor der Kaserne
Vor dem großen Tor
Stand eine Laterne
Und steht sie noch davor
So woll'n wir uns da wiederseh'n
Bei der Laterne wollen wir steh'n
Wie einst Lili Marlene.

Martin had taken a crash course in German, learning mainly military terms and phrases like "Drop you weapon." He did not understand enough to follow the lyrics. Still, the English words ran in his mind in time with the song the soldiers sang.

Underneath the lantern,
By the barrack gate
Darling I remember
The way you used to wait
T'was there that you whispered tenderly,
That you loved me,
You'd always be,
My Lili of the Lamplight,
My own Lili Marlene

When they were done, he joined in the applause and raised his glass to the young men. And for the moment, he almost let himself forget the grim requisites of war and the imperatives of orders. Almost, but not quite, because Odette was not outside the horror, standing in the light like Lili Marlene; she was deep in the folds of the night that spread its gray wings over all the city of

Lyon, and over all of occupied France, *aux uns portant la paix, aux autres le souci.* To some bringing peace, to others, worry.

19

"Where the hell did you rent the Peugeot?" Gerry asked, sliding onto the leather seats.

"I did not rent it. Gerard Nemo has let me to use it."

"Geronimo?"

"Gerard Nemo, the French Consul General in Boston."

"Very nice." Gerry directed him to the condo in the rehabbed mill building. He saw Gina's green Subaru Forester in the lot, "I'll introduce you to my . . . " He never knew what to call her. Significant other? Please. Lover? Worse. Girlfriend? High school. " . . . to my friend."

Gerry showered while Gina made coffee and her son, nine-year-old Matt, brought Alain Honein a steady stream of artifacts from his room. A turtle shell, an arrow head, a model airplane, a soccer trophy, a large magnifying glass, all of which seemed to delight the Frenchman, particularly the yo-yo, which he rose to play with, speaking French in his excitement: *Attends! Attends! Voilà, regarde, eh?"*

Matt observed this rare specimen Gerry had brought home inquisitively, while he waved a deck of cards in front of him. "Hey Mister, you wanna see a trick? Wanna see a trick, Mister?"

Gina laughed at his emotional involvement with the yo-yo, expressing his disgust in rapid French when he failed to execute whatever maneuver he was attempting, and while the coffee brewed, she went into the bedroom where Gerry was putting on his jeans. "Where did you find that one? He's too much for T.V."

"He found me. The French government is interested in a case that's unfolding here in Lowell."

"Why?"

"I have no idea. I still haven't gotten any details from him. Sorry, Gina, but could you entertain Matt while I catch up?"

She nodded absently, but her eyes narrowed, and she raised a hand toward his face. "Honey, you have a bruise on your cheek. What happened?"

"I had a scuffle with Alain before I found out who he was. I'll explain later."

"That little guy gave you that?"

"Excuse me. He's a tough little bastard, let me tell you. National Lebanese Judo champion or something. He's from Lebanon originally. And he's not a midget for Chrissakes, he must be five nine. Very wiry, too."

"Sorry, Gerry. He does look wiry."

"Very wiry. Strong, too. And very tricky." He smiled and slapped her butt.

"Mr. O'Neil!"

"I'm sorry Miss Santtuchio! I don't know what got into me!" Miss Santtuchio was what he always called her in the little games they played.

"*Oh là! C'est pas possible!*" they heard Alain shouting in the kitchen. "Y'are very good! How you do that, eh?"

"It's magic, Mister," the boy said gravely, shuffling the deck of cards.

Alain took his coffee black with two sugars; they went out to the table on the deck. Gina offered to make ham sandwiches, but Gerry said he'd make something later, wondering if Alain were a Muslim, in which case he would not be welcoming a ham sandwich. For now, though, he was more interested in what had drawn an agent of the GIGN to Lowell, Massachusetts.

Alain sipped the coffee, nodded approvingly, and began. "Martin LeBris, during the war, was work with Resistance group in Lyon and the region around. *Bon*, as you know, it is a bad time in France, and especially in Lyon. Klaus Barbie, you have heard, *non*?"

"Of course, the Butcher of Lyon. He was extradited from South America."

"Yes, from Bolivia. They have a trial in France in 1984 and he die in prison in 1991. He is very bad man. He like to make the torture very much to the people he arrest. He have kill four thousand. You know about Jean Moulin. It's a brave man of Resistance, and he tell Barbie nothing, which is the reason his dust is in *Le Panthéon*. Just to tell you."

"What's that got to do with Martin LeBris?"

"Recently, *il y a deux choses qui . . .* two things 'appen. First, a retired General Buckley is write a book about O.S.S. And he finally convince someone to release the record is sealed. You see, is sixty years pass, they begin to, how you say . . . "

"Declassify?"

"*Exactement*. This is bad, because the General, and everyone think that the war is long time ago, it's not matter. Now is on internet lists of code names of Jedburgh agents, insertions of OSS, names of missions, drop zones, you see? And you can see agent Patrice Quenton, also known as Trevor, he take off from RAF base Keevil. Still they don't list his real name."

"I don't think Martin knows he's being declassified."

"Yes, it's typical government. Now the second of the thing, on twenty-first March, Bruno Lohse is dead; he has ninety-five years."

"Who was Bruno Lohse?"

Alain took a deep breath and shook his head. "Ah, okay. Before the war, he was art dealer in Berlin. Then he join the Nazi Party, eh, *enfin* he is Deputy Chief of the *Einsatzstab Reichsleiter Rosenberg.*"

"Which was?"

"I'm getting tired to speak so much English, Oh *Mon Dieu*, my brain is 'urt. Is ha-*hurt*." He took a deep breath. "Have you aspirin if you please?"

"Hang in there, Alain. Just take it easy. Let me get you an aspirin. Remember, you're a tough little bastard."

"I'm tough leetle bastard, oh *mais ça c'est dur, dur.*" He sighed heavily and shook his head. "I can use your vaysay, your twalette?"

"My vaysay? My twalette? Oh, my toilet!" He laughed at Alain's pained look. He slapped the Frenchman on the shoulder and said, "Of course. I'm sorry, pal."

Gina came in and slipped her car keys off the rack. Matt followed her, saying, "Mom is taking me to Larry's Comics!"

"What a good Mom!" He kissed her and said, "I'll be done with this in an hour or so."

"We'll do something tonight," she said brightly, and Gerry thought, man, I lucked out with her. She's bright, she's cute, she's a good mother, and she even likes to watch the old 40's movies with me. And as he watched her at the door waiting for Matt to grab his baseball cap from the rack, he felt a love for her surge like an incoming tide across the dry flats.

The three of them froze as they heard Alain washing his hands and singing in the bathroom:

Au clair de la lune,
Mon ami Pierrot,
Prête-moi ta plume,
Pour écrire un mot.

Ma chandelle est morte,
Je n'ai plus de feu;
Ouvre-moi ta porte,
Pour l'amour de Dieu.

"Gerry, is that guy kinda crazy?" Matt whispered.

"No Matt, he's just kind of . . . French."

When Gina and Matt were gone, Alain took a couple of Tylenol and they continued at the kitchen table. "Okay. What I was saying?"

"The Einsatz something?"

"Yes, *Einsatzstab Reichsleiter Rosenberg.* They were the Nazi thieves who was charged with stealing the art from the Jews, and from *les musées.* So Bruno Lohse is died, is dead, and some of his *cahiers* . . . the notebook, go out and art dealers maybe get information about the paintings or artifact that has been disappeared. And even the notebook of 1945, they don't know where it is."

"Who doesn't know where it is?"

"Nobody doesn't know where it is. Is missing."

"O.K., but how did you connect all this vague supposition with Martin LeBris?"

"Sorry?"

"I still don't see exactly what this has to do with Martin."

"Well it's a . . . coincidence strange, *non*? That after Lohse die and his notebook is missing, suddenly there are two men who

die, separately. They don't die. One is shot-the other is, eh . . . "
He put his hands around his throat and stuck his tongue out to
illustrate.

"Strangled," Gerry said.

He nodded. "Old men. They are name Valentin Flandres and
Martial Baudry. They are both connect, eh, connected with the
group of Resistance, CCL: *Coeur de la Croix de Lorraine*. You
see that is group Martin LeBris is like *le chef de reseau*. The chief
of the network. We don't like . . . France don't like these people
to be kill. They have *Legion d'Honneur*, like does Martin. We
don't like the peoples kill our Legionaires, eh? So we check on
other member of CCL, Martin's friend, Jean Michel Corvoisier,
and even here in America I'm come to explain you. Because now
I think this guy at night is come to get information from him, or
to kill him."

"If Brunho Lose was so interested in looted art, could these
killings have to do with a missing or stolen piece of art?"

The Frenchman nodded. "Yes, of course. It's what I think."

"Any idea which one? Are there many missing?"

"*Oh là*, I can show you the registry on internet. Is thousands
of pieces still missing from just between '41 and '45. You go to
the looted art dot com. Is some recover all the times, too.
Recently is recovered gold cups from Goluchow Castle in
Poland. And also processional cross from Limoges, all
disappeared by Nazis during the war."

"So Martin's visitor is somehow connected with his past."

"It's logical, no?"

20

Gerry couldn't get in touch with Larry Vega until late Sunday afternoon. He picked him up and brought him to the Café Paradiso; they sat at a table in the lowering sun.

"This is a classy place, Officer. I ain't never been here."

Gerry thought, yeah, you ain't never been any place where some penny ante dealer wasn't selling eight balls of coke in the bathroom, or where one of the patrons had a full set of teeth, or where the women didn't wag their heads at each other and swear like sailors.

"You seem, I don't know, depressed, Larry."

He nodded, twisted his neck, and stroked the Fu Man Chu, but without his usual spasmodic energy. "You know, you said that Al Lekakis is a loser scumbag . . . "

"Yeah, but I meant that in a nice way," Gerry said.

Larry didn't smile. "You know what I realize? That's what I am. I'm a loser scumbag, let's face it."

Gerry was letting him get to Al Lekakis in his own time, but Christ, he couldn't take the Marlon Brando *On the Waterfront* redux. He sighed. "If you're waiting for me to tell you you're not a scumbag, Larry; well, you'd have to do something to prove it. You gotta change the way you live."

"I know," he said. "I know. I'm gonna change."

"The waitress doesn't seem to be coming out here. Let me go get you a beer."

"I'd just like a ginger ale, please."

He went inside to the bar and ordered a ginger ale and a gin and tonic from a very young bartender with the *de rigeur* exposed tattoo over her ass; the "tramp stamp" Ray Cox used to call it before it became mainstream. He carried the drinks out to the table. He was off duty, but he couldn't seem to get off the job. Larry was staring at the cobbled street and looked like he was about to cry. I should have brought Frank McGuin's counselor, Gerry thought. I never know what to say to guys who are going to cry.

"Cheer up, Larry. You look like your best friend died."

Apparently, and not surprisingly to Gerry, that was the worst thing he could have said. Larry Vega pressed his lips together hard and shook his head. Gerry thought, I could be here all day, "I'm sorry you're feeling bad, Larry. You want to give me some information? If it's good, I can slip you a double sawbuck. Go get a steak dinner; you'll feel better."

"Al Lekakis was just another asshole. He hung out all over at the Tap Room, Captain Jack's, Melanson's, The Savoy, West End Club and the Rainbow for a while before they threw him out. He'd go in the bar, and he'd hire whoever was sitting on a stool and put 'em up on a roof. Just tap tap tap up there; then he charges the customer 30 bucks per man per hour and shows them a pile of broken slate and shit. Or he says, 'Lemme get up there with my camera and take a picture of the roof.' Then he gets up there an' rips the shit out of the roof and takes pictures of it. Only rich people fall for that. Like that pretty boy pol who pays eight hundred bucks for a haircut. That's why Lekakis don't work in Lowell; that shit don't work here. And when he got a check, he blew most of it on booze and coke, and no broad that's a coke head is gonna turn down free blow; that's how he ends up with broads like your friend's wife. I met her. She's whack, man."

"So what do you mean he *was* just another asshole."

Larry seemed not to have heard the question; he continued. "I ain't had good luck with women, as you can see." He pointed at the skull and crossbones on his arm above the name 'Alice.' "She was my wife, but we just signed the papers for the divorce. I fucked up her life, too, I guess, not to mention I got a little boy, Davey, who is only five, and he already knows his dad is no fuckin' good. Alice wasn't really bad either, but I was into dope, and then she

 divorced me, and I did that tattoo to piss her off."

He laughed weakly. "You see, now I'm older, I'm startin' to realize I am a fuckin' loser. And my mother, she's real sick with cancer, and she's alone. She always prayed a lot for me, you know, lit candles at St. Anthony's, and I guess I musta really disappointed her. So, I went there the other night, and I prayed with her, like I ain't done since I was a kid, and I promised her I'd straighten out, and that's a promise I gotta keep."

He was getting choked up again, and Gerry sipped his drink while Larry slipped the napkin out from under his ginger ale and blew his nose. "So, I don't want to screw any more people up. I'll help you; maybe it will help that woman to get away from Lekakis 'cause he's bad news. And he's fuckin' with the wrong people, I'll tell you that." He leaned forward, his elbows on his knees, stretching his neck and flexing the muscles of his face into a strange mask for an instant. "What I'm telling you today, I'm not telling you because I want something for me. What I'm telling you, I'm telling you because you are a good guy, and I did have it comin' when you whacked me that time."

"I'm sorry about your mother, Larry. I really am."

"I had a job for a while as a short order cook at the Eagle Diner. Al used to come in a lot, always ordered the Market Street Special, and if it was slow I'd talk to him 'cause I kinda knew him from the Savoy and the Tap Room. Once he came in, and he was holdin' heavy . . . wads of cash." He told me to meet him over at the Savoy, and I did. We were drinkin' shots of tequila, and he got pretty fucked up. He put that song on the juke box where they yell 'Tequila!'"

"Yeah, yeah," Gerry said. "What did he tell you?"

"I'll tell you, but I can't testify or nothin'. I'll give you the info, that's it. He said he did this roofin' job for a rich old lady in Newton. He told her she had mortar mites. He had to rip her chimney down, then he told her that the wood under the slate was rotted. Anyway, he was driving her to the bank so she could make withdrawals. He took her for thirty, forty grand. So he had a chunk of change, and he knows these Colombian dealers, I don't know their names. They hang out at The Tic Toc Club, and he was using the cash, you know, to parlay into the big-time cocaine business. He wanted to be a player. Like the song says, 'your money for nothin and your chics for free,' right? He asked me to carry some stuff into Boston for him. I did, once. Just handed it to a guy at North Station wearing a shirt that said *Millionarios*. That's a Colombian soccer team. And there was like a password thing. I don't wanna do that again. It's scary."

"You know where he keeps his stash?"

"Probably not where he lives or in his truck. He's crazy, but he ain't dumb."

"Larry," Gerry said, "don't ever repeat what you just told me – to anyone. Especially about the Colombians. You might end up in the trunk of a stolen car."

"That's why this is just between you and me. I ain't told no one. The doctor says my mother won't last too much longer. A few days maybe. Then I'm outta Lowell. Shoulda done it a long time ago. That's why I don't even mind bein' seen with you here. Anyway, nobody I know comes around here."

"No one is going to put this together. Where are you going, Larry?"

"I got a good friend in Florida. He got a business, installin' pools, takin' care of pools. He's been askin' me to go down there an' work with him. He's doin' real good. And my mother is gonna leave me her car. I want to send some money up to my little boy. Maybe someday he won't hate me. I'm really tired of bein' an asshole."

"That's good. I like you, Larry. When you're not loaded, you're not a bad guy. I'll never repeat your name in association with this."

"I trust you. Hey, I do feel bad about your friend's wife. She got a taste for the *perico*, that's what the Colombians call the coke, and it was one of those Jekyll-Hyde situations." He drank the rest of his ginger ale and stood up. "Are we square, Officer?"

Gerry stood too, and said quietly, "No, Larry. I owe you. Come by the station before you leave. There'll be an envelope for you at the desk; just bring an ID. To help with your gas money."

"To be honest, I could use it."

"Sorry for your trouble," he said. "Losin' a mother is never easy. You need a lift?"

"Nah. Thanks."

They shook hands, and Larry turned, his hands in his pockets, and walked off down Middle Street, turning his head reflexively to spit between his teeth on the cobbled street. Gerry wondered if he would keep his promise. Years on the force had made him cynical; he doubted it, but you had to admire the guy for trying.

He was walking back to his car on Merrimack Street. The downtown was nearly empty on this Sunday afternoon, but he noticed an old Cambodian woman, her head wrapped in a scarf, leaning on the arm of a young girl who appeared to be her granddaughter and speaking to her in Khmer. Her cheeks were sunken and her eyes clouded. His conversations with others in the Cambodian community left him in little doubt that this old woman had seen some bitter days; scenes that she could never make the young girl understand.

The children and the grandchildren of the refugees, raised in the new land, could never understand a world where death stalks the innocent in forgotten hamlets; where silent columns of smoke rise at dawn; where death arrives on sudden wings from soaring machines, or is dealt by children led by children, armed with AK-47's and blind hate; where demons shovel millions into the all-devouring and ever-famished jaws of the war machine of a failed ideology — to build a paradise on a Golgotha of skulls. But the old woman had survived those days to walk here in the strange brick-reflected light of the old New England mill town. He recalled the lines he had read in the old book in Martin's apartment, "drawing his last breath in the halls of the stranger," and so it was for many as the tides of war drew in and hurled back millions to the far shores of the world.

As he was approaching his car, his cell rang. It was Alain. "Jeh-REE," he said, "I'm at the Double Tree 'otel wiss Martin LeBris. You need to come 'ere. Room sree sree seven."

Gerry stood outside room 337, listening to Alain and Martin conversing in French. Despite his six years of French, he could make out nothing; they spoke too rapidly. He knocked on the door and said, "It's O'Neil."

Alain let him in, no longer boisterous, but subdued. Martin was standing at the window in the fading light, holding a cup of coffee, looking out over the canal below, the channeled water rushing between granite block walls to join the Concord River.

"What's up?" he asked.

"A friend . . . a good friend of Martin's, Jean- Michel Courvoisier, from CCL Resistance group was kill in France. Shot, wiss his wife."

The name registered. Alain had mentioned him as a Frenchman who had fought beside him. That made three dead — four with his wife. "I'm very sorry, Martin."

"Thank you, Gerry. Can I have my guns back?"

"I'll get on it. When did this happen?"

"They have daughter in Brussels. She call for about a week and only she get the...the responder."

"The answering machine."

"Ah, yes. She say some time they go away like that, so she wait to call police. So they are dead at least a week."

"Plenty of time for the same killer to get here," Gerry said.

Martin shook his head and turned from the window. In a quiet and matter-of-fact voice, he said, "I can't believe I let that son of a bitch get away. It won't happen again."

Gerry felt obliged to remind Martin that the police would investigate the matter and apprehend the intruder, and that he would have to stand trial, and then, perhaps be extradited to stand trial for crimes in France. Neither Martin nor Alain looked convinced.

"Of course," Martin said. He opened the suitcase on his bed and pulled out a bottle of Glenlivet. Gerry found some plastic cups by the sink. "Alain?" he asked.

"Yes, I have a small amount, please," the Frenchman said, almost apologetically.

"So you are not a Muslim, Alain?"

A pained look came over his face. "I am not *good* Muslim."

"Well, I'm not a good Catholic," Gerry said. He sat on the edge of the bed, while Martin and Alain took chairs at the drop leaf table.

"I explain Martin about the ah . . . declassify, declassification of OSS records. I am call back to France now to investigate murder of Courvoisier there. Of course we know, thees directif is stu-peed because is *here* the killer. You take care of Martin. Also, I have the name of man you must to talk with is in jail in Massa-shoosett." He opened a notebook and tore out a page, which he handed to Gerry. *Dermot Burke, MCI Concord.*

"I remember reading about him. He was a suspect in the Isabella Stewart Gardner Museum heist, but he was finally caught with a John Singer Sargent painting stolen from a Beacon Hill drawing room. Shot a couple of people, including a cop, trying to get away."

"Burke is spend time in Berlin and Munich in seventies. It was very good place to try to buy or steal the looted art. He know all the peoples is traffic in stolen art treasure from the war. We sink Martin's visitor is German. Maybe Burke know someone who give the good information."

They left Martin watching the History Channel in his room. "I never get tired of watching Hitler lose," he said.

The two detectives went downstairs and into the bar off the lobby and ordered another drink. Gerry asked, "What name did we check him in under, again?"

"Daveed Burns."

"David Burns. That's OK. Listen, Alain, this killer, or these killers, seem pretty sure that Martin knows something. You think he's hiding something from us?"

Alain tilted his head to one side, pursed his lips, and nodded slowly. He inhaled through closed teeth, an odd smile suggested not mirth, but the recognition of a problem. "You don't go to all these troubles just because you suspect something. Martin know something, or he have something, or there is reason that someone really want him dead. *Really.* It's what I think. And you?"

"I agree. Unless the treasure in question were something extremely valuable. Then you might just take a chance, go fishing, as we say."

The Frenchman nodded. "Yes, I understand. This is possible."

The bartender placed a napkin in front of each of them and set their drinks on it. Gerry placed a hand on Alain's arm as he reached for his wallet, and drew out his own. "You're a guest of *Les Etats Unis.*"

"*Merci, mon ami.*"

"Can I ask you another question, Alain, just out of curiosity, a personal question?" Gerry asked.

"Sure."

"All right Alain, so you're a Muslim. Tell me what happens when you die."

"Well," he began, as his eyes took on a serious aspect, "I believe I will stand before Allah."

"All right."

"And He will say, 'Did you try to do the right sing?' and I say, 'Yes.' And He ask me, 'Did you develop your mind and get education?' I going to say, 'Yes,' And then he going to ask me 'Did you help your family?' and I say 'Yes,' 'And you tell the true?' I say, 'Yes.' 'You help the poor?' I say 'Yes.' And then he going to ask me, 'Did you drink?'"

Alain held up his glass of JB and soda and shook his head sadly, "And Gerry, I don't know what I am going to say."

Gerry tried to look sympathetic, but after a few seconds he burst out laughing and slapped his friend on the back, "You may be a bad Muslim, but you're a good man, Alain. I'm glad we met."

Three stories above them, Martin Le Bris was watching the black and white films of General Omar Bradley's First Army capturing the bridge at Remagen and pursing the retreating remnants of the German army into the Ruhr. Joyous faces of liberated French men and women filled the screen. They climbed atop Sherman tanks and waved American flags. They threw flowers at the advancing troops who broke ranks to receive the embraces and the kisses of the women. As the camera panned the ecstatic inhabitants of that vanished moment, Martin studied the faces of the young soldiers and read the common expression there. It said to him: "Now we know why all that blood was shed. Now we see why our comrades fell on these foreign shores and in fields whose names we could hardly pronounce."

And he spoke to another ghost who had joined the ranks of spirits he felt around him in the night. Jean Michel Courvoisier. "If there is a God to judge us, Marius, He will forgive us, I'm sure, because someone had to do what we did. Someone had to liberate Europe from those bastards and tear down the gates of Auschwitz and Buchenwald. And valor must be honored even in heaven. And if we are condemned, we'll resist even in hell. *Que Dieu vous bénisse, mon vieux copain.*" He drew the Cross of Lorraine in the air before him, a single vertical line, crossed twice. "God give me the strength to avenge you and Linde and the others."

And then, his face set in a hard mask, he spoke to the visitor whose presence he also sensed somewhere in the night, nearby. "You want the cross, *maudit chien sal*? Come and get it." In his glasses, the VE Day celebrations were reflected, tiny gray squares of the light of other days, and the narrator said: *Years of war have left millions dead, and Europe in ruins, but this is the time to celebrate the end of the Nazi regime, and to begin to think about the new world that is beginning.*

21

It soon became clear to Martin that Odette was BEC 22. Perhaps at first there had been another, probably her husband, Serge; in any case, *the man* that London imagined, had either been arrested or killed. Odette was running the network. She sent orders to "patrols" in various parts of the country: Monaco, Marseilles, Pau, Nice, Lyons, Paris, and Normandy. She organized letterboxes for pickups and gave out code names. She received the information and decided what was urgent, what had to be coded and transmitted by radio, and what would be sent by courier.

One of Martin's missions was to help train selected members of the Resistance to "play the violin," that is, to operate radio transmitters for clandestine communications, as well as ciphering or encoding messages. London would be sending new transmitters which would be distributed across an underground intelligence network, a network through which the Special Operations Executive hoped to receive daily reports on enemy movements and troop strength throughout *France-Sur*, including ship movement in and out of ports, departures and arrivals of submarines from their pens, locations of fuel dumps, truck convoys and freight trains, and, if possible, the fallback positions of retreating German troops in the event that the Allies were successful.

When and where the new transmitters would arrive, Martin would know. The message was not long in coming. Two weeks after arriving in Lyon, while the rain fell on the city and streamed down the panes of the windows of his room at the Hotel Napoléon, he lay on his bed staring at the garish flowered wallpaper and listening, not to an illegal ANC-1 transmitter, but to a battered radio he'd bought at the *marché au puce*. The BBC was broadcasting a Duke Ellington concert live from the Edgewater Hotel in Chicago. He could imagine smoke swirling about the whining muffled trumpet, the cigarette girls carrying their trays in short ruffled skirts and pert pillbox hats.

He lay back, making out patterns in the cracked plaster of the ceiling, and finally dozing for minutes at a time, waking to check his watch, never allowing himself to sink completely, drifting in and out of the music in half-conscious reverie to the time before the war, when he had paddled his old red canoe up the Merrimack River, past the Tyngsborough Bridge.

Ah, those days of peace. Lying in the bottom of the canoe, the stars scattered across the black field of the sky, he drifted downstream, slipping by the ballrooms that dotted the banks toward the bend in the river that was his hometown of Lowell, listening to the dance music with its undertones of voices and laughter rolling out over the tranquilly flowing expanse of the water as he slid along in the darkness, beyond the wavering slips of light that stretched out from the banks.

The Ellington concert ended, and a classical program began with a nocturne of Chopin. God, that music would make your heart ache and more: tragic, portentous, like a funeral dirge for the last hero of a beleaguered people.

The canoe slid over the water. He drifted there now – The Riverview Ballroom, The Passaconway, The Belmundo Lounge. Johnny Lambert said there were springs under the dance floor at The Keith, and that was why you could dance all night and never tire. He opened his eyes and looked at his watch. He drew a hand over his face, and leaning on one elbow, picked up a pencil and notebook from the night table.

He listened for a while, leaning toward the radio. The Chopin ended, and another piece began. The music merged into the sound of the rain. "Two piano classics there for our late night listeners. That was Franz List's *Lovedream Number Three* in A flat major played by Josef Reuben, preceded by Chopin's *Opus 27, Number 1, Larghetto*, in C sharp minor, Peter Shumaker on piano. And we have a message for Trevor. 'We will meet you at Apple. Three, first seven, 2, 49 dash 50. Three, first seven, 2, 49 dash 50.'"

The numbers were incomprehensible, except to an agent who knew the master list. Book three was *La Bible en Espagne*. He dug it out of the pile of books that lay against the wall. First seven. That would be page seven of the introduction as opposed to the body of the text. Two-second paragraph, forty ninth and fiftieth word: April 27th.

On the morning of April 27th, five members of the thirteen-man cell left early in the evening from Lyon Part-Dieu station in separate cars, posing as commercial travelers: insurance agents, wine merchants, a design engineer for Renault. Martin traveled with Odette, a young couple in love, a cover which was all too easy to simulate. She laughed carelessly as he took her picture in front of a fountain, not with the tiny Minox, but with a tourist's Falcon Bakelite Twin Flex. She arched her brows suggestively and raised the hem of her skirt a few inches, smiling as he imagined she must have smiled so often before the war.

They disembarked an hour and twenty minutes later at St. Étienne Chateau station in Le Puy. They left their compartment, where a bespectacled woman with her nose in a book watched them out of the corner of her eye. They stood smoking in the narrow, rocking aisle.

"How did you come to take all this on yourself?" he whispered.

She had denied it for a while, but he had spent too much time with her not to understand. "I was working as a secretary in Paris in June 1940 for a large publishing house. My husband, Serge, was a member of the Army Intelligence Service. On June 11th, we left our daughter with my mother and fled south with half the city toward the unoccupied zone. We immediately began our business. Serge organized the network."

"BEC 22?"

"The original. But I knew everything, mainly because my memory is almost photographic. We never wanted to carry incriminating papers. I carried everything in my mind. After he was arrested, I continued to communicate with London and the network using his code name." She crossed her arms and shrugged. "Some men might not have confidence in a woman. Who knows, London might not even want to work with a woman."

"You have my confidence," he said.

"Now, yes. But at first . . . " She put on a gruff man's voice: "'Are you sure you know how to read a map?' And, 'You make me take my mind off my work.'"

"Well, that's still true," he admitted, "but it's not your fault."

"Oh, it's not? Thank you very much." She smiled, and her cigarette glowed red as she inhaled.

He shrugged and caressed her cheek, "Men are men, no matter what, *mon amour*."

"No, Hitler can't even change that, thank God."

The door at the end of the car slid open and a stout woman in the gray uniform of the auxiliary police walked toward them. Martin squeezed Odette's hand.

"Papers?"

"Of course," Martin said.

He held Odette's cigarette while she searched her purse and finally handed the forged *Ausweis* to the woman who now raised a clipboard and checked it against a list of names. Martin saw that the blinds were pulled down on the doors to the adjacent compartments. If somehow their names appeared on the list, he saw himself breaking the woman's neck in one sudden movement, carrying her to the door at the back of the car, and dropping her body between the cars. He smiled good-naturedly at her while she checked both identity cards, her eyes sliding down the list, but then she nodded and moved along, knocking on compartment doors.

They were met by a man called Renard, their liaison with the local *maquisards*, who, as evening fell, ushered them along the wooded trails toward the drop zone Martin had specified as Apple, a grassy plateau beyond the village of Cayres on the Allier River.

Marius was with them. He trudged along, shoulders bent, with a light machine gun slung over his shoulder that Martin recognized as the one he'd taken from the dead German weeks before. One of the locals sung in a low voice as they traced the narrow path:

Friend, do you hear the black flight
Of crows over our plains?

Friend, do you hear the muffled cries
Of our country in chains?

An hour after they had scouted the terrain and taken up their places, they heard the throbbing of engines drawing near in the darkness above them. The Lysander's lights came into view, flashing M-M-M in Morse. Martin directed his flashlight toward the sky and responded C-C-C.

The plane wagged its wings in confirmation, and as it passed overhead, chutes billowed above the dim starlit plain, and the Lysander veered away southward, probably to Algiers, climbing, the hum of its engines fading into the silence of the night.

The engineers in London had designed a package for the radio transmitters that would in theory withstand the shock of landing, but of the five An/PRC-1 suitcase radio transmitters, two appeared to have been damaged. The five smaller British MCK-1 transmitters, designed to fit into biscuit tins, were undamaged. In addition to the transmitters, there were explosive detonating devices designed to be attached to railroad tracks, acetone time-delay fuses, pencil fuses, a box of .22 caliber automatic pistols with silencers, gas tank charges, and forged ration stamps. It was a guerilla's Christmas.

There was a box marked "Trevor," in which he found three million francs, counterfeit, but indistinguishable from the genuine, and a ten by twelve silk sheet on which were written numerous sentences, each of which was assigned a four letter code for rapid communication. The silk was chemically treated so that a cigarette would incinerate it in seconds. Martin had been taught that whenever he broadcast with a silk code sheet, he should have a lit cigarette in his mouth. There was also a Minox camera, a box of phosphorous grenades with the fuse assembly removed and packed separately, and a box of twelve disposable .22 'stingers,' three inch tubes equipped with a firing button. They fired a single .22 caliber round and could not be reloaded. There was also a cigarette case that could be set to explode when it opened. The OSS design engineers were clever.

Odette was ecstatic about the radios. She turned to Lucien, a young man in a slouch hat with an unlit, half-smoked cigar between his teeth and said, "Now you can start your violin lessons."

Still holding the cigar in his clenched teeth, he said, "Much easier than running courier all over the country with messages in the heel of my shoe."

They gathered the chutes and tossed them in the Allier, weighted with rocks. Bending under their load, they retraced their steps. There was an open truck waiting in Cayres, and much of the drop was packed among crates of vegetables, covered with potatoes, endives, carrots, and onions. They would be spirited away from the farmer's market into the *traboules*, or secret passageways, of Lyon the next day.

Odette directed the operation, and he knew that she had plans for each link in the network and how the transmitters would be distributed. She had ceased to pretend, with him, that she awaited orders from BEC 22. She was a natural organizer, and he sought her advice on distributing the money. Men and women who took to the hills or went on reconnaissance patrols needed money and ration stamps for their families.

Marius, Lucien, and a third courier named Martial would take portions of the money to contacts within other Resistance groups: Combat, CDLR, COMAC, and the MLF.

There was soup and bread served by an old hump-backed woman for the six or seven who remained, and Martin and Odette fell asleep in the loft of the barn of the old farm in Cayres. It was a cool night, and they slept huddled together with their coats over them, like gypsies. When he awoke in the night, he saw that she was awake, her eyes on him.

"What's wrong?"

She pulled him closer and said, her mouth close to his, "It's a dangerous game you play with Grahamar. He is not a fool, you know. And you have been inside the Berthelot Center. In his office, and come out again. What if they look for you tonight, and you're not at your hotel room?"

"I've confessed to him that I'm a bit of a womanizer. The owner of the hotel has told me that they've searched my room twice as well as the adjoining room I rent. They've found what I told them they'd find. Books. The library of Marius. And so I think Grahamar believes me. Moreover, he likes me. He wants to like me because he thinks I can provide him with valuable things and that his possession of certain artifacts will give him the air of culture he's so desperate for. Last week I provided him, for a nominal fee which he was happy to pay, with a love letter written by Gabriele D'Annuncio, the Italian writer, and a letter by Victor Hugo to the English poet Swinburne. I bought the first, but the other was one of Marius' treasures."

"Has Grahamar other treasures stolen from France?"

"Oh yes. France and elsewhere. They've emptied churches, museums, and private collections of Europe. Grahamar is friends with that great pig Göring, and has received some gifts from him; what is not destined for some Fuehrer Museum in Austria, Linz, I think he said."

"I hope that what you get from Grahamar will be worth the risk. Be very careful. I worry for you, Patrice. He beat a thirteen-year-old girl nearly to death with a club, in front of her parents. She will never walk again. Her back is broken. He will do anything to get information, if he thinks you have it. Anything."

"It's worth the risk. I've seen him put documents with the OKH stamp in his desk."

"*Obercommando des Heeres . . .* " she murmured, "German High Command."

"It would be easy to photograph them if I were alone there. He trusts me, Odette. Besides, I don't think he believes that any Resistance fighter would willingly go into Berthelot."

A small cry of fear escaped her lips at the thought of her lover in that fearful place. She held him hard against her. "Think carefully, Patrice, of your plan before you try it."

'

22

As he had several times before, Martin LeBris walked toward the archway that led to the cobbled courtyard of the Centre Berthelot. He showed the pass that Grahamar had written for him to the sentry, who gave him a halfhearted pat-down while continuing his conversation with an attrative young woman who had leaned a bicycle against the wall and come over to inquire about a work voucher for a visiting relative. She took no notice of Martin, nor he of her, though they knew each other well and had rehearsed the moment for a long while before falling together on the bed in a room in the Hotel du Dauphin. The sentry cast a quick glance at the pile of books Martin held wrapped in twine. "Shall I untie them?"

The soldier stepped aside and nodded him through the arches, still chatting with the woman, who, he thought, seemed to be smiling at him. Colonel Grahamar walked toward Martin in the corridor, his heels clicking on the tiled floor. "I've been looking forward to seeing you, Patrice." It occurred to Martin that this German officer had taken a genuine liking to him, but that would not save him if he were caught tonight. Grahamar ushered him into his office on the second floor and closed the door. As he dropped the bundle of books on the desk, Martin glanced casually at his watch. Seven fifteen. He had to hold the colonel's attention for fifteen minutes.

However, it was the German officer who spoke, "I have recently acquired something I think will interest a collector of any kind." He unlocked a drawer in his desk and withdrew a wooden box with a graven heraldic device of some kind on the lid. He unlocked the box with a smaller key. His hands rose from behind the opened lid, draped in a gold chain from which hung a gold cross as long as a man's hand, from wrist to fingertips. The end of each arm of the cross held an emerald, which seemed to radiate outward along golden branches from the large pear cut diamond at its center. "*La Cruz de Nueva Granada*," he said proudly.

Martin looked the piece over with unfeigned awe. "Well, I have nothing to compare with that. Now I feel like a fool. My books are worth thousands, but this is worth millions. Where did you get it? If you want to tell me, of course."

"I wouldn't say this to anyone else, Patrice." He smiled and pretended to look about nervously. "You know, an American company, General Electric, is making a portable wire recorder. It records sounds, voices. You don't have one of those, do you?"

Martin laughed. "Oh, that would be a good way to get myself shot."

Grahamar smiled at his own good humor and set the cross back in its box. Martin glanced at his watch. Ten minutes. "You know," the German said, "The Third Reich will last a thousand years. So the SS is stripping Europe of her treasures with impunity. Göring gave me a Raphael, as a gift. Imagine that. Here, have a Da Vinci. Here, take this Rubens. Twelfth-century illuminated manuscripts. Crown jewels. Göring's personal collection is housed at Carinhall, in the Schorfheide Forest in Brandenburg, named in memory of his first wife, the Swede, Carin von Fock-Kantzow. His collection will rival the *Jeu de Paume*, but as I told you before, most of the masterpieces of Europe will go to Austria for the *Führermuseum*."

Martin shrugged and said, "To the victor go the spoils, eh?"

"Yes, but what if the Reich does not last a thousand years? Maybe it will last a thousand years. What if it lasts five years? Then the artwork will be loot, and the victors will be forced to return it, or to hide it somewhere and be unable to show it or sell it."

"And your solution?"

"I exchanged the Raphael for the cross, which is not stolen. The bill of sale says I bought it, and its provenance is unassailable. It was forged in Cartagena, in the Spanish colony of Nueva Granada in the 17th century, and later given by Philip IV to María Theresa upon her marriage to Louis XIV. It was bought by a Russian Princess in 1826, and her family sold it to a Jewish industrialist in Switzerland in 1933, from whom I bought it, or exchanged for it, legally." He replaced the cross carefully and shut the box. "Of course I cannot keep it here. It's far too valuable. The diamond is fifteen carats, color grade D, perfect white! The insurance papers are pending."

"What was the Raphael like?"

"Oh, it was wonderful of course. *Portrait of a Young Man.*" Grahamar stared into the space between them, his arm outstretched, as if he could see it there. "It was taken from the Czatoryski Museum in Krakow. If we lose the war, the world will be looking for that painting. It's not that I think we're going to lose, you understand. But the cross is mine, no matter who wins the war."

"You think ahead, Colonel." He waved his hand over his books as if he were swatting at a fly. "I'm sorry to waste your time with these little treasures I've found. They're nothing, really."

"No, no. I assure you. I relish our conversations and the so-called little treasures you bring me."

"Well," Martin smiled ingratiatingly, "you are very kind to say so. I do have something that . . . does the Fuehrer speak French?"

"No, the Austrian Corporal speaks only German." He winked and added, "You didn't hear me say that."

"I understand. Well, you said your friend Göring speaks French. He might appreciate this. *A Treatise on Physical, Intellectual, and Moral Degeneration in the Human Species and Causes, 1857.* Twelve lithographs present 37 degenerate adults and children."

Grahamar flipped through the lithographs, his brow wrinkled in disgust. "Look at the mother and child. Both imbeciles. Why should people like that be allowed to procreate?"

"I ask myself the same question. Keep it if you find it interesting. Now you may not find the structure of the organ of the ear interesting. But this rare volume was published in 1638. The author, Du Verney, was the tutor to the Dauphin, and most interestingly, the sixteen fold-out illustrations are attributed to the famous Sebastion LeClerc, very rare . . . " He glimpsed the minute hand of his watch. *Now, Odette.* " . . . first original edition. Look at the ornate binding and the . . . "

The explosion rattled the walls of Grahamar's office and sent a thin spray of white dust from cracks in the plaster ceiling. "What the devil was that?" Martin cried.

"Sounded like a bridge blown over the Rhône." Truck engines were roaring to life in the courtyard, and Grahamar was quickly replacing the locked box in his desk and turning the key, while Martin gathered up his books, leaving the treatise on human degeneration. Grahamar put on his cap, the silver *totenkopf*, or death's head, above the glossy visor reminding Martin, if he needed reminding, with whom he was dealing. "Regrettably, I must go. Come back tomorrow to show me the others."

In the corridor, Grahamar turned to lock the door. He had left the light on. Martin glanced again at his watch. He imagined the acetone eating through the celluloid disk, releasing the firing pin. The second explosion was nearer, and as Martin cowered against the wall shouting his French curses, Grahamar set off at a run. Some others flew out of offices and toward the stairs at the end of the corridor, while Martin walked slowly along. Within seconds he was alone, and he turned back. He set the books down by the door and slid out the volume at the bottom. He opened it and removed from its hollowed interior a set of burglar's tools. The door was open within ten seconds. In OSS training, he had been second in safe-cracking and lock picking only to the teacher, a man who had worked for John Dillinger. He kicked the books inside and entered. Kneeling, he retrieved something else from the hollowed book: a tiny Minox camera.

He worked quickly. The center desk drawer sprang open, and he withdrew the manila folder he'd seen Grahamar studying as he entered one evening. He rifled quickly through the pages until he found something that might save Allied lives. Here was the OKH stamp: *Positionsbestimmung zuruckfallen Frankreich.* Positions of retreat for Southern France. He photographed the six pages rapidly and replaced the folder in the drawer and the camera inside the book. He was gathering up the books when he heard steps in the corridor outside. He froze, waiting for them to pass, but instead heard a key in the door. There was no place to hide.

Colonel Horst Grahamar was perplexed to find that the door was not locked. He stood staring at the door handle for a few seconds as the door opened, until he looked up and saw Patrice Quenton standing in his office, backing slowly away from his desk.

"Ah, I hoped I was wrong, Patrice. But on my way to investigate these explosions, it did occur to me that if someone wanted to be alone on this floor, it could be attempted with such a diversion."

Martin sat down in one of two winged chairs on either side of a small table, upon which chess pieces stood in mid-game. "After those explosions I found myself alone. The cross was too much for me. I was going to steal it. I admit it – you can shoot me. I wouldn't blame you."

Martin knew that once he was in a cell it would be too late; whatever chance he had to escape must be taken in the next two minutes. Grahamar walked to his desk, opened the drawer, and withdrew the box once again. He opened it and smiled.

"I don't believe the explosions were a coincidence. There's something deeper going on here. You know I will get the truth, my friend. That's what we do here. I'm afraid you have revealed yourself as a spy." He closed the box, and casually withdrawing his Luger from its holster, took the seat opposite Martin. "Speak," he said.

"All right. *Les jeux sont fait*, as they say. I'll tell you what you want to know. May I have a cigarette?"

"Of course."

"Would you care for one, Colonel?"

"After you. Very slowly, if you please." He steadied the Luger on the armrest.

Slowly, Martin fished out a slim silver case and a box of matches from his pocket. There was only one cigarette in the case, which he removed. When he closed the case again, the detonator was armed. "Oh, I'm sorry, Colonel. You wanted one." He handed the case to him and slid the matchbox open. "Silk cuts, Colonel. Very nice. I got them in England."

"So you were in England?" He opened the cigarette case. There was a dull crack and a phosphorescent flash. Martin caught him as he fell sideways and set him down softly, unconscious, on the floor, his face peppered with small bleeding punctures, his left eye a hole from which ran a glutinous mass of pulp. Martin picked up his books quickly, ready to resume his role as the antiquarian. When he was about to make his exit, he saw the open case on the colonel's desk, and reached over. He drew out Grahamar's precious antiquity and hung the chain about his neck, stuffing the golden cross under his shirt. Then he blessed himself.

He saw what looked like a personal letter protruding from under a blotter pad, and he threw it inside the hollowed book. Closing the door behind him, he made for the stairs, and was soon passing under the archway where he saw a new guard, very young, to whom he said, "That's the last time I'm visiting the colonel. It's dangerous around here!"

The sentry shrugged and said, "*Ich spreche Deutch*!" and while jeeps continued to roar out of the Centre Berthelot in the direction of the river, Martin strode along Le Rue Berthelot in the opposite direction. He took out the pass signed by Grahamar and tore it up, dropping the pieces into a storm drain. If the German officer was found dead, or even more if he survived, the Gestapo would be hunting for Patrice Quenton.

The streets were deserted; tonight it would be impossible to cross the Rhône and get to Vieux Lyon to meet Odette. As he passed the cemetery Saint Michel Saint André, he heard a whisper in the darkness: "Quenton!"

A figure emerged from behind a dimly outlined obelisk in the cemetery. Patrice never tensed, because even in the dark he knew the voice and the man. It was Marius, who always seemed to materialize in the darkest hour. In one movement, he grasped the spikes of the wrought iron gate and vaulted over. "Come," he said, and they arrived shortly at the chiseled stone façade of L'Église Saint Étienne, the door of which opened quietly on well-oiled hinges to let them enter and closed again.

A short, stocky priest led them into the sacristy, and indicated a couple of blankets laid over a Persian rug. He lit a candle for them, and then said, "The WC is down the stairs, at the back of the church. It's open. *Dormez bien.*"

He retreated softly as Marius whispered, "*Merci, Mon Père.*"

The priest returned briefly and said, "Come and go carefully. If they find out you were here, it will go hard for me."

"We will. God protect you *mon Père.*" Marius' face, as he turned to Martin, was etched with worry, dark shadows flicking about his eyes in the candlelight.

"Why are we here?" Martin asked.

"We can't use the Rue du Boeuf. It's not safe."

"Why?" he asked, though his heart already told him.

"Odette is taken," Marius said. "She will try not to talk, but you know what they say about Grahamar. He could make a wall talk."

23

Professor Dermot Burke, Irish émigré, art thief, and killer, was sitting in the prison library, or media center, as it was called, of MCI Cedar Junction in South Walpole. He was reading the German newspaper *Sueddeutsche Zeitung* online. The overhead light shone on his bare cranium, which glistened as if it had been polished; he wore tinted glasses; he was the only prisoner in the media center sporting an ascot.

Another prisoner, dressed in blue denim like the professor, leaned over and said, "You can read that shit?"

Burke, without taking his eyes off the page, responded, "It's not shit, Mr. Foster, it's German."

"What's it say?"

"It says that Camille Pissarro's *Le Quai Malaquais, Printemps,* has been found in a bank safe registered to the recently deceased Bruno Lohse at the *Zeurcher Kantonalbank* in Switzerland. It has been missing since it was stolen from a Jewish publisher named Samuel Fischer in 1938."

The other man laughed. "It don't even make sense in English."

"A lost painting has been found in a safe. It's worth 6.7 million dollars."

"Holy shit."

"You understand that."

"Oh yeah. That I understand."

A guard approached the men and said, "Burke, you have a visitor." His eyes narrowed and he stepped closer. "What the hell is that around your neck?"

"It's an ascot. I was allowed to receive it."

"Well, take it off. You see anyone else wearin' a fuckin' asscot at Cedar Junction?"

The guard held out his hand and Burke untied the ascot and pushed it into his outstretched palm.

"Get with the program, professor, or you'll be back in the segregation unit." The guard led him, not to the common visiting area, but down a separate corridor lined with numbered doors.

"Where are you taking me?"

"You have a special visitor." He passed his I.D. card through a slot. A buzzer sounded, and he pulled the door open. Burke eyed the stranger, who was sitting at the table. He was a cop. It was in his manner, in the short graying hair, and in the cheap suit. In the manila folder on the table in front of him. He rose and extended a hand. "Mr. Burke, my name is Detective O'Neil of the Lowell Police Department."

Burke ignored the proffered hand and flopped in the plastic chair at the Formica table. The guard indicated a button on the wall and said, "Just ring if you need me. I'll be right outside."

When he closed the door, Burke ran a hand over his smooth scalp and said, "What the bloody hell do you want?"

"It was suggested to me that I talk to you. I see you continue to communicate with various art dealers in Europe. You've received cards from Hagen Shatz in Amsterdam; another from a Hansi Varhein in Munich. What do you communicate about?"

The man glanced around and leaned over the table as if he were nervously imparting a dangerous secret. "You're from

Lowell, Massachusetts, right? James McNeill Whistler's home town. You know his *Arrangement in Gray and Black, Number One*? Eighteen seventy-one?"

"Whistler's mother."

"Precisely. It's in the Musée d'Orsay in Paris. My friends in Europe are going to get me out of this human zoo, and we're going to steal it, together, and bring it back to Lowell where it belongs." A low laugh, like the sea washing a gravel shore, seemed to issue from deep in his lungs. He was enjoying himself. "Seriously, Detective, who talks about anything of consequence on a prison phone? Innocuous holiday greetings and idle art gossip – infrequently."

"You won't be out of this zoo for a while, Dermot, because you're one of the more dangerous animals in it. People imagine an art thief as somehow an elegant kind of criminal."

"Ah yes, Cary Grant in *It Takes a Thief*. You don't see the resemblance?" He took off the tinted glasses and gave Gerry a profile.

"There's no doubt you're more highly educated than the average criminal. You've passed yourself off as a college professor on more than one occasion, right?"

His expression turned sour as he replaced the glasses. "I've forgotten more than any Ivy League professor ever knew. Only my family didn't have the money to send me to study art at the university. 'You've got to live by your wits, Dermot,' the old fella told me. And so I did."

"Living by your wits. Is that what you call it?"

"What do you call it? I was nicked, yes. But I lived like royalty for a while. I spent more money in one year than you'll see in your entire police pension."

"You left out the part where you kill people."

The convict shrugged. "Self-defense."

"The jury called it murder. And you wounded an officer who was trying to take you into custody. That makes you, not a charming Cary Grant jewel thief, but a genuine bad guy."

"Well, I'm not going to rehash these old charges." He turned sideways and leaned over, coughing into the crease of his elbow. "I need a cigarette. Do you have one?"

"Sorry. Other than the great Whistler heist, what did you and your friends have to talk about?"

"Difficult as it may be for you to believe, Detective, I do have friends. There's even a woman who says she loves me."

"Ever hear of Bruno Lohse?"

The aging art thief said nothing for a second, and Gerry could almost see the wheels turning behind the pale eyes. Slowly, he began to shake his head and said, "I'm going to say no, just so you lay your cards out."

"And you're the genius who's forgotten more than the college professors ever knew?" He laughed. "The IT department here has been kind enough to print up a list of some of the web sites you like to visit, and some of the pages you've viewed. Now look at this. I highlighted the important part: *'Hat Hermann Göring's oberster kunstraouber Bruno Lohse kraftig in die eigene Tasche gewirtschaftet' . . . "*

"Your pronunciation is awful. Just surfing the web, as they say, Detective."

"An online translator renders that particular line literally as: 'Has Hermann Göring's most important art robber Bruno Lohse forcefully lined his own pockets?' Funny how when you surf the web, you catch a lot of waves that contain references to Bruno Lohse. You've also searched a lot of OSS sites."

"Lohse was an art thief, one of the biggest ever. I'm an art thief. I'm curious about him. As for the OSS, well they ran a group called "the Monuments Men," who were charged with recovering the art that was looted during the war. Their records are interesting because I like to stay abreast of what has been recovered and what is still...out there."

"You worked in Germany for a while, correct? You know the art scene?"

"God's teeth, Detective. Whom do you think you're talking to? Listen, the Harvard Yenching Library was robbed of forty-one Chinese books and two scrolls, from the Song, Yuan, Ming and Quing periods. Some are over a thousand years old, 960 A.D., if memory serves. Taken right out of the Rare Book Room. They're valued at well beyond a million dollars. They've not been located. I proposed to help the police to recover them in exchange for my freedom. They were not even willing to discuss it. So what could I possibly get out of telling my secrets to a cop from a backwater precinct of a washed-up mill town?"

"What is it you want?"

He leaned back and laughed, or wheezed, mirthlessly. "Ah, what do I want, so. Ironically, all a sophisticate like me really wants is the usual cliché. A very large gin and tonic on a deck overlooking the Caribbean, with the woman who loves me, or if she's not available, any fine thing will do, though the one I think I'd really like to meet is the *Unknown Woman in a Blue Dress with Yellow Trim*. She existed once, as real as you and I, and now all that is left of her having passed this way is a piece of canvas on which Fyodor Stepanovich Rokotov mixed and brushed some paints in the 1760's. The love of art is nothing more than an attempt to escape oblivion, Detective. I cling to it, steal it, die for it, kill for it they say, and am locked in a cage for it—and then I die and am forgotten, but the unknown lady in a blue dress lives on."

"You don't want a deal, Burke. You want absolution and a ticket to Puerto Rico. No, they won't talk about that, because a human life is more highly valued by some people than paints mixed on a canvas. But I'll see what I can do. And by the way, you and I and Shakespeare, Mozart, Michelangelo, and the woman in the blue dress – we're all bound for oblivion. You're too bright not to face that fact."

"*Ars longa, vita brevis*, that's all I mean." He sighed and looked around the room. Pale green walls. No windows. His face reflected the barrenness he found there. "I'm tired. Make me an offer if you like. I expect to die in this place, so there's really nothing you or anyone can threaten me with, Detective O'Neil." He stood and stretched.

"I'm sure they've finished searching my cell, and I'm ready to return."

"You know people in the Munich underworld?"

"I can only repeat the eternal question of the criminal mind, Detective: What's in it for me?"

"Let's see what's in it for you, Burke." He pushed the button and the guard opened the door. Another man came in. He was in his mid-forties, wore a gray suit, dark hair combed neatly back, a sparkling white shirt and red tie. He had risen through the ranks from guard to warden by dint of education and political savvy. He was well over six feet, and wore what looked like size 12 wingtips. Dermot Burke did shake his extended hand.

"Good morning, Burke."

"Good morning, Warden."

He nodded at Gerry, and said, with simple gravity, "Detective O'Neil." They shook hands, and all three sat around the table. The guard exited and closed the door.

"Warden Guthrie, I'm wondering how we can reward Mr. Burke if he assists us in an important ongoing investigation."

The warden took a pair of reading glasses out of an inside pocket of his suit coat and put them on. "Let me see his folder, Detective."

Gerry slid it across the table. The warden pulled a pen out of his top pocket and clicked it open. He scanned the sheet and said, "You've been here in Supermax for five years, Dermot. What do you think of it so far?"

"What do I think of it? Well, Oscar Wilde summed it up well." His eyes took on a distant aspect and he recited:

All that we know who lie in gaol,
Is that the wall is strong;
And that each day is like a year,
A year whose days are long."

Gerry thought it ironic that Burke should be quoting the man who wrote: "All art is quite useless," but he said nothing. This was not the time to shatter the con's comfortable feeling that his was by far the superior intellect in the room.

"Yes," the warden said, "twenty-two out of twenty-four hours in a cell. It's hard time. And you spend most of your free hours in the library. Where would you like to go if you could be transferred?"

"How about Framingham?" Dermot asked.

"Oh, the women's prison, of course." The warden laughed. "You might not like the women you meet there. They are not generally connoisseurs of art. I've spoken to Norfolk. This is level six, as you know. They're level three. A job in the library? Windows? A walk in the yard? And when you're eligible for parole in 2014, provided you've stayed out of trouble, and Detective O'Neil says you were helpful, we'll make sure the right people on the parole board know about it."

"Provided I'm alive. Can you move up my parole eligibility date, Warden?"

"Not unless they elect me Governor of the Commonwealth. You know my reputation, Burke. Anyone ever tell you I was not a straight shooter? I say what I mean, and I stand by my word. That's who I am. You want the deal?"

Burke removed his glasses, and swiped at an eye with the edge of his cuff. "I'll take it, Warden."

"You want your lawyer as a witness?"

He shook his head. "I hate lawyers, even my own. I believe you, Warden. When will the transfer happen?"

"I'll fax the papers over this afternoon. Two weeks, maybe less."

"All right."

"I'll give you a chance to talk to Detective O'Neil." He shook hands with them once more and rose. Gerry rang the buzzer, and the guard opened the door.

"One more thing, Warden. I need access to an outside line. You think anyone I know is going to talk when they see MCI Cedar Junction, or whatever cage I'll be in on the caller I.D.? They have to think I'm out. And I need a computer that's not filtered. I had the Louvre Museum blocked on me the other day."

Gerry cast an inquiring glance at the warden. "Can you do it, Warden?"

"We'll get him a private line and access to a computer if that will help. Communications will have to be monitored."

When they were alone, Dermot Burke said, "I have a confession to make, Detective."

"What's that?"

"I have no idea what happened to the forty-one Chinese books from the Harvard Library."

"While we're being so honest, Mr. Burke, let me just tell you that if the info you give us is bullshit, you'll be back here in short order."

Burke shook his head and said, "Oh ye of little faith."

"Ah, it's not that I don't trust you, Dermot, it's just that I don't trust you that much."

The haggard Irishman laughed at that and said, "Well, maybe I'll surprise you then."

24

Down. Down. Their footfall on the worn marble steps echoed in the stairwell. An odor of disinfectant hung in the air, barely masking a nameless and frightening odor that seemed to permeate the dampness and emanate from the stone walls bathed in electric light. Down. Down. Into the cellar of *Le Centre Berthelot*. She knew what happened here. She had imagined this dread descent many times. Her thoughts turned to the white Virgin, *Notre Dame des Neiges,* on the mountain above St. Luc, casting a pitiful glance earthward from the height where the mistral swept the clouds from the face of the stars. "Be with me," she whispered to the serene white lady in her mind.

The young man in the impeccable gray uniform and wire-rimmed glasses led the way past a cell where she glimpsed a dark figure huddled in the corner, rocking back and forth. He opened a door, and stood aside, erect and officious, as the man in the long leather coat pushed her inside. He might have been handsome, she thought abstractedly, with his fair hair neatly trimmed and combed back, and with the clear gaze of his sapphire eyes.

He might have been handsome if one had seen him at a café or strolling across the Bellecour, but here there was only ugliness. Beauty in this place was like the rose that wound its way about a scaffold. It only augmented the horror by the contradiction of its presence in a place where there could only be pain and death. As if in answer to these thoughts, the light bulbs in the corridor suddenly dimmed and she heard, from the interior of the basement, the sort of howling scream that she had only imagined as she read Dante's depiction of the Inferno. She shivered and steeled her heart, a heart whose every beat she could feel, and count, as it drummed within her.

The two men appeared not to hear the screams, however. Torture for them had become banal, it seemed—just another civil service job. The man in the leather coat pulled a notebook out of his pocket and said, "Your name is?"

"Odette Langeron."

"No, it is Odette Prieur. Try again. What is your name?"

She knew it was hopeless, but she continued. "You have confused me with another Odette. You see my papers. My name is . . ."

The blow hit her so hard in the face that she flew backward, her head striking the stone wall. Everything went white as she slid to the floor, tasting blood. Then, without knowing why, she drew herself up and stood again before the man who had struck her. There was a ringing in her ears. She wanted to scream at him. *It will not be so easy to make me talk.* But he would see that soon enough.

"Do not lie. What were you doing outside this building tonight?" The uniformed man yawned and looked at his watch.

"I . . . I . . . I . . . " She sensed his sudden movement and raised her arms in front of her face instinctively. She was not strong enough to block the blow. It drove her own hands into her face and slammed her backward against the wall. Her breath caught, and she crumpled to the floor, gasping.

The man with the wire-rimmed glasses asked the Gestapo agent something in German.

The one who had struck her did not respond. He put the notebook back in his pocket and clutched a handful of her hair tightly. He hauled her roughly to her feet. "An officer was attacked here tonight as you no doubt are aware. He is recovering. He wants very much to be here tomorrow for your interrogation. You will tell the truth about what you were doing here and about the identity of the man who entered while you spoke with the guard. You will tell everything you know about everyone you know. You will spill your guts, like a whimpering little child, because if you do not, you will be praying for us to kill you, begging us to end it by killing you, but rest assured, *petite garce*, we will not kill you, not even when your own mother would not recognize the battered, torn, blood-soaked, disgusting . . . *thing* that was her daughter. Sleep well – we will see you in the morning."

He looked her over critically and said something rapidly to the younger man in German. Then he left.

She shrank backward into the corner of the cell as the man stepped up and pulled her belt off. "Don't worry," he said in heavily accented French, "I'm not going to rape you. However, it would matter to no one if I did." He patted her body down, and then leaned over, untied her shoe laces, and tore them out of the eyelets. "He doesn't want a suicide." He paused, crouched there with his forearms resting on his knees. "Listen, tell them whatever they want to know tomorrow. Your friends will not blame you. I've seen big strong men crying for their mothers. You think a little woman like you will be braver?"

His eyebrows formed two arcs over his round glasses. "I doubt it. Grahamar is not a man to be trifled with, and it appears your friend wounded him, put his eye out. He will be here tomorrow, still raw and bandaged. I hear he will take you to the Hotel Terminus to use some of their special equipment for

Versharfte vernehmung. That is, what do you call it, enhanced interrogation? Believe me, it will go very badly for you if you do not tell him everything."

The screaming that they heard from somewhere in the interior of the basement resumed with horrifying intensity. "I'm no sadist. I don't enjoy these screams, but what else do terrorists understand? Good night, Odette Langeron, or whatever your name is. You see, these games you've been playing at are dangerous." He shrugged and shook his head, as if to say, "It's your own fault."

He locked the door and went out, whistling Lili Marlene, and she heard another door open and close at the end of the corridor. The screams, somewhere, had turned to moans and babbling sobs, and Odette broke out in a cold sweat. The cell was empty save for an iron bunk, a pitcher of water on a wooden box, and a filthy bucket. Her face was sore, and the skin around her eye felt tight where she knew it was swelling. She wondered what time it was and thought about the coming day. A wave of nausea swept over her and she staggered to the bucket and vomited.

She had to think. She felt the walls and looked quickly around the room for some means to kill herself. She needed air. There was one window at the top of the low wall across from the cell door. She tried to move the bed, but it was clamped to the floor.

She set the pitcher on the floor and moved the wooden box under the window. She put her hand through the bars and felt what was left of a window frame outside. She paused at one point, running her finger back and forth over what was a small piece of glass protruding from the frame. She tore a splinter of wood from the frame and began to work it in the crevice that had held the pane until, a few minutes later, she had extracted a piece of glass, not so large as she would have liked, but large enough to do what had to be done. Odette said a brief prayer, not for her own soul; the Virgin would understand, but for her daughter in Chambrel who would not see her mother again in this life.

Standing at the window, she felt the air on her cheek, and a longing love for the night outside the barred windows grew in her, for the moon that sailed above her dreaming daughter, for the rain that was beginning to fall on the sidewalk and perhaps on the roof of the country house where Amélie slept.

Furiously, she pulled at the remainder of the wooden frame that had once held an exterior window, and it fell away piece by piece until nothing remained between her and the world outside but two iron bars across a rectangle of space.

The space between those bars was large enough for a girl to pass through. Her daughter, if she were here, could escape, but Odette did not think that she would ever be able to do it. She searched the cell frantically for something she could use to dig at the bars. She pulled the mattress onto the floor. Underneath, it was supported by a thin sheet of wood nailed to a frame. She knew there was no way to extract a nail, but she pulled hopelessly with bleeding fingers, and she cried because she knew she must either escape or die tonight. If she were here in the morning, Horst Grahamar would exact a horrible revenge on her body, and she would have to prepare herself to endure pain beyond comprehension because she could never talk. She would never talk. Never. But it would be so hard. It would be a hard, hard way to die.

She looked again at the window, hating the smallness of the space between the bars. I must try, she thought. She waited, listening at the cell door for a moment. The screaming had died, or perhaps the screamer had died. There were voices. They could be heard but faintly, as through walls or doors of iron. Then closer, in a nearby cell, she heard a faint, almost whispered voice, singing the song she had heard among the maquisards:

Friend, do you hear the black flight
Of crows above our plains?
Friend, do you hear the muffled cries
Of our country in chains?

The song, barely audible, renewed her courage and resolution. She moved quickly now, trembling with desperate energy. She removed all of her clothes and pushed them through the bars, except for the long skirt, which she hung over the edge of the stone before the recessed window. She took what water was in the pitcher and poured it over her body.

Her eyes widened as she noticed a small corner of something white on the floor beside the pitcher of water. She picked it up and held it to her nostrils. Nothing had ever smelled so good. It was soap. Quickly, she rubbed the small piece into her palms and began to spread it over her head, her torso, and her hips.

Two bars, three spaces. She studied and compared them, and decided that the middle was the best; the iron would not move, but it would not rip into her like the stone.

Odette blessed herself and pulled her body up toward the window. She began to push her head into the space between the bars, but realized that her arms would have to go out first. She put her arms through, as though she were diving upward and sideways, and then began to push her head through the iron bound space, looking skyward, driving with her elbows against the outside of the bars.

She felt the vice-like pressure of the iron closing on her head, a dull blinding ache, and feared that her skull would crack, but still she drove forward, slowly, the bars now tearing at her ears, and at the swollen skin around her eye. Her instinct was to pull back, but she drove harder. She felt as though her ears were torn, but her head was through, and she gasped as she felt the rain falling on her face, falling from the sky outside the cell. Her back, which was hanging at an awkward angle, still inside the cell, felt as though it would break. She wriggled her body forward slowly, taking an inch at a time, two inches, the unyielding bars extracting a toll of pain for her passing.

The iron tore at her breasts, and compressed her ribs, squeezing the breath from her. She stifled her cries of pain, knowing that what waited for her if she were in that cell in the morning would be far, far worse. The parallel iron bars now grasped only her hips in their tortuous narrows. She twisted her pelvis, her slick body compressed until her legs felt numb, and then she was out, on the rain-spattered sidewalk, reborn under heaven's rain.

She lay for a few seconds in the darkness, feeling the cool rain on her naked body, but driven to fly by the soul of fear itself, a fear that reached out to her from the other side of the dark rectangle. She pulled her remaining clothes from the inside ledge through the cell window, and still aching from the iron grip of the bars, limped to a shadowy corner of the building where she dressed quickly and set off through the darkness and the rain, her breath shortened by the pangs that shot through her ribs, thanking the Virgin of the snows. "I may die for France," she thought, "but not tonight. Not yet."

25

Gina had fallen asleep on the couch. Her reading glasses framed her closed eyes, and a David Daniel mystery novel lay on the floor beside her. Tony Bennett crooned softly over the kind of piano that brought slow dances and the smoky cabarets of forties films to mind. Gerry stopped to look at her, her head tilted amid a tangle of dark hair, the image of peace, and he watched her as he listened to Tony Bennett singing "I'm Glad There Is You."

In sleep she seemed to feel his eyes because she stirred and opened them, at first slightly, and then wide. "Hi, honey," she said, stretching her legs, and arching her back. She pulled off her glasses. "My God, I was reading, and I couldn't hold the book up anymore. Is something wrong?"

"I'm afraid so," he said. She raised her legs while he took a seat at the end of the couch, and lowered her feet on his lap. "I just came from Frank McGuin's house. Cheryl died of an overdose this afternoon. We don't know exactly what killed her until the toxicology report comes in . . . probably a mixture of booze and drugs. Her so-called friends, including Al Lekakis, said that they thought she was sleeping at a booth in the Tap Room. By the time someone decided to check on her, she was gray . . . dead."

Gina closed her eyes and shook her head. "Well, you did all you could, Gerry."

He sighed. "I suppose. I just feel bad for Frank and his kids."

"How are they taking it?"

"It's a nightmare."

She sat up and put her arm around him. "You know I've been thinking. You need to take a weekend and go do some guy thing with Hugh."

He sat up at the mention of his son's name as if awakening from a dream and said, "Yes, you're right. I have to do that. As soon as this case is resolved, we'll go on a fishing trip up to Maine."

"Do it, Gerry. Your job can take a psychological toll. You need to get away."

"You know, it was a strange day. I saw in the obits that Agnes Vega died, survived by her son, Lawrence Vega. Larry Vega is that sad sack I told you about, *gonna change his life*! Right. And then there was Cheryl. I'm talking to this old guy, Martin. He's a lot like me, you know. It's strange, and it makes me think." He got up and went to the liquor cabinet in the kitchen area of the great windowed room that was almost the entire apartment. "There are things . . . what did he say, 'I wonder if God will forgive me.' You know I'm not the most religious person, but I wonder sometimes, what if I'm walking around, trying to do the right thing, and I'm already damned?" He poured a large Jameson into a tumbler and splashed a little water over it at the tap.

"Is there something you want to tell me, Gerry?"

He leaned against the counter for a moment, shaking his head. "I don't know if I really want to. I've never told anyone. Not even my first wife in all those years."

"What happened, Gerry?"

He came and sat down beside her and raised the whiskey. She saw that his eyes were tired, and for the first time since she'd known him he looked his age. "Was it something that happened on the job?"

He shook his head. "It was in Viet Nam." He looked her in the eyes. "I'm afraid you will see me differently."

"Horrible things happen in war, Gerry. I know that."

"But it wasn't in combat. It was in Saigon. I was a crazy twenty-year-old. We were high." He exhaled deeply and drank some whiskey. "We had snorted some . . . I don't know if it was heroin or opium. And we had more in the jeep. There was a South Vietnamese policeman. They had white uniforms, and we used to call them white mice. He stopped us, me and this guy called McKidd, and told us to get out of the jeep, and I started to argue with him. I don't remember if he had his pistol out, or if he was getting it out. God forgive me, Gina. I picked up a twelve-gauge flare gun and fired. I can't tell you why I did that. The flare ripped into his stomach. I drove away, but I saw him there, screaming on the ground, with a burning hole in his gut. I murdered him."

She had never seen Gerry cry, or even imagined it, but the tears fell, and his voice was choked with the grief that he had tried to bury in the darkness of shame and under the weight of years. "I always thought that M.P.'s would come and arrest me – that someone must have seen, but life was cheap there. It never seemed to matter to anyone, except to the family of that policeman who never came home."

Gina leaned toward him and rubbed his back. "Gerry, blame the war. Even if it wasn't combat. You can't change the past, but that's not who you are now. You're not a violent person. You don't get out of control on drugs. It *was* the war, Gerry. War and youth."

"But who can forgive me? And what penance can I do that will ever put me at peace with myself?"

"Your long regret has been your penance. What else is there? What good would it do?"

He nodded slowly, turning the glass in his hands. "I found McKidd about five years ago. He was living in Mississippi, where he was from. He was dying of colon cancer. He said, 'It's buried, Gerry, like I will be soon. Leave it there.' But you can't keep things like that buried."

"You have to live with it."

"That's what Faulkner meant: 'The past isn't dead. It isn't even past.'"

"No, it's not. It's part of us."

26

He had hardly slept, thinking of Odette and for the first time since he was a child, praying, for hours, feeling the pain of helpless rage. He should have killed Grahamar. He tried to think of a way to trade the cross for Odette, but Grahamar would never release her until he had it, and once he had it, he would never release her. Moreover, there was no way to communicate directly with the Gestapo. In the small hours before dawn, he rose, and lit the candle the priest had left. Creeping out of the sacristy, he went down the stairs into the cavernous, silent church. He began to look around, and found a ladder in a crawl space behind the altar, and an old candle-lighter, about four feet long. He pulled a rag out of an empty bucket. Opening his shirt, he slid the heavy chain and jeweled cross over his head and hung it in the crux between the two short curved arms of the candle-lighter. There was a wick at the end of one arm, and a bell-shaped snuffer at the end of the other, which he unscrewed, and pushed back in space under the altar. Then he tore the rag in strips and tied the chain and the cross tightly to the hardwood handle.

Quietly, carefully, he pulled the ladder out, and set it up against the wall adjacent to the organ. He climbed up and was able to sit on the ledge of a window beside the organ pipes. He lifted the long handle of the candle-lighter and lowered it down into the fluted organ pipe, like a ramrod into a barrel, turning the candle-lighter so that one of its curved arms hooked over the back of the organ pipe. Hardly noticeable, he thought, even from this vantage.

After dawn had begun to color the darkened stained glass windows with rich wine and blue and gold, Martin heard low voices in the nave of the church. He shook Marius, but he knew it wasn't the Gestapo. They always arrived before dawn, and they arrived in numbers, shouting. Père LeBrun knocked and opened the sacristy door. "There is someone here to see you," he said.

It was Lucien, carrying a satchel full of newspapers. The priest reached over and pulled off the cap he wore tilted over one eye, and pulled an unlit cigar from between his teeth. "You're in God's house, young man," he said, handing him his cap and cigar.

"Sorry, *mon Père.*"

The bespectacled priest mumbled something and walked out. Lucien put the satchel down and said, "Odette has escaped. She is at the Rue Denuzière, recovering." Martin was on his feet embracing the young man before he knew what he was doing, while Marius dragged a sleeve across glistening eyes.

"Is she all right?" Martin asked.

"She's a little beat up, limping, but all right. Marius, she wants new identity papers. I have her new information, and a photo." He reached under the papers. "*La Voix du Midi.* I hate delivering this shit." He handed Marius an envelope.

"I'll have her new papers before she moves out of Denuzière. But she must leave Lyon."

"You can try to convince her of that. She wants to deliver a radio first to someone from MUR at La Tour Rose."

"Why is she running around the city with radios when she just escaped from Berthelot?" Martin demanded.

"She says BEC 22 wants the network running as soon as possible."

"Right."

The priest came back and said, "There is some commotion in the square. You," he said, pointing to Lucien, "go out and kneel by the candle tray. If anyone enters, you wanted to say a prayer for your mother, which I hope is true. Marius, you and your friend leave by the back door, that way. Leave singly, and carefully."

"*Au revoir*," Lucien said, following the priest to the door, where he paused and said, "Patrice, Odette says that the new radios are better. Why?"

"Better range, and for example, you can tune the receiver to a different frequency than the transmitter, so that you can listen for incoming messages while you're transmitting. Cuts down on air time and makes it harder for the direction finders to locate us. I'll show you, but you must go now."

"Good. By the way, they're tearing your rooms apart at the Hotel Napoléon. Lyon will be very dangerous for you now, too. Get new papers. Stay with Marius in Vieux Lyon, Presqu'ile, and the Croix Rousse. He knows the alleys and the *traboules*." The *traboules*, a network of hundreds of medieval passageways that led through the oldest parts of the city; a labyrinth in which the uninitiated were quickly lost.

27

As darkness descended on the city of Lyon, Martin was walking along the Rue Ravat toward the Rue Denuzière, carrying a bottle of wine, like a young man on his way to see his girl, which was, after all, what he was. It might be a mistake, but he couldn't wait to see her. He rounded the corner, and watched for a stranger lingering about, or a black Citroën with tape across its headlights. Nothing looked amiss, and he took a deep breath and walked on. The Gestapo sometimes allowed prisoners to escape so that they could follow them to their comrades, but Odette would have made sure that she was not being followed.

He walked into the bar on Rue Denuzière, where he asked for a cognac. It was almost empty; a few elderly gents played dominoes at one table. Arnold, the barman, was a member of a Resistance group called Combat, and he and Odette had met upstairs with him and others a month ago about the plan to penetrate Berthelot.

Martin placed what looked like a matchbox on the bar and said quietly, "The film is inside." It had been agreed that it would leave with a downed RAF flyer and his guide who would cross the Pyrenees within two days.

Arnold pushed a rag over the well-polished marble counter top, and the tiny box disappeared. He said softly, "You are a brave man, Monsieur. When you finish your drink, you know where she is."

"*Merci, Monsieur.*"

The cognac warmed his heart, and after a moment he left the bar and walked under the arch and into a stairwell that smelled of urine. At the top of the first flight, he gave three knocks, then two, then one. A moment later, he heard her voice, "Who is it?"

"Patrice."

The door opened. He entered quickly, and she locked the door again and looked at him. For the first time since her capture, she allowed the tears to fall. "Patrice, I never thought to see you again." Her left eye was purple and swollen, and her dark hair, drawn back, showed that one of her ears was covered in a white ointment. Martin wrapped his arms around her, the bottle hanging from his left hand. "Don't squeeze," she said.

He froze and stepped back. He touched her face gently, and her shoulders, and kissed her lips tentatively, as a grammar school boy might kiss his girl behind the bleachers. "They said Grahamar would interrogate me and that my friend had put out his eye. What happened?"

"He found me in his office after I photographed his papers. I gave him a cigarette from a booby-trapped case. The mistake I made was not finishing the job. How were you taken?"

"Oh *mon Dieu*, what bad luck I have. My bicycle fell into a rut, and the rim was bent. The first bomb went off, and I couldn't pedal the bicycle, and I threw it aside and started running, and just then a patrol passed by, and some *collabo* pointed me out. I was very unlucky and very stupid. And the guard at the gate recognized me."

"I didn't think he'd forget you soon."

Martin opened the wine and poured some into teacups he found in the cupboard. He handed her one, and they sat on the tattered chintz of the couch. She closed her eyes and sipped the wine, and then she told him of the experience she'd had in

Berthelot. He stroked her hair as she related the fearful passage from the cell to the sidewalk. "And you're all right?" he asked.

"Just a little sore. Nothing broken. Look." The blinds were already drawn, but she rose and drew the curtains together. She pulled her sweater off, and then unbuttoned her dress and let it fall on the couch; she pulled her slip over her head and stood before him naked, and he saw the raw scrapes along her breasts and ribs, and the purple bruises where her hips had been racked in iron. Her body was a testament to vulnerability, he thought, and yet her spirit was a monument of invulnerability. So fragile, so beautiful, so delicate, and so strong.

He wished he could protect her, forever, from every threat, but he felt a sadness blossoming in his heart and in his eyes, knowing that he could protect her, and himself, from very little. They had both been extraordinarily lucky, but the storms, the hate, the hard steel and hot lead, and now the implacable vengeance that pursued her and him would never cease. From here on out, it would be *le ratissage*, the rat hunt.

"Make me yours," she said, unbuttoning his shirt.

"I'm so afraid to hurt you any more, Odette. Let's wait until you've healed."

She laughed and then bit her lip and put a hand on her rib. "Come, I would not take off my clothes if I were not ready for combat, a very mild combat, because I know a man is not made of wood, eh? *Doucement, Patrice, doucement.*"

His hands slid gently over her body, sensing its fragility, and softly he kissed her bruised and tender breasts. After a while, they picked up their cups and she guided him to the bedroom and laid him down, and like a woman at the seaside entering the cold water warily, she straddled him slowly, and reaching between his legs, she guided him into her as she settled over him.

"My name is not Patrice, anymore, Odette. It is Paul."

"Ah," she said, her slender body rising and falling on him slowly, "My name is not Odette anymore. It is Carmen."

The bedroom itself seemed to breathe faintly in the air that stirred in the window curtains, allowing a thin streak of light to fall across her body and then fade into dimness. He touched her swollen face and her contused breasts as one might touch a tiny wounded bird, filled with pity and love. He felt her cry of pleasure that was almost a cry of pain, and his heart was pierced with the thought of what might have been this day, and he kissed her, perhaps a little too roughly for a moment, and said, "It's not at all like the animals!" She laughed and held her ribs, while tears ran from her dark eyes. "I love you, Odette."

"Carmen."

"I love you."

She smiled, and winced once more. "I do love you too," she said. And if there was some reserve in her voice, Martin sensed exactly what it meant. *I love you, but I have sworn to serve France. And until we are free, that is where my first allegiance will be.*

They sat up in the bed and Odette leaned over him to pick up their cups of wine, but her breath caught, and Martin said, "Let me get them." Slowly, she straightened out and leaned back on the pillow.

"You have to go to Ardeche to recuperate. You'll be safe in the hills around Colombièrs."

"Yes, after tomorrow. I'm meeting a man who repaired one of the radios that was damaged in the drop. The others have all been distributed. I'll bring this one to La Tour Rose, and then I'll leave for a while." She raised the wine to her lips.

"I'll meet the man."

He felt her hair move over his chest as she shook her head. "No," she said, "he doesn't know you. If he doesn't see me, he'll leave the radio somewhere and disappear. I'll do this. I must. Things are moving fast, and there is so much to be done; intelligence gathering on the harbor at Nice for U.S. naval forces, an Allied landing in Southern France, the clearing out of glider areas, the reporting on troop strengths and movements. Every radio in every sector will be vital."

He rose and went to find his jacket. He pulled from some tiny pocket in the seam a small paper pouch. "Take this," he said. "If you're captured again, I don't think you'll be so lucky. Swallow it, and you'll be dead in seconds, painlessly."

"Patrice, if I'm captured I will try to survive; there is always hope while one is alive, to find a way out. If not, I will show them what a free French woman is made of. That I swear."

A mist began to cloud his eyes. "It's the Catholic teaching, right? You think you'll be damned? It can't be."

"I just want to play out whatever hand is dealt to me."

"Even if you could bear your torture, how could I?"

"You would have to bear it, and all things, for our cause. But I've survived many missions here in Lyon. This will be my last."

Martin remembered his father, Jean LeBris. During prohibition, he used to make bootleg runs to Canada. He was paid to guide the smugglers back through the woods on unmarked and unpaved lumber roads recrossing the border with a truckload of whiskey.

It was dangerous, though, and he had told Martin's mother that he was done. One night two men came to the front door, and his father had gone out to talk with them. After a while, he came back in, and, as she twisted her hands in her apron, he said, "One more run, Molly, and I promise, it's over."

He left the next night, and he never returned. The FBI was waiting for them in the woods near the border. From what Martin learned later, there was a shoot-out. His father had taken to the woods. Whether he bled to death under the dark ceiling of branches, or was lost in those vast forests, no one ever knew. He lay there, remembering his father; how as a boy he'd run down the hill on Wiggins Street to meet him coming home from the mills and take his empty lunch pail to carry for him, swinging it happily as they walked. And for many years, Martin searched the face of every lanky stranger, hoping for the smile of recognition and the strong arms of his father around him. One of his friends had even sworn he'd seen him on a ferry between Portland and Halifax. But if he could have returned, he would have. He had died alone in the forest. And so Martin did not like the sound of Odette's words. *One last time. Once more.* Those were unlucky words, and he blessed himself quickly in the dark and drew close to her and breathed the warm fragrance of her tangled hair while she slept.

28

Marius and Martin Le Bris waited in a room on the third floor of La Tour Rose for Odette. The chamber of the Spanish Llama pistol hung open while Martin cleaned it.

Marius was leaning against the frame of the window, half watching the intersection outside the courtyard, and half reading Shakespeare in English. "Listen, Patrice," he said. "Even if you don't understand, it's a beautiful language. Listen to the sounds!"

In peace, there's nothing so becomes a man
As modest stillness and humility.
But when the blast of war blows in our ears,
Then imitate the actions of the tiger.

Martin feigned incomprehension and began to laugh. "What? He's talking about piss?"

Marius was annoyed, suspecting that Martin understood him well enough. "No, that's how "*la paix*" is pronounced in English! Peace! *Dans la paix* . . . in peace."

Martin continued to chuckle. "Sorry, it sounds like '*Dans la pisse.*'" He always doubted whether he was fooling someone as bright and as good with languages as Marius, but he had to give it his best attempt.

But Marius was no longer interested in Shakespeare. "Look at this," he said, nodding toward the window. A German transport vehicle stopped, and four soldiers clattered down onto the cobbled streets, leaving another ten sitting in the back. They were setting up patrols at various intersections in the old city. When the truck had pulled away, two of the Germans pulled out cigarettes and began to mill about. One of them unslung his rifle and peered through a sniper's scope at roofs and windows of the surrounding buildings. The two men in the small room, without so much as a sudden shift of their weight, moved out of the frame of light. "That's damned bad luck," Marius said.

"She won't come walking right by them with a suitcase. Odette's too smart for that."

"Carmen," Marius said, "Carmen Guerin." He chuckled. "She thinks I'm a miracle worker; the truth is I already had new papers prepared for such an emergency." They sat on the floor by the window for a while, taking occasional glances at the scene below. Martin loaded and holstered his pistol, and stepped out in the hallway to a water closet to relieve himself. When he reentered the room, the Frenchman did not turn away from the window, but waved him quickly over.

A young boy had come into the *carrefour*, riding a bicycle. Pannier baskets full of potatoes hung over the back wheel. He was headed toward the courtyard of La Tour Rose, but he stopped to turn and look back. Odette came into view, pacing quickly, eyes downcast, a kerchief pulled tightly over her head. The two men in the room of La Tour Rose guessed immediately what was going on. "Keep going!" they murmured urgently, as if the boy on the bicycle could hear them.

The soldiers had stopped Odette, and one of them was talking to her, while the others, who probably did not speak French, looked on idly. The soldier seemed to be asking her what had happened to her eye. She stroked it and shook her head, smiling, giving them whatever story she'd prepared. They hadn't asked for her papers, and she seemed about to move on, when one of the other soldiers pointed at the boy on the bicycle. He was circling back toward Odette. Martin's heart sunk. "No," he thought. "No, no, no."

It happened quickly. One of the Germans said something to the boy, then reached into the basket. He pulled out the transmitter, scattering potatoes on the cobbled street. Odette turned to run, but a soldier had her by the arm.

"This will be our only chance," Martin said. He tore the mattress off the bed and grabbed an MAS 36 7.5mm bolt action carbine and tossed it to Marius, with two extra five-round clips. He picked up the other weapon, a Petter sub machine gun with a thirty-six round magazine. He was flying down the spiral staircase of the tower and across the courtyard before Marius could say, "*On y va.*"

One of the Germans was leaning over the brown leather case he'd carried. Martin knew it was a *Feldfernsprecher*, a Field Telephone, but didn't know if he was just getting it out, or had already called and was putting it away. How long did it take to get someone on the line and say: "Come to La Tour Rose. We've caught a spy."

"You do the fine shooting with the carbine," Martin said. "I'll get anyone who's not near Odette. Now."

He sprang into the sunlit archway and opened fire on the soldier with the field telephone and the one near him. One fell immediately, convulsed for a few seconds, and lay bleeding in an awkward pose of death. The other was crawling for cover, his rifle abandoned in the street. The little boy was running away, screaming, his bicycle lying in the street with its front wheel spinning. Marius had killed one of the other soldiers, but the last one clutched Odette around the waist and crouched behind her body as he backed toward the corner. They saw the muzzle of a rifle rise under her arm, and heard her scream at them to run. They dove back into the courtyard as the barrel flashed and the cobbled street smoked with stone dust. They heard the wild high pitch of bullets ricocheting around them.

"What now, Patrice?"

Even at this critical moment, it passed through Martin's mind what courage this slim intellectual possessed. He was breathing heavily, probably full of adrenaline, but he'd been ready for any fight since the day they met. Martin peeked out quickly, and the rifle blasted the edge of the stone wall, stinging his face with rock chips. Their only chance had been to take her immediately. A standoff was no good, and by now the German had backed around the corner and could watch their position with some security. There was a last game they could play. *Les traboules*. The passageways.

"Can you bring me through the traboules to the other side of the street?"

"Yes, I can," Marius said, "but it will take some time."

"Maybe we shot the radio man before he communicated with HQ." And once again the two men were running. They entered an old wooden door by the side of a medieval well and ran along a passageway that seemed to run parallel to the street. Its walls and floor were stone. They ran down a sloping ramp and passed between the facades of old houses and another stone wall. Marius paused and then turned sharply into a dark passageway that seemed to pass under a street.

When they began to rise, Martin saw what looked like the courtyard of a nunnery, with arched porticoes and a cloistered garden. An elderly woman in a gardener's apron was pruning plants with a pair of secateurs, apparently oblivious to the sound of gunfire that had shattered the calm or the morning. She nodded at the two men armed men and continued her work. They walked across the garden, and Marius indicated a gate half hidden in the arched and ivied trellises that led to it. He opened the door a few inches and scanned the scene.

"My God, Patrice. It's too late."

He caught a last glimpse of Odette as *Wehrmacht* troops threw her into a truck, and he saw them shut and lock the rear door. Other soldiers were stationed around the square. The dead men and the wounded man were being loaded into an ambulance, while about ten soldiers were running toward La Tour Rose, rifles raised.

They reentered the *traboules* that Marius knew so well; soon they were far from the scene. They did not speak, but as Martin heard the echoing of his footsteps on the stone, passing along the damp, cool dark, he had never felt so alone, not since his father had disappeared into the northern woods to die.

The two points in time seemed to converge in his soul, and he stopped in the dark, while Marius stood in a rectangle of light at an open doorway; his back slid down the stone wall, and he sat in the narrow passageway with his head in his hands and cried like the little boy had cried long ago, standing at his father's workbench in the cellar of the house in Pawtucketville, sobbing, "Come back. Come back." Marius looked over his shoulder at him, closed the door, and stepped back into the dark. He sat on the ground, against the stone wall, as silent as the ancient stones.

There had been no coming back for his father, and there would be no coming back for Odette this time, either. He'd had to bear his father's fate. But where was the strength to bear this?

Pity and rage twisted his heart when he thought of what would happen to Odette, and he would give anything to stop it, but he couldn't. Still, if Odette could survive long enough for them to find out where she would be sent, he would try.

29

Martin and Marius waited on the corner of the Avenue Berthelot and the Rue de Marseille. Lucien and Antoine waited with them, as well as a young woman Martin knew only as *La Parisienne*. Darkness was descending over the old city. They learned that Odette had been taken from Berthelot to the Hotel Terminus, where Klaus Barbie often led interrogations on the elegant fourth floor. If she survived, she would be taken either to Montluc Prison or back to Berthelot. Two groups lay in wait, one at each of the most likely routes from the Hotel Terminus to both Montluc and the Centre Berthelot.

"Are you nervous?" Martin asked *La Parisienne*.

"Yes, a little."

"When you've played your part, just put your coat on and walk away."

She glanced toward the doorway where her coat lay on the ground. "I understand." She did her best to smile, pushing her fair hair behind her ears. Where do they find such women, Martin wondered. She couldn't be more that twenty, and ready to risk it all against armed men.

On the corner, a man holding a leash began to call loudly for a dog. "*Viens, viens, mon p'tit chien! Hugo! Hugo!*" He continued to call and whistle. It
was the signal.

"You're drunk!" the young woman screamed at Antoine, and Marius and Martin crossed the street as a light Kübelwagen, the

German version of a jeep, and a lorry rounded the corner. Marius held a stack of newspapers under his arm and pretended to be selling one to Martin.

"You're a liar! And a damned whore!" the slim Antoine shouted back. As the German vehicles approached, their shouting increased in volume. *La Parisienne* slapped the young man's face. He clutched at her dress below her neck with both hands and tore hard downward, so that her bare breasts were revealed, and catching a glimpse, Martin remembered the famous painting of Delacroix, the bare-breasted Liberty brandishing the tricolor at the barricades.

The light four-man vehicle had stopped, and the lorry behind it. The man with the leash had already disappeared.

"*Tu me fais chier!*" she cried.

"*J'en ai plein le cul avec toi! Putasse!*"

The Germans in the Kübelwagen watched the scene, nudging each other and smiling. "*Dank fur das Erscheinen!*" the driver called. Martin took a deep breath, nostrils flaring and jaw set. *Be bloody, bold, and resolute.* He stepped quickly to the passenger side of the small car. The newspapers fell as Marius ran to the lorry; they both fired at point-blank range. *La Parisienne* had donned her coat and was walking away. Antoine ran to the back of the lorry, pulling a pistol from inside his jacket. "*Dich abgesetzt Waffe! Einen Lastwagen verlassen!*"

Martin saw the muzzle of a submachine gun jut through the canvas flap. He shot into the side as the air resounded with rifle fire. Shots chewed the cobbled street and ripped into Antoine's body as he stood firing the pistol. A German soldier in a green uniform tumbled out of the back of the truck. His rifle clattered on the street. Antoine lay dead beside him, blood spurting from his neck.

Another German in the back could be heard shouting "*Ich übergebe! Ne tirez pas!*" He pulled back the flap slowly, hands raised. Marius and Martin shot him and leaped up on the back of the truck as he fell, hanging over the door for a few seconds before tumbling over and thudding to the street. In the distance, across the Saône, they heard the diversionary explosions.

There were three prisoners in the truck. One had already clambered off and was hobbling away in torn, bloody clothes. Another was unconscious. The third, a mute shadow, stirred, and Martin gasped as Odette raised her head. One of her eyes was gone, sunken or pushed into her head; the other dangled on her cheek. Her hands, wrapped in bloody gauze, were fingerless, and her skin was blanched and swollen.

"Grahamar had her injected with bleach," Marius whispered.

"Odette!"

She raised a bandaged hand blindly as if to ward him off. "Patrice! Run!" Her words were thick and slurred.

"You're coming with us. You need a doctor."

"No, no. Run! Find my daughter at . . . "

"Yes, at Chambrel. Rue du Lauriers, 29. Amélie Prieur."

"Tell her I'm dead, but not the truth! Tell her I love her and I want her to be—to be brave."

Martin was choking on tears of helpless rage. "Trust me, *mon amour*." He tried to lift her, but she cried out; he could feel the shattered ribs beneath her torn and filthy dress.

"Please, kill me. Amélie can never see me like this."

"I'll find your daughter."

"They say everyone talks. But I never talked, Patrice."

"I know you didn't."

"*Le Bon Dieu comprendra. Tue-moi je t'en prie.*"

God will understand. Kill me, I beg you.

"Decide, Patrice, *now*. There's no time." Marius was standing at the back of the truck, looking anxiously down the street.

****

Gerry O'Neil watched as the old man took off his glasses and began to wipe them with a handkerchief he'd pulled from his pocket. Martin shook his head slowly, swallowing hard, and dabbed at his eyes. Finally, Gerry asked, "What did you do?"

"I put my pistol to her temple, and I shot her."

The two men were quiet for a moment as the weight of the words and of the years settled about them, like a suffocating blanket over the present. Finally, Martin looked up, put on his glasses, and said, in a hoarse whisper, "That's why I never slept very well after the war."

"Martin, do you have anything valuable that you brought back from the war? Anything someone would kill for?"

Martin hardly heard the younger man. He was hearing once more the sound of the shot shattering her skull and feeling her hot blood splattering his face as her last words hung in the air. "*Le Bon Dieu comprendra. Tue-moi, je t'en prie.*" He had heard those words again every day and every night since the first of June, 1944.

30

Martin forgot everything. He forgot his training, his duty, his orders. His only thought was revenge, to go to the Café du Petit Coin armed with a machine gun and a phosphorous grenade. But by the time he got back to the hideout in the old city, he had begun to think again. He knew that Grahamar would not be at the café now, or if he was, he would be ready, waiting for him. And to offer himself up as a lamb to the slaughter, that was not his idea of revenge. He must be the lion that tore this Nazi lamb to pieces.

He also remembered his promise to Odette, and before morning lit the square of the village of Thizy-les Bourgs, where he had been meeting with leaders of the MLF, he donned a pair of goggles and was out of the city on his way to Chambrel on an Italian motorcycle, a black 1939 Moto Guzzi horizontal single cylinder he'd bought with counterfeit money. He showed his new papers, which identified him as Paul Rainville, and was waved past a few sentries at a roadblock near L'Arbresle. He was a railroad worker, going to visit an ailing mother in Paris; they made a cursory search of his canvas saddlebag.

It was early afternoon when he arrived in the village of Chambrel, and found the house at 29 Rue des Lauriers. All was still. A large gray cat slept in the sun on the front stairs. The dark green shutters were closed. A small plaque beside the front door said "*Maison de Secours Aux Enfants.*" He rapped on the door, but heard no movement inside. Finally, a gate opened at the side of the house, and Martin saw an elderly gentleman in a wide-brimmed hat holding a watering can.

"*Bonjour Monsieur*. I'm looking for Amélie Prieur." He held out the photo of her that he'd taken from the Rue Denuzière. "I have a message from her mother."

"Yes, I know little Amélie, *Monsieur*. I'm so sorry, *Monsieur*." He was leaning heavily against the garden fence, his hat bobbing on his white head as he seemed to struggle for breath.

"You're sorry for what? She's out?"

"She is gone. Sweet girl. They are all gone," he said. Martin saw that his face was twisted with pain, his eyes vacant, staring into memory. "The Germans came here two days ago. There was an armored car and a big truck. They said that Madame Soulat was hiding Jews, and they took her away and all twelve of the children. I lay down in the bushes, here, and Mademoiselle Tardieu jumped out a window and ran away, too."

"Where? Where did they take them?"

"They said they were going to put them on a train. I heard a German officer tell Madame Soulat that the mayor himself, Massart, had informed the Gestapo that there were Jewish children here. I'm all alone now. I don't know if Madame is ever coming back. I don't know if I should keep tending the garden." The old man began to cry. "The children were frightened," he said, "they were calling me, 'Uncle Picot!' they cried out, but what could I do?"

"You could do nothing, *Monsieur*." Martin reached inside his pocket and drew out a roll of notes. He stuffed five hundred into the old man's trembling hand. "Take care of yourself." He pulled the motorcycle inside the fence and said, "I'll be back for it." He set off down the street, passing the pot-bellied shop keeper sweeping his sidewalk, and the two young girls arm in arm singing merrily, *"Sur la chemin de l'école,"* and the gentleman sitting at a café table reading a newspaper. It was as if nothing had happened in the village, and he wanted to take all of the people he saw by the hair and shake them and scream in their faces, "Why are you not in mourning for the poor innocents you saw being hauled away? Whose screams you must have heard just two days ago?"

The street he was on led directly to what he was after. A long brick building with rows of windows and a mansard roof, graced by a cupola on which a clock told him it was just shy of 3:00 pm. Above the ornate doors, the words were written in blue tiles on a white backgkround:

Le Mairie. City Hall.

He walked up the stone steps and into a large office where a young woman sat typing under a map of France. *"Bonjour, Monsieur,"* she said pleasantly, "can I help you?"

"It would be my honor to see the mayor if he is in."

"He's just returned. Whom shall I say is asking for him?"

"Marcel Anglade, of the French Academy. I'm doing a history of this region."

"Oh, how interesting."

He had already seen the office door on which the words "Le Maire Gaston Massart" were printed on the pebbled glass. She knocked softly and opened the door. He heard a brief conversation, after which she returned, smiling. "Yes, he will see you now for a short time."

She inclined her head toward the open door, and said, "Monsieur Le Maire Massart, allow me to present Monsieur Anglade of the French Academy."

The man sat at a mahogany desk, his spectacles on his nose. He was wearing a dark suit with a *fleur de lis* pin in one of his lapels. "I'll be with you in a moment, sir. Please, sit down." He indicated a chair in front of the desk. "Just let me sign this." He paused and looked over the lenses, "Is it the fifth or the sixth?"

"June 6th, 1944."

"Ah, well, I would have to be a fool indeed not to know the year." Finally, Massart rose to greet him, stretching a hand over the cluttered desk. His dark hair lay flat against his head and smelled of pomade as he leaned toward Martin. He set his glasses on a pile of papers and rubbed the bridge of his nose, "A member of the French Academy, eh? I must tell you I have the highest regard for that organization, Monsieur Anglade. The preservers of our French language and culture."

"Thank you, Monsieur Le Maire. It's a difficult job today preserving French culture, when, frankly speaking, it is undermined by Jews and communists at every juncture."

The mayor nodded gravely, his mouth turned down judiciously, "I understand your sentiments perfectly. The problem with the Jews is that they are a nation within a nation. This cannot be. And they are the cause of a lot of our problems with Germany now."

"Didn't I hear they rounded up some Jews hiding hereabouts a few days ago?"

"Yes, and good riddance to them. I can't . . . we can't have them here causing trouble for law- abiding French people."

"What do they do with them?"

"I believe they take them to Drancy, a collection center of sorts. From there, who knows? They can send them back to Zion or to the devil for all I care." He smiled and folded his hands on the desk. "In any case, what is your book about, sir?"

Martin paused, and then asked, "Did I say I was writing a book?"

"Yes, I mean, Jeanne, my secretary, said you were writing a book. A history, I believe?"

He shook his head. "No, in fact I'm not writing a book."

The two men sat looking at each other for a few seconds. Gaston Massart, Mayor of Chambrel, was beginning to look uncomfortable. "Well is there anything else I can help you with?"

"Have you ever read Homer, Monsieur Le Maire?"

He shifted in his seat. "I fail to see . . . "

"You see, while Odysseus is away, the suitors do whatever they want, whatever they can get away with. They lay waste to his stores, court his wife, abuse his son. And Homer says that they are like fools who threaten some small lion cubs, you see . . . but then one day the lion comes home." The mayor's eyes were large now, and he drew back, swallowing hard, because this stranger's eyes were filling with tears, and yet smoldering with a kind of fire he had never seen in a man. "You betrayed those little cubs, and one of them was dear to me. You murdered them Massart, but now the lion is staring you in the face, and you must be a fool indeed not to know what that means."

Martin LeBris flew over the desk at the man, who hardly had a chance to give voice to the shout of panic he felt welling in his chest before he was driven backward over his chair and slammed onto the floor. He felt the hard grip of two hands on his head, fingers wrapped in his hair, and then a sudden twist, a flash behind his eyes, and nothing more, because his neck had been snapped like a dry branch.

Martin almost ran into Jeanne on his way out. "*Mon Dieu!* What happened?" she cried.

"He began to clutch at his chest, Madame! I didn't know what to do. I think he's had a heart attack. My God, I'm afraid he's dead!"

She cupped her hand over her mouth, trembling, and said, "This is terrible. I always tell him he works too hard, Monsieur."

"I'll go find a doctor! Maybe he's only unconscious!"

Other people were streaming in from the wings and down the stairs, tip-toeing toward the mayor's office as Martin ran out the front door and toward the *Maison de Secours Aux Enfants*. A short time later, the Moto Guzzi was whining along a gray ribbon of road that snaked through the hills west of Chambrel. A red scarf streamed out behind him like wings outstretched in the wind, and in the rose light of the descending sun, his hair flew about his face like a halo of fire.

"You can't go off on any personal quest now," Marius insisted. Representatives of the *Franc-Tireurs, Mouvement de Liberation National*, the CCL and other Resistance movements were to meet in the basement of L'Église Saint Étienne to coordinate their efforts and to organize commando missions by GF or assault units. "The invasion in Normandy has begun, and the best way, maybe the only way, to save Odette's daughter will be to do everything we can to help that invasion succeed and push the Germans back across the Rhine. Think of your duty to your country, my friend."

Does Marius suspect that my duty is to another country, Martin wondered. Sometimes he thought he did. Duty. What had Grahamar said to him? *Duty is implacable.* He remembered the OSS recruiter who, on learning that he spoke French fluently had asked, "Do you want to serve your country on a dangerous mission?" His brash and naïve reply: "That's why I signed up,

Sir." Would he answer that way now, knowing what he knew, having seen what he'd seen? He wondered. And yet, to have met her . . .

Marius gripped his arm and said, "Odette, above all others, would understand."

"I'll stay, but I want Martial Beaudry dispatched to Drancy. He's smart, and he speaks German. Let him see if he can find out if Amélie is there; if not, where she has been sent and if there is any way to buy her back. Tell Crépin to sign him out for ten thousand francs in a money belt. Make it twenty."

The men arrived, singly and in pairs, and Martin spread maps on the stone floor. The assignments were meted out based on orders from London and from *Le Conseil National*.

The mission of the CCL was simple and required immediate action. German troops and Panzer divisions would be called to the North to assist in repelling the invasion. They had to be slowed down. They would take to the hills and begin their war in earnest: the cutting of telephone and electric lines with paratrooper hatchets; the demolition of railroad tracks and bridges, for which they had detonating devices that resembled railroad signals; sabotage of fuel dumps, and of German vehicles with gas tank charges, and the primitive but effective tire spikes.

Other weapons from a recent drop were handed out. There were sleeve daggers, garrotes, and .22 caliber silenced automatic pistols for the close range killings of sentries. And there were the lethal cyanide pills for fighters who were taken.

When dawn spread over the city, outlining the Basilica of Notre Dame against the pale sky on the hill above the Rhône, the men left; again, singly and in pairs, mingling with citizens on their way to work, or to wait in line for food rations, or see if

there was bread to be had at the *boulangerie*. They slipped away like the mist that dawn found clinging
to the Rhône, and that melted in the day, but one
had been recognized exiting the church, a piece of intelligence that was reported by a collaborator.

Their numbers grew with their successes. The *maquisards* slept in a different place every night. They cheered when they heard that Rome had fallen, and then grew somber at the news that the German 2nd SS panzer Division *Das Reich*, led by Sturmbannführer Adolf Diekmann, had massacred six hundred and forty-two men, women and children in Oradour-Sur-Glane in Haute-Vienne as a reprisal for Resistance acts of sabotage and ambushes of military convoys. And Jean Michel cried when the news came that Père LeBrun at L'Église Saint Étienne had been visited by the men in black uniforms and hung from his choir loft.

The fighting continued all summer as the Allies pressed on. The Seventh U.S. and First French Armies established a beachhead on the southern coast and moved into the Rhône Valley. The CCL provided tactical intelligence and, with other French Forces of the Interior, helped to protect the Southern flank of the 3rd Army by harassing the enemy and interrupting communications. In September, the last German troops abandoned Lyon, and were pursued not only by the Americans and the British and their allies, but by 300,000 members of the FFI.

Martin LeBris and Marius hounded the retreating troops like the Furies, because Beaudry had followed the children of Chambrel to a camp in Poland called Auschwitz. The liberated prisoners reported that the children had embarked and arrived on the same train, but that they were never seen again. When he asked what had become of them, they pointed to the massive smokestacks that rose from the camp's incinerators. Amélie, too, was dead.

By February, the German homeland was ablaze, and in the Spring of 1945, her final battles fought, Germany surrendered; Jean Michel and Marius joined the crowds that spilled through the streets of Lyon and drank madly the red wine of victory while Martin stood in a fountain and sang "Take Me Out to the Ballgame" for the drunken throng, and explained to Marius, in a very suddenly acquired English, the game of baseball. The latter stood with mouth agape, but insisted that he was not at all surprised.

Martin was hung over, even after sixteen hours in a real bed in a small hotel near the Bellecour. He was awakened by the radio. He could hear its murmuring squawk coming through the headphones that sat on a table near the bed. There were no codes written on flammable silk held in nervous fingers. Only, as he picked up the headphones, the repeated message: "Patrice Quenton, please report your location Q5."

He opened the window that gave out onto a narrow cobbled street, and after peering about, and seeing no one below, gathered up the radio set and tossed it out. He watched with satisfaction as it crashed and bounced on the street. Two little boys appeared from nowhere, excitedly carrying off the pieces. Report to Paris, they would tell him. My ass. From his pocket, he drew the crumpled letter he had taken from Grahamar's office. It was from his wife, Erika; Marius had translated the domestic inanities it contained. Zur Ibs Mühle, Jahn Strasse, Freudenstadt. *They say the war is over. It will be over when Grahamar is dead. Not before.*

Marius tried, half-heartedly, because he knew it was useless, to dissuade him, but as the rivers, flushed with the melting Alpine snow, rushed into the valleys, and the earth reawakened as if in sympathy with Europe's new awakening, Martin roared northward on the Moto Guzzi. The Swiss border, he had heard, was heavily guarded and difficult to cross, so he rode on toward Chalon sur Saône, where he spent the night in a room above a bar.

Early the next morning, he drank a *lait fraise* and a *demitasse* of coffee, with a crust of bread and a piece of cheese and set off for Bensançon, and then Mulhouse, where he intended to slip across the border. The Allied 6th Army Group held the town. It included elements of the U.S. Seventh Army and the French First Army. Martin explained to the Americans that he'd been hiding in France since escaping capture on a stolen motorcycle. He was trying to rejoin his unit which was part of the 6th Army under General Devers in Bavaria.

He was allowed to pass amid a cacophony of shouting civilians, exasperated troops, and forlorn refugees on horse-drawn wagons, or pushing barrows and carts. Wealthier Germans, with their belongings strapped to the roofs of their cars, waited in endless lines for M.P.'s to give their trunks a cursory search so that they could return and see what, if anything, of their homes had been spared by Allied shells and marauding Soviets. Their faces were drawn and heavy with defeat and perhaps regret, so different from the jubilant faces he had left behind in Lyon, though there, too, there was fear; for the daughter who had dated a German; for the husband who had supplied the German army of occupation, and for all those who had complied with posted warnings and military directives, whether from Vichy or Berlin, a little too assiduously.

Martin was tired, but at Breisach am Rhein he consulted his map and set off North along the Rhine, slowed for a time by a convoy of American and Canadian troops. He stopped in Offenburg, where he was able to buy gasoline, eat dinner, and rent a room at the same stop, all from a sad-looking couple who spoke neither French nor English, but who counted out his money very carefully and slowly, as if to assure him that all was fair, though how they calculated the exchange rate was more than Martin could fathom. In the morning, the old man offered Martin the use of their bath before breakfast, which he could not refuse. In any case, the remaining road was short.

As the sun banished the fog that lay over the lowlands, he headed east just north of Offenburg, through greening mountains, which toward noon became veiled in dark clouds that hid deep gorges and stone walled ravines that fell precipitously away from the road, and Martin was forced to move more warily. Still, his heart picked up its pace that afternoon when he saw a road sign ahead that said *Freudenstadt 5 km.*

Zur Ibs Mühle. Martin had forgotten to ask Marius to translate that, but he knew that Mühle meant mill, and so when, from Jahn Strasse, he spotted the paddle wheel in the stream beside the neat stone house with its window frames painted blue, he pulled the motorcycle off the road beside a hillside cemetery full of tilted and weathered markers, and leaned it against the stone wall at the back under overarching trees. The sky had been threatening all afternoon, and now it began to rain. He put on an *impermeable*, or waterproof poncho that he pulled from a pack that was tied to the fender rack of the motorcycle. He also took out bread, cheese, sausage, and a bottle of water. He shoved the pack under his poncho. He chewed grimly, the rain running off the hood in front of his face, a knife lying on the wet ground beside him. He imagined Grahamar in the house below. He prayed that he was there – already planning a future, putting the war behind him, forgetting the agonized cries of a woman stronger than either of them.

He drank some water and leaned back against the wall. The rain murmured its eternal song in the leaves of the old trees that leaned into the stone wall and crouched over the damp graves on the other side. He drank again and closed his eyes, listening to its whisper. He wasn't aware he had slept until he awoke with a start. Darkness leaked out of the mountains and filled the wet hollows. The rain had let up; the last drops ran lazily from the higher leaves onto those below and onto the sodden ground. But there was another sound: voices, and car doors closing. He sat up, stretching the painful knot in his back. He folded the impermeable, and disconnected the tailpipe of the motorcycle. From it, he withdrew a silencer that he screwed into the barrel of a .22 caliber pistol. A silencer was always difficult to explain, even to American soldiers.

When the pipe was reconnected and the bag packed and stowed, Martin scrambled down the hill. He saw that the downstairs windows of the Mühle house were illuminated, casting streams of light over the mill pond beyond. A moment later, a rectangle of light appeared upstairs as well. Figures moved dimly behind lace curtains. He approached the narrow rushing channel. The raceway must be closed, he thought, because the mill wheel did not turn. The house was actually on a small island. A wooden walkway crossed over the mill stream, connecting the driveway to a deck where the door to the house stood beside the water wheel. On the far side of the house was the mill pond.

At the end of the driveway were two vehicles. Martin ghosted toward them, the pistol raised beside his right ear, looking in the windows, circling to the front. The first was a VW Kübelwagen. The outline of a *Wehrmacht* black cross, or *Balkenkreuz*, was still visible on its door under a thin coat of paint. His breath caught when he saw the slat grill and familiar recessed headlights of the second vehicle. It was a Willys MB Jeep, and the hood was adorned with a white, five-pointed star in a circle. U.S. Army. The thought crossed his mind that Grahamar was being arrested for war crimes. If that were the case, he should be escorted out shortly. He saw that the keys were in the ignition of the army jeep; he removed them and put them in his pocket. Then he unfolded his knife and slit the tires of the other vehicle.

He was accustomed to watching for sentries, but he knew there were none. The war was over. Instead of wading across the stream, deep in the shadows, he walked directly over the bridge, the pistol at his side, and up to the back door, which he turned and found to be unlocked. He entered the kitchen and heard voices speaking in English in an adjoining room. He listened for a moment to their voices.

"We also have contacts in *La Jeunesse Communiste.*" The language was English, but the voice was Grahamar's.

"We'll want notes on their meetings, too," another voice said. He could smell the cigarette smoke as he moved toward the passageway. "Post war France is breaking into factions. Those who united to fight you are now battling separately for power, and we are afraid that since the Right was discredited in the eyes of most of the French, that the elections, when they come, will give unprecedented power to Communists like Maurice Thorez and Pierre Villon . . . "

"Puppets of Moscow."

"Yes, and so the work we are doing will be vital . . . "

He paused, and stood suddenly, staring at the armed man who was framed in the doorway. Grahamar, his left eye covered with a patch, had to swivel his body and look along his shoulder to see the intruder. He said nothing, but his American companion, who wore the double silver bars of a captain, said, "What the hell is going on here?"

Grahamar said, carefully, "This man is one of your agents. American or English, I believe. A very good one. He's come here to settle an old score with me."

"Is that right?" the captain asked.

"That's right. My name is Martin LeBris, OSS, and I've come here to kill this bloody bastard."

The army officer heaved a sigh of exasperation and sat down again. "I'm afraid you'll have to put that thought out of your mind entirely," he said. He leaned forward to extinguish his cigarette in an ashtray on the coffee table. "My name is Captain Paul Gibbons. General Edwin Sibert, Chief of Army Intelligence in Europe, has authorized me to recruit German intelligence specialists. This man comes highly recommended by General Reinhard Gelen as a potential . . . ." He paused and sighed again, shaking his head wearily. "Well, that's really all you need to know, LeBris. Put down the pistol. That's an order."

"Well, I've got a star and two bars in the Navy, Gibbons. So I don't take orders from you." Gibbons looked to him like a man whose talent for organization had been recognized and utilized. He was an officer clerk, with prematurely thinning hair, an Errol Flynn mustache, a clean uniform, and an exaggerated sense of his own importance.

"In this matter, I represent General Sibert. Don't forget it. Now you're making me very nervous with the pistol. The war is over. We backed the Resistance with men like you. Now we will be backing men like Grahamar against the Soviets. It's a new world, a new reality. For Chrissakes, at least the Nazis were capitalists!"

Martin looked at the insignia on the captain's shoulder. It represented SHAEF, Supreme Headquarters Allied Expeditionary Forces. General Eisenhower's headquarters. A flaming sword on a black field. The sword of freedom dispersing the Nazi night. A rainbow arching over that device, below a thin stretch of blue sky. Hope for a better future.

Finally, Grahamar spoke. "We've all lost things in the war, Mr . . . . LeBris. And yes, we've all done terrible things. But now I am making an oath of loyalty to your side. A pact to protect your children and mine from the common enemy."

"You've read *The Iliad*, Grahamar?"

"Of course," he said, as if humoring a child.

"Then you may remember Achilles words to Hector:
Nor oaths nor pacts will I make with thee
Such pacts as lambs and rabid wolves combine
Such leagues as men and furious lions join."

He saw Grahamar's single eye grow wide, and as he raised his hands before his face, uselessly, Martin fired three shots at point blank range into his heart.

"You've fucking killed him, LeBris!" Gibbons cried, jumping up and standing over the crumpled figure. "You'll spend twenty years in Leavenworth for this!" He stepped backward disgustedly as the pooling blood began to edge across the varnished floor.

"I told you I'm a Navy man, Captain. Portsmouth Prison."

"It will be some hell-hole I can assure you of that."

"Better a hell-hole with Grahamar dead than a sunny verandah drinking cocktails with our Nazi pals in your fucking new world."

Martin heard doors opening upstairs, voices, and a rapid footfall on the stairs. He backed into the kitchen, but saw a woman and a child. The little girl surveyed the scene, looked quickly at Martin, and ran from the room. The woman threw herself at the body on the floor, kneeling in a dark pool of blood. Gibbons spoke to her apologetically in German, but she looked up at Martin, her loose blonde hair shading her kindled eyes, and screamed "*Der Meuchelmörder!*" She spit a stream of German imprecations at Martin before breaking into sobs and burying her face in her bloodied hands.

"You've made a fine mess of things, LeBris."

"Tell her she never knew him. If she did, she wouldn't miss him. I'm sorry the little girl had to see it." He left the house, tossing the jeep keys into the millpond as he passed over the bridge.

****

"So how come you never went to prison, Martin?"

Gerry and Martin had left the Doubletree Hotel, where Gerry had stopped on a stroll through downtown, and were walking to the Coffee Mill. Gerry had invited Martin to try a Mill City Blend. "I'll tell you, but first, I'm getting my guns back today, right?"

"Yes, yes. They're in my trunk."

"All right. Well, I went to prison for three days when I arrived in Paris. Finally I was released and ordered to appear at SHAEF headquarters in London, to see General Eisenhower."

"To see Eisenhower?" Gerry stopped short. "Are you kidding me?"

"No, I'm not."

"What happened? Do you remember?"

"Do I remember? Do I remember Pearl Harbor? I went in, and there was Ike himself, sitting at his desk, large as life. He looked up at me, took off his glasses, picked up a few sheets of paper on his desk, and said, 'Lieutenant LeBris, I have a report here from Captain Paul Gibbons that you liquidated a spy recruited by a duly authorized representative of General Sibert, this office, and the United States Government.'

I said, 'That's all true, Sir.'

He said, 'What do you think I should do with this report?'

'I think you should throw it in the trash, Sir.'

He nodded. Then he got up, ripped up the papers, and threw them in the trash. At a kind of side table, he grabbed a bottle of, what the hell was it called? Ah yes, Buffalo Trace Bourbon and a couple of glasses. He also had a bottle of what he called branch water, and poured a splash in each. 'Can't get this in Europe,' he said. We drank for a minute, just savoring the bourbon, and Ike said, 'At least Gibbons had the presence of mind to swear to the woman that you were an unknown member of the French Resistance who had tracked her husband to his home. The lie was for us, not for you.'

I thanked him, and when I was about to leave, he said, 'LeBris, I really don't give a damn about that Nazi son of a bitch. There are far too many good men to weep over. And I have another report here about what this Grahamar did with a couple of downed U.S. pilots before he hung them. George Patton and I visited a place called Ohrdruf, a liberated concentration camp. You know what a battle-hardened old bastard he is. He went around the back of one of the buildings and vomited. It's something you can never forget. Never. That having been said, the war is over, and we may find ourselves with strange bedfellows in this new contest with the Soviets. I just hope it's worth it.'

I said, 'It won't be worth it, Sir.'

He walked me to the door and said, 'I thank you for all you did. But we can't afford any more of your loose cannon antics. It's over. Enjoy the peace. That's an order.' He shook my hand, and I left."

Martin and Gerry were halfway up Middle Street, the sun washing the old red brick walls of the late 19th century buildings and the gray cobbled street.

"That's quite a story, Martin."

There was an Army Recruiting Office at the corner of Middle and Palmer. A sergeant had about fifteen new recruits, and was marching them down the sidewalk toward the two men.

Martin noticed that Gerry seemed to tense up, and as they approached the sergeant and the double column of inductees, he said to Martin, "I hope he doesn't think we're getting off the sidewalk."

Martin was amused, but Gerry suddenly barked at the officer, "Sergeant! You need to remove these recruits to an approved parade area immediately!"

The sergeant, who Martin thought, looked like he might have just returned from Iraq, spoke calmly to the confused group that followed him. "At ease," he said. Then he turned to Gerry, and said respectfully, "I'm sorry, sir. The captain ordered me to take them out and give them a little march. You're welcome to go inside and take it up with him. In any case, I'll be happy to transmit your concerns."

Somewhat taken aback by the sincerity of the young man's response, Gerry continued, "Well, as a veteran, I don't think it's right for the military to be encroaching on civilian . . . "

"I understand your concern, sir. I'll talk to the captain about it. Thank you for your service, sir."

"All right. Well, thank you, Sergeant."

When they had walked a little farther, Martin began to chuckle, "I thought you were going to arrest him. That would have been interesting. Seems like you have a bit of a problem with the Army, O'Neil."

"Yeah, little bit of a problem. I took one look at that guy, and I had a flashback of this C.O. we had in Vietnam, real gung-ho type. He came into our hooch one night, and I had the lines from "Dover Beach" pinned over my bunk. *We are here as on a darkling plain...*"

"*Where ignorant armies clash by night.* He must have loved that."

"You would think I had sold secrets to the Viet Cong. He was in my face screaming for five full minutes about how I was a fucking cancer creeping into the morale of the group. Maybe I was. The Army just rubbed me the wrong way, but this guy we just met seemed to be solid, a gentleman."

They turned up Palmer to the Coffee Mill and Martin insisted on paying for the coffees – two Mill City Blends to go; they continued walking to Gerry's car, which was near the police station. "We'll stop by the hotel and pick up your bag, and I'll give you a ride back to the apartment."

"I miss my Hannibal," the old man said.

"Who?"

"My cat."

"Right. Can I ask you something? Do you ever feel bad about the killing? I mean, I know it had to be done, but does it ever get to you?"

"There are a couple of things I'd rather forget. I did what I had to do, and as I told you before, I just hope if there is a God, that He forgives me."

"What about killing Grahamar with his wife and daughter there, did that bother you?"

"It's not my fault that he was married. As for the daughter, it's too bad, but what about the children who died in the concentration camps? What about the children he and Klaus Barbie tortured, sometimes in front of their parents? No, his death doesn't touch me. Not at all. He got off easy. I'd find it much more difficult if I knew he were alive."

"Don't get me wrong. I'm not blaming you. He had it coming all right. But what if during the war you killed someone who didn't deserve it. Wouldn't that bother you?"

"Well, I don't know the circumstances, but I'd say when you're in a violent and irrational world, violent and irrational things happen. And that you are probably a better man than I am."

"If you knew the circumstances, you wouldn't say that."

"Listen, Gerry. I'm old enough to be your father. I've never had a son, but if I did, I'd be happy if he were very much like you, even with whatever it is that troubles you. That's the truth."

"Thanks, Martin. You're very kind."

They reached Gerry's car, and when they got in, he slid a CD into the slot. "I picked this up just for you." He handed him the CD cover, on which a G.I. sat under a striped awning at a café table, holding hands with a young woman. "Songs of World War II." A lonely accordion wound into orchestral strains, and the deep and languid voice of Marlene Dietrich rose out of the past:

> *Underneath the lantern by the barrack gate,*
> *Darling I remember the way you used to wait;*
> *'Twas there that you whispered tenderly,*
> *That you lov'd me, that you'd always be,*
> *My Lili of the lamplight,*
> *My own Lili Marlene.*

"Do you remember that song, Martin?"

The old man said nothing. He stared straight ahead, seeming not to have heard. The years fell away, and he heard her voice once more. *We can't afford to dream now. Too many have died.*

> *Even tho' we're parted,*
> *Your lips are close to mine.*
> *My Lili of the Lamplight,*
> *My own Lili Marlene*

He saw her again in the back of the lorry, the pitiful, broken body, and the nearly infinite force of her faith and her will, hammered into tenuous thinness, but still integral; her soul stronger than the tools of her torturers; stronger than death; tempered into something beyond what was possible in the fire of her love of country and her unshakeable commitment to set it free from the invader. "*Le Bon Dieu comprendra. Tue-moi.*" *I'm sorry Odette. I couldn't help you. I'm sorry.*

Gerry saw that Martin had pushed up his glasses and was pinching the bridge of his nose, his head bowed and angled away. He switched off the CD and put on a sports talk show. When they arrived at the Pollard Mansion, Gerry popped his trunk, pulled out a shoe box, and handed it to Martin.

"Your guns."

Together they walked up the broad staircase to Martin's apartment. The cat wound about his master's legs as soon as they entered. "I have to run, Martin," Gerry said. "I have a friend around the corner. His wife was with Lekakis at a bar when she died of an overdose. Just want to see how he's coping."

"There's just one thing that bothers me. Are Luz and her daughter safe? Is Lekakis dangerous? I worry about them."

"I don't know if he's dangerous, but he's in danger. He's involved with some drug dealers who I hear operate out of The Tic Toc Club. I just wrote a request to my boss that we put the place under surveillance, so we may nab them all soon. Al's supplier, if it is Carlos Luna, doesn't play by any rules. He's a little cartel boss wannabe. Lekakis could get caught up in that and end up in jail for a long time, or worse. Just call us if he comes around. Don't try to handle it yourself!"

"Of course not," the old man said as he set the shoe box on the kitchen table.

31

Frank McGuin's house was like a funeral parlor. The lid of the Baby Grand Piano was down, and littered with cards and vases of flowers. The ceiling of the kitchen where Gerry sat with his old friend reflected the shifting light of the pool outside. Looking through the curtains, the detective saw an occasional sparrow skim the water; whether to drink or to swallow an insect, he couldn't tell.

Frank was changing the strings on his Martin acoustic guitar. He shook his head gravely and said, "I never expected it, Gerry. Maybe I'm naïve, but I never expected it."

"I'm so sorry it turned out this way. How are the kids dealing with it?"

"My boy has been crying for days. As for Ashley, I don't know. If she cries, she cries alone." He strummed the six strings and began to turn the pegs, so that the tones bent upward, until a harmony was achieved. He struck a few more chords as he fine-tuned. Then he laid the guitar on the table and said, "You want some coffee?"

"Hell no," Gerry said, and Frank managed a smile.

****

After his mother's funeral, Larry Vega was ready to leave town. He had picked up the forty bucks O'Neil had left for him at the desk and had another fifteen hundred left over from what his mother had saved to pay for her funeral expenses. Al Lekakis had asked him to stop by and see him before he left. He took his mother's '98 Civic with the plastic Jesus stuck to the dashboard. Al might ask him to carry something to Florida. "I ain't gonna do it," he told himself. But then, it wouldn't hurt to listen to what he had to say. If he was holdin' heavy, he might slip him a C note for the road.

He rang the doorbell, but no one came. He waited a minute and walked around to the side porch. The back door was open, and he called through the screen. "Al? Hey Al, it's Larry!" He opened the door and stepped into the kitchen. It was nearly bare, just a couple of chairs and a fold-out poker table littered with empty bottles of Bud. He thought that Al must be lying in bed with a bad squash on. He peeked into the barren living room, where half a pepperoni pizza sat in an open box on the floor. He walked along the passageway toward the bedrooms, calling out, "Al? Al, it's Larry."

The bedroom door was open. There was a king-sized bed, and on it, a blood-soaked body in boxer shorts and a torn Hawaiian shirt. At first, he wasn't sure who it was. The jaw hung gaping, and the eyes were open, covered with a dull film. His neck was slit, and the blood loss had left his face gray, the skin stretched over the bones so that already death's head had appeared. He didn't see any knife near the body. Larry could feel his heart pounding in his throat, and he had a sudden urge to urinate.

Yet he stared at the body, rooted to the floor. For a second he thought he saw the chest rise and wondered if he could be alive. But a few seconds later, he decided that that was an illusion. He remembered Mack, the crazy drunk at the Tap Room, who said to him one night. "When you're dead, you're deader than you'll ever be." Yeah, Al was deader than he'd ever be.

He scanned the room quickly. There was a pistol on the night table. It was black, but Larry didn't know what kind it was. He wasn't into guns. He spotted a bag of coke on the dresser, beside a mirror on which was laid a small pile of the white powder and a razor blade; he picked up the bag and felt it. Must be an ounce. The room was humming with the buzz in his ears. He remembered that he shouldn't leave his prints on anything. He stuffed the coke in his pocket. He knew he had to get out of here soon, but he peeked warily into the closet. Nothing but a pile of dirty laundry. He picked up a T-shirt and held it over his hands while he opened the drawers. Empty. A voice in his head was screaming at him to get out even as he knelt at the end of the bed and looked under it. *A briefcase.* Shit, it was near the head of the bed. He didn't want to kneel in blood to get it out. He picked up the end of the bed and swung it out over the blood pool, and then he stepped up on a dry section of floor and gripped the handle of the briefcase. He felt its weight. It was full of something. Quickly, he swung the bed back and made an exit. He looked back and saw no blood tracks.

There was a Red Sox cap on top of the refrigerator. He put it on. He wiped the handle of the back door and stuffed the T-shirt in his pocket. A car was passing out front. He tossed the briefcase behind a barrel and stooped to tie his sneaker, tucking his chin so that the bill of the cap obscured his face entirely. When he heard the car move on down the street, he picked up the briefcase and carried it to the car, tucking it down behind the passenger seat before driving slowly away, wondering what he had done.

It was 11:00 a.m. when he put the key in his mother's door for the last time. He had told the landlord he would vacate the apartment by 1:00 p.m. because the guy was sending some painters. Three suitcases of his own, and a box of things he'd salvaged from among Agnes Vega's meager possessions, sat just inside the front door. He'd sold the kitchen table and a bookcase to a Puerto Rican he knew from the Eagle Diner, and tossed just about everything else. He carried the briefcase into the bathroom and locked the door, closing the blinds in the narrow window. While he pissed, he looked at the briefcase lying flat across the sink. There was a combination lock at the clasp on each side. He took off his belt, put the buckle under the latch and pulled. The clasp on each side broke with one tug. He opened the briefcase.

There were several more ounce bags of cocaine; five "fingers" of what he suspected was raw, uncut, heroin, and a lot of cash stacked and secured in elastic bands. He picked one up and thumbed through it. They were hundreds. There must be fifty in each packet, five thousand dollars. About twenty packets. A hundred grand, plus the coke. And you could get about two thousand bags of heroin from one finger, usually sold on the street at about six bucks a bag.

He knew that the Colombians would kill him for much less than this. He could go by The Tic Toc Club, and hand it over to Carlos Luna, that was the guy Al dealt with. They would thank him for getting it to them before the cops found Al's body. They might even give him a reward. *But no one knew he had it.* And what perfect timing. He'd be in Florida.

He threw everything in the trunk of the Honda and jumped on the highway: 495 to 95 South, breathing easier as the miles flew by. Only when he was south of New York did he begin to wonder. *Who would kill Al and leave the money, the gun, and the coke? Who would do that?*

32

Gerry joined Dom Trivedi at a table near the back of the Club Diner. *The Boston Herald* crossword puzzle was open in front of him. "A San Francisco hill," he mused aloud.

"Telegraph Hill?"

"Three letters."

"Hmm. Nob Hill."

"How the hell do you know all this shit?"

"It's my business to know . . . "

"Yeah, yeah. It's your business to know what other people don't know. Sherlock Holmes. That's all the bullshit answer I ever get out of you."

"The truth is I stopped in San Francisco on the way back from Nam, stayed for a while with a buddy I met in the service." The pencil moved in Dom's thick fingers: N-O-B. The waitress, with the exasperated air that comes at the end of a double shift, passed by and refilled Dom's mug. "Coffee?" she asked Gerry.

"Please."

She poured the steaming coffee, pulled a handful of cream cups from an apron pocket, and slapped them on the table. She pulled an order book out of her apron and a pencil from behind her ear, blowing a loose strand of hair out of her face. "Do yiz know what yiz want?"

Dom ordered the Club Supreme Omelet, and Gerry a Western on rye.

"Nasty business about Lekakis, not that the community will miss him much. What do you hear, Dom?"

"I hear there's a lot of cash missing. There's your motive."

"You know how much?"

"No. A lot."

"Any ideas?"

He shook his head and put his pencil down. "They say Lekakis was with a young broad with long, dark hair at the Savoy earlier. No one noticed if he left with her, though."

"That's what I hear. You know Larry Vega?"

"Skinny? One of those mustaches, what do they call 'em? Fu Man Chu? Used to cook at the Eagle?"

"Yeah, that's the guy. He left town the same day Al was murdered, or very close to it."

"He strike you as a throat slasher?" Dom's expression suggested that Larry Vega did not strike him as a throat slasher.

"No, not really. Just a misguided dope. He told me his mother had one foot in the grave. He was going to leave town when she died. She died, and he left, like he said. Start a new life in Florida. I don't think he's smart enough, or quite bad enough, to put all the pieces together and carry it out. It's just that I saw Al's cell phone records. He called Larry the day before he was killed."

"Well, you never know. Vega could be dumb like a fox. But if he does have the money, he'll be lying low for a long time. Could be hard to find."

"He said a friend was getting him a job cleaning pools. Must be hundreds of them in Florida. Anyway, it's a long shot. I can put a bulletin out. Apparently he's driving his mom's car."

Gerry helped Dom with the crossword puzzle for a few minutes. He folded the paper and put it to one side when their breakfasts arrived. "Well, you won't be the only one looking for him. If he knew Al, other people are going to notice that he disappeared at the same time the money disappeared."

They put forth various theories and speculated about the kind of murderer who slashed a throat, especially when there was a loaded gun on the night table. The waitress came by and laid the plates on the table. "Can I get yiz anything else? Lemme see. You want ketchup?"

"Sure," Dom said. She leaned over the neighboring table to retrieve a red plastic bottle while he memorized her ass. When she had put the ketchup in front of him and marched off, Gerry, with raised eyebrows, said, "Why don't you take one of those cell phone pictures, Dominic?"

"Come on, Gerry. I'm married, but I ain't dead."

33

Insurance. That was why Martin had taken the box and sent it to his mother's house after the war, addressed to himself. If the echoes of these events ever reached across the Atlantic; if shadows took substance to pursue him, he would be ready. Once, he had almost turned them into the police for disposal. But something held him back. It was warm in the attic of the old manor, though the sun had hardly risen over the rooftops of Venice Avenue.

He pried up two dry, old floor boards near the chimney and knelt beside the opening, running his hand under the loose insulation. After a moment, he bent low and pulled out a box. A label on the top said, "Welwyn Experimental Lab Station IX." Those were the boys in the Frythe Hotel in Welwyn Garden City who produced some of the most ingenious and deadly devices in the OSS arsenal. He replaced the boards and stowed the pry bar behind the chimney.

Carrying the box in his arms, he descended the narrow, creaking stairs slowly. They were steep, and he felt the cooler air as he reached the bottom. He unlocked his door, and in a few minutes the contents were spread on his bed. He returned to the door and turned the key once more on the new deadbolt; he switched off Liszt's *Evening Harmony* so that he would hear anyone approaching.

Though some of the weapons were simple, they had saved the lives of more than one agent in the days of the rat hunt. There was the flat sleeve dagger. Taped to the forearm, it was easy for the enemy to miss when one was frisked for weapons. There were coins with fold out swivel blades, pencil daggers and lapel blades. He sorted them, and considered for a moment. At his age, garrotes, brass knuckles, punch blades, and weapons for hand to hand brawling would be of little use. He picked up the .22 Enpen. It was, to all appearances, a fountain pen. In reality, it was Enfield's smallest gun, firing a single .22 caliber bullet. There was the Welfag, a similar firing tube disguised as a cigarette. And there was the Stinger, an easily concealed three-inch barrel with a firing button: a miniature disposable gun, deadly at close range. One shot – no reloads.

Ah, but as the old Irish rebel had said, there are no bad shots at ten yards range, and he hoped to get even closer to the man who would come to rob him and then to kill him. He chose the weapons he needed, hid them in hollowed books, and returned with the rest to the attic.

****

"Who the hell is calling me at 11:15?" Gerry wondered. He and Gina had taken Matt and a friend of his bowling at Brunswick Lanes, and had started watching "From Here to Eternity" when he went to bed.

"O'Neil me oul' flower, how is it with ye?" The voice was Dermot Burke's, but in his well-oiled condition he seemed to have slid back into some previous Dublin self.

"Are you drunk, Burke?"

He heard the gravelly laugh and the cough, "A bit mouldy to be sure, Yer Honor. Yes, there's a lad here, an unnamed official. I gave him some advice on a bit of a family heirloom he had, and bejasus if I didn't find a pint of what I strongly suspect to be John

Jameson's twelve-year-old beneath me pillow. I say I strongly suspect because the blessed liquid had been transferred into a plastic soda bottle so that I wouldn't do meself or someone else mischief with a broken bottle."

"Any luck with your research?" he asked hopefully. Dermot had called a few times before, but it was usually to get more information rather than to share any.

"Fair dues to you, O'Neil. Ye got me in here, and I like it well enough, better than that other oul' kip house. And me own phone and a quiet room for me *police work*. I just requested it to call you."

"Well, that's good. Is that it? You called me to tell me that you're drunk and happy?"

There was silence, and then a low and knowing chuckle. "Ye put a challenge to me, O fuckin' Neil, did ye not? Y'expressed a lack of confidence in me fuckin' abilities, though in what words, I seem to disremember."

Gerry sat up, and winking, raised an index finger to Gina. He grabbed a pen on the counter and an envelope and opened the sliding door, stepping out onto a porch overlooking the river. The white foam flashed in the darkness as it broke over the rocks below. "Did I challenge you, Dermot?"

"That you did. Ye had but little faith in the cute hoor that I am. That I *still* am. And while yer police investigators are arsing about, and coming up with fuck-all, yer man Burke has got a name."

Gerry wanted to ask what name he had, but he sensed that he would have to humor Burke's vanity a bit more. "How did you do it?"

"Well, the best way I can describe it to the curious mind, in the words of the immortal bard, the fuckin' Swan of Avon, is . . .

" He paused, and Gerry could almost see the plastic bottle raised, the long-missed golden brown *uisce beatha,* or water of life, filling Dermot's gut with fire and his brain with musey fumes. "Huyeah. The fuckin' what was I saying? Ah yes, as the bard put it, 'to find direction through indirection.' You can't learn that kind of thing in the fuckin' Police Academy. It's instinct. It's understandin' the criminal fuckin' mind and how to make them feel at ease, and most of all it's havin' the palaver and fuckin' hard sense that you take with mother's milk when yer bred between the canals in the heart of the Hibernian metropolis."

"Good man, Dermot. What did you find out?"

"Ah, he's a clever dodger himself, a right cute artist."

"Who?"

"Adlebert Lustig, Munich art dealer, gombeen man, and one who knows. Close with the boys in the Schönart Anstalt."

"Who are they?"

"Ah, never mind that. I laid out a line of blather based on our several colloquies, implying that I might be in the possession of, or have access to, some information that I'd be wanting to unload at less than fair market value. Who would be interested in that sort of information, and all that."

"Did it go over?"

"Like snuff at a fuckin' wake, O'Neil. And in an ass's gallop, I had three names. I've eliminated two, by a process that it might belabor me mind to explain in me current state, unused as I am to a drop or two of the pure. Be that as it may, there's one name left."

"And that is?"

"Will you bring us a few Robusto cigars one day soon?"

"Yes, I will."

"That would be lovely, but no matter. A deal is a deal, and there's honor among thieves and all that arseology. The man you want to talk to is called Karl Hoetger." He spelled it out as Gerry wrote.

"If this is our man, I'll bring you a box of cigars."

"Well, I'll be right here at fuckin' Ha'penny Place." He hung up. Gina was already asleep on the couch in front of a blue screen. He went into their bedroom to turn down the covers. She clutched his neck like a child as he carried her to the bed and laid her down. "I have to brush my teeth," she murmured, but rolled over and was asleep again.

Gerry turned off the TV. He wondered what time it was in France. Five-thirty or 6:00 a.m. Good enough. He picked the folded paper out of his wallet and went back out on the porch to call Alain Honein.

34

Lekakis' parents took care of the arrangements. Luz and Ana went to the funeral at St. George's; they sat quietly in the back, heads bowed before the great mosaic of Christ the Savior with golden halo, hand raised in blessing between the alpha and the omega until Al's mother, Nitsa, approached her, face dim behind a black veil, and invited them to sit with her and her husband. Later, outside the church, she said, "I'm sorry he treat you bad. He was my son. I loved him, but he was not a good man. We know that. Please bring Ana to see us. She's a good girl, and she's our blood."

Her husband, Basileios, nodded, but was suffering too much to speak. He had sat in his Broadway tailor shop with a tape measure hanging around his neck, laboring at a sewing machine while Nitsa had stood, pushing the damp strands of gray hair out of her face, in a cloud of steam at the pressing machine for all those years, for what? To see their only son fall in some useless war he could not begin to understand. And what would be the point of all their labor now? Everything had been for the young man whose casket had just been rolled into the gleaming, black hearse. They could only put their hopes in Ana now.

They would have preferred their boy to marry a Greek girl, but what was done was done, and now they knew that his choice of a woman was not what went wrong with his life, and her dignified presence at the church was evidence of that. Luz and her daughter traveled to the Westlawn Cemetery in the Pappas

Funeral Home limo. After they had lowered the flower-strewn casket into the ground, Luz said to her mother-in-law, "They say it may have been Colombians who killed him. I'm so sad, so ashamed."

The older woman raised the veil, and shook her head, looking intently into Luz's face. "It has nothing to do with you," she said. "You are a good person. I can see that. God can see that." Nitsa dabbed her swollen eyes with a crumpled Kleenex and lowered the veil once more.

"Most Colombians are good people," Luz said, "but the ones who are bad are very bad."

Ghostly, from behind the dark veil, the mother of the slain son said simply, "Isn't that true everywhere?" And squeezing Luz's arm, she added in a whisper choked with pain, "I'm sorry he did not treat you better."

They drove her back to her car at St. George's, while Nitsa coaxed answers out of Ana about her school and her friends, and when she said that she got a ninety-seven in math, old Basileios smiled and said, "You keep studying, Ana. We want to help you with college some day."

Nitsa Lekakis took Luz's hands and squeezed them in both of hers. "You don't have to come to the house, Luz. They will all be speaking Greek. But call me soon. *Zoo-ees esas*. Life with you, both of you."

Martin had avoided contact with Luz Morales and Ana. He didn't want them to happen to be nearby when the killer returned. He had gone downstairs once to have dinner with them, but Gerry had agreed to keep an eye on the perimeter of the house. The day after the funeral, a Friday, Luz began a novena for Al Lekakis' soul, reciting the rosary and the prayers for the dead.

Upstairs, in the City of Books, Martin, old and armed for war, read Tacitus: "The story I now commence is rich in vicissitudes, grim with warfare, torn by strife, a tale of horror even during times of peace. However, the period was not so utterly barren as to yield no examples of heroism." He nodded slowly, thinking that in every tale of horror and grim warfare, there were also tales of heroism, and how at the darkest hour, the finest spirits were revealed. Wasn't that what Churchill had reminded us so often during those years?

The phone rang, and he dropped his marker into the book and closed it. It was Luz. He sensed that she was still dealing with the death of Lekakis. He was a bad lot, as the English said, but he was still the father of her child. Through the phone, at this distance, he could ask her. "How did you end up with him, Luz? You seem so gentle, so full of kindness."

"Thank you, Martin. You are a gentle man, too." He was silent, squeezing the receiver, and wondering what she would say if she could see what he carried inside him. She continued. "I came here to see my aunt and uncle for their fiftieth wedding anniversary. I went to a party with some cousins who lived here, and I met Al. I was so impressed with an American who could speak Spanish, even bad Spanish, and he could dance, too, *salsa* and *merengue*, even *cumbia* almost like he was from Medellin. Oh, I was not the first Latin girlfriend that he had." She laughed, mirthlessly, at her own blindness. "I said, 'Hey you're a good dancer,' and he said, you know, very arrogant, '*Por eso me llaman El Muchachito.*' 'That's why they call me The Kid.'

I was younger then, and I suppose I was *inocente*, or I should say, *estupida*. I could see he wanted to be . . . " Her voice took on a deeper tone as she said the words, "*a macho man, a tough guy.*

But in my culture that is not unusual. All the guys are like that." Martin heard her sigh, and in that sigh he heard wisdom won by hard experience and scorn for her youthful exuberance. She concluded, *"That's why they call me The Kid.* Right. I don't want to meet any more macho men."

They talked for a while longer, the old story of disillusion, as one finds out that the beloved is an invention, and that the real person is so very different. She told him about her job at the hair salon, all the hours on her feet, cutting hair. "It's hard sometimes, but it's not so bad. I don't mind doing it for my daughter." Finally, Luz said, "Ana wants to speak to you."

He heard a few words in Spanish as she passed the phone and then the little voice, "Martin, I miss you."

"I've been so very busy, but I miss you too, Ana."

"Martin?"

"Yes, my dear?"

"When will Jesus come again?"

"I don't think anyone knows, child."

"Because it's so hard to picture him in our clothes. Or will he come dressed in those long robes they used to wear?"

"I think they taught us that he would come again at the end of the world."

"I think he'll come before that."

"Well, you may be right."

"Can I call you sometimes, Martin? On my own? I know your number, you know."

"Any time you like, sweetheart."

35

She did call. The next morning, when Martin was getting ready to walk to the Windsor Shop for the morning paper, a bespectacled old gentleman armed with the weapons of a distant war that lived yet a while in the collective memory of a fast-fading generation. He picked up the phone and heard the little voice, even littler, whispering. He pressed the receiver to his ear. "Martin. There are two men here my mama doesn't know them . . ." He heard voices speaking Spanish, and Ana's voice away from the phone. He heard the words "*la plata*," silver: the money. He dropped the phone. His instinct was to run, but the trick knee gave out and he stumbled. "*Putain de bordel!*" he cursed, his heart beating the old tattoo of war as he lunged for his jacket, covering his lean frame and the Llama pistol at his breast.

As he turned on the landing under the great stained glass window, he breathed deeply, focusing his thoughts on what he must do. The door was unlocked. He pushed it open and stepped in, taking in the scene with quick eyes: Luz on the couch, under the image of the Sacred Heart. Ana with her arm around her, leaning into her, and two men, one standing over them, the other, hard eyes glaring out of a shaved head, holding a pistol aimed at his head.

"*Quien es este typo?*" The man at the couch asked Luz. He was wearing Nike sweat pants and a soccer jersey stretched over a slight paunch. His dark hair was spiked. There were dark circles under his eyes, and he wore a piece of rawhide around his neck with what looked like religious images in tiny frames hanging from it. Martin felt the familiar weight of the pistol under his arm. They would not think to search him. An old neighbor. A nobody. I am nobody.

She spoke in English for Martin's benefit. "A neighbor, a friend. He has nothing to do with Al. Neither do we."

He nodded. "Hey, old neighbor, you got bad timing."

"What's your name?" Martin ventured.

"Nevermind my fucking name. I call you '*viejo*,' old man, an' you call me . . . you jus' call me 'sir.' I got to take these girls to help me find my money, and my *perico*. We gonna look for it together. Because you know, my money can't just disappear like that. Not without somebody gotta pay. *Es asi*."

"But didn't Al already pay?" Martin asked.

"He pay somebody. But he don't pay me. Some *hijo de puta* is laughing at me, *Viejo*. People gotta see there are consequences when you lose my money. Even if already you're fuckin' dead."

"You know they had nothing to do with Al."

"It's none of your business anyway, so shut your mouth." He turned to Luz and said in a low and menacing voice, "He came here sometimes, right? He talk to you? What he say? You need to tell me what's going on here."

Martin heard Luz begin to sob and saw her daughter kiss her, as if she were the mother, comforting her. But Martin knew that Luz was crying not for herself, but for Ana. "I can pay you the money," Martin said. "More than you lost."

The man approached him, looking into his face intently. He smelled as if he'd doused himself with a half-bottle of cologne. His eyes narrowed; his brow creased. "How do you know how much I lost, *Viejo*?"

"I don't think you lost more than I have."

"I don't think *you* got a hundred grand."

"I've got a diamond worth ten times that. You can have it."

"Ten times! *Que hijo de puta piedra!*" He ran a hand along the stubble that darkened his chin. "I think you're full of shit, but I like diamonds. I got a friend, he's a . . . *joyero . . . como se dice joyero?*"

"A jeweler," Luz said.

"He got a little machine he put on the diamond. I seen it. An' if it's a diamond you get a green light and it goes 'beep.' An' if it's some other shit you get a red light. Then we got a problem. You got a problem."

The man with the shaved head was still holding his gun on Martin. The other pushed his arm down, and leaned in, his mouth beside Martin's ear. He said, "If you are full of shit, or if you go to the cops, *Viejo*, an' I tell you what. They die. You know the last person who mention my name to a cop. Then he ran back to Colombia. So my friend Flaco here went down the next week. Found him in church, prayin'. That didn't do him no good at all." He laughed, and Martin felt his breath on his neck. "We understand each other? All I want is what is mine. Like we say in Medellin, *plata o plomo, ves?* I get the silver, or they get the lead. You seen *The Godfather*, right? That's me right there."

"I'll be back in half an hour."

"Wait a minute. Where you get a diamond like that? I mean no offense, but you don't look like a movie star."

"I stole it during the war."

The killer with the holy images hanging around his neck nodded. "This *Viejo* is a thief! Better be real and fuckin' big. We not gonna wait here." When he heard those words, Martin thought he should kill them both. He could get the man near him with the stinger that was already in his palm and then turn the big gun on the kingpin. There was no reason to take the hostages anywhere else.

Nike man went to the kitchen table and picked up one of Ana's crayons. He wrote in black under a smiling sun, 551-0306. "Flaco, give him the cellular. You call this number when you have it, *Viejo*, an' then like they say in the movies, nobody gets hurt. That's the only way right there." He shrugged. "It ain't fair, but thas' no my problem." He smiled broadly. "*Adios, pues.*" He waved his hand, dismissing him.

Flaco handed him a phone while his boss held out the paper to him. "I don't need that. I have the number."

"You sure?"

"I've got a good memory. Listen, sir . . . *Señor*, I said I'd be right back. Why are you taking them somewhere else? That makes me very nervous. Stay here. I get the diamond, bring it back, and we're done, no?"

Luz was watching him with wide eyes, as if she were afraid to breathe, clutching her daughter. Nike man reached into his pocket and pulled out a pack of gum. He unwrapped one and popped it into his mouth, chewing quietly for what seemed like a very long time. "It makes *me* nervous waiting in someone else's apartment, for a guy I don't even know. Call the number. I not gonna kill people for fun, *Viejo*. I need a reason. I got no reason to hurt them if I get my payback. This one is Colombian." He inclined his head toward Luz. "She ain't gonna talk. She knows. I get this big valuable diamond, and everything's cool. You all keep your mouth shut. You live longer that way."

He saw one of Ana's elastic hair bands coiled like a tiny cobra on the kitchen table beside her crayons. He stood on the edge of decision. When bullets started to fly, Luz and the child could be hurt. The quality of the rounds in the Stinger was excellent, and he'd kept it dry, but after all these years, would the powder burn efficiently? He wouldn't mind taking a chance if only his life depended on it, but what if it misfired? Luz closed her eyes and nodded almost imperceptibly, her dark eyes moving toward the door. *Go.* He turned and left, slipping the stinger in one pocket and the cell phone in the other.

"It's just business. I give you an hour, *Viejo, no mas.* Then I gotta take care of business with your little friends."

The bastard talks about business the way Grahamar used to talk about his duty. Martin knew he couldn't make a mistake here. He *could not* make a mistake. Time had turned the massy wheels so that he had a chance to do what he had failed to do the last time. Revenge didn't matter. He would take no joy in killing the drug dealer and his quiet friend if he could not save Luz and Ana. If they took the lives of those innocents, he would kill them; he would try to kill them, but it wouldn't matter. It wouldn't matter to him, and it wouldn't matter to the world. It seemed to him now that there was always a certain amount of evil in the world, and when you killed one bastard, the evil just flowed into some other being.

He had to go back upstairs to get the car keys. His knee hurt as he mounted the stairs, but he didn't pause under the stained glass window to rest while he drank its beauty. He hadn't driven the old Buick LeSabre for a couple of weeks, but it started up. He saw the Lincoln Navigator pull out of the front driveway, but he could see nothing through the tinted windows. He ran scores of possible scenarios through his head, some with good outcomes, others with bad. He forced himself to consider them coldly, without reference to the two people who were so dear to him. It was a mission, and emotion was what Conan Doyle had once compared to "grit in a sensitive instrument, or a crack in a high-power lens."

The Navigator turned left on Westford, and he turned right, toward the Enterprise Bank. Martin knew that he could only deal in probabilities. He could only weigh possible actions, could only interpret words and attitudes and motivations and reactions. And he knew that all missions were, as Tacitus had said, *rich in vicissitudes*. He remembered Luz's signal with her eyes, the quiet affirmation. He hoped that she understood the mindset of these people better than he did. He could not fail, and if he failed, he could not live. There was room for no more ghosts in the City of Books.

36

Alain Honein was not long in getting back to Gerry. A photo of the suspect growled out of the fax machine while Alain explained by telephone. Karl Hoetger was known to the police in Munich and to Interpol. He had begun with a small gang in Hamburg, hijacking trucks and smuggling contraband, usually cigarettes, to the Balkans. Later, he began to traffic in stolen and looted art. He had been questioned in the theft of Claude Monet's "Poppy Field Near Vetheuil" from the Bührte Collection Museum in Zurich. Suspicions could not be confirmed with evidence, and he was released. The painting had not been recovered.

He had also been a suspect in the death of a Hamburg businessman who had recently purchased a 14th century samurai katana said to have been forged by a legendary artisan called Goro Nyudo. The theif must have been disappointed when the Japanese government declared, upon the disappearance of the sword, that it was not forged by Nyudo, but probably by a later smith known as Muramasa. Still valuable, but not a national treasure.

Gerry was sitting at his desk at the Lowell Police Station, scribbling notes. "So Alain, there can be little doubt that Martin LeBris is holding something of value that this Hoetger wants."

There was a brief pause, and Gerry imagined his voice, trapped in an electric current, passing over the Atlantic and through hundreds of miles of wire or maybe bouncing off some satellite to Alain's ear. "That is posseeble."

"Wouldn't you say it was probable?"

"I would say, except for one theeng. The father of Hoetger was name Otto Hoetger. He was marry to Tina Grahamar, the daughter of Erika Grahamar."

Gerry's hand froze over the notepad. *Martin had killed Hoetger's grandfather*. A young intern, looking pleased with herself, peered into his cubicle. She was holding a thin folder. "Alain, I'll call you later."

"*Allez bonsoir*. And Gerry, be careful. He will not mind to kill you."

"Thanks, Alain." He hung up the phone and swiveled in his chair to face the intern. "What have you got?"

"Well," she said, opening the folder, and pushing a lock of blonde hair behind her ear, "I checked all the car rental places. Karl Hoetger rented a car from Commodore Rental on Route 38. The plate number is there, and the car is a 2007 Toyota Camry, silver. And I checked all the hotels. They get nervous when they see Lowell Police Department on the caller I.D., but . . . "

"Yeah?"

"He's staying at Room 47 of the Caswell Motel in . . . "

Gerry was already on his feet. "Excellent job, Kate. I'm going to recommend you for a raise."

She handed him the folder. "Yeah, right."

"Well, I'll at least buy you a coffee."

"I don't drink coffee."

"Then you're shit out of luck!" he called as the glass door swung shut behind him. In the sunlight of the JFK Plaza, he called Ray Cox. "Ray, I need you to drop what you're doing. Can you? Great. Go out to the Caswell. Keep an eye on Room 47, suspect is driving a silver Camry, license plate . . . " He flipped open the folder: "Eight, two, zero, delta, romeo, tango. If he arrives, let me know. If he's there and tries to leave, detain him for questioning in B&E and assault with a deadly weapon on Martin LeBris."

"The old spy with all the books?"

"You got it. I've got to type up an affidavit for a search warrant. Judge Downes is usually pretty good about these things. Let the Tewksbury Police know that I hope to have the warrant in about an hour, and they can send one of their guys over to go in with us."

"Righto, Gerry O."

"You're the best, Ray."

"You're only saying that 'cause it's true."

37

"This way, Mr. LeBris." Everything about her suggested discretion: the pale blue dress, the silver, well-coiffed hair, the reading glasses hanging on the dark cord, the light scent of lavender perfume, and above all her voice: precise, clear, and pitched at a perfect 'for your ears only' tone.

She had him sign his card and escorted him into a room walled with rows of numbered deposit boxes. He handed her his key, number 1366. She opened the corresponding door, and handed him a strongbox. A video camera mounted in the corner monitored and recorded their actions. The bank worker indicated a private booth, and left him as he entered. "Just push the buzzer when you're done, sir."

"Thank you." In the private booth, he opened the box and withdrew a cloth sack, feeling the familiar weight of its contents. He opened the sack briefly and looked at it, for the last time, he thought. He would not miss it. *La Cruz de Nueva Granada.* "Ironic," he thought, "Nueva Granada was the old name for Colombia." He remembered the gold chain flowing over the hands of the Nazi Grahamar, the diamond at its center reflected in his complacent eyes. Martin had always hoped that some day he would be able to do something good with the bejeweled cross, even if he had to break it up. This was it. If its diamond heart could rescue the lives of Luz and Ana from early graves, then the curse he had associated with it would be broken, and it could take its bloody provenance and bad luck to people who deserved it.

He stuffed the cloth packet back in the box, unbuttoned his shirt and hung the cross once more about his neck. He rang the buzzer, handed the box to the discreet woman who replaced it, locked the small door, and handed him the key. He signed his card again, thanked her, and left.

Once in the parking lot, he leaned against the LeSabre and took the cell phone out of his pocket. A car pulled into the space beside him as he punched in the number: 978 55 . . .

The passenger door flew open, hitting him hard so that his legs buckled, and he fell to his knees, groaning. He heard the phone clatter, and scanned the ground quickly for it. But a man was over him, hauling him quickly toward the open rear door of a car. He now recognized the leather jacket, the pony tail, the square jaw of his visitor, the man who had killed Marius, he thought, and a rage grew in him. He made his hand flat and stiff and jammed his fingers into his attacker's solar plexus, an old OSS trick that had always served him well. He heard him gasp, but he did not go down. Time had sapped the strength from Martin's arm.

He reached for his gun, but was struck in the temple and dazed. He grappled awkwardly with his assailant, who wrapped him in his young, strong arms and began to force him into the back of the car. As he did so, he felt the cross, and when Martin's legs went out from under him, and the floor of the car rushed up to his meet his face, he felt it being torn over his head. The killer was on him again, punching him in the ribs and tearing his coat off. He pulled Martin's gun out of its holster and threw it on the front seat. He ran his hand over his pants pockets, whispering, "I know you're a tricky bastard, Quenton." Duct tape wrapped his hands, and a blanket was tossed over him.

A drunk walking a pit bull through the parking lot stood wavering like an aspen in the wind, watching the scene with a cigarette in the air in front of his face. "Hey, you should take it easy on the old guy, Bud. He's old, ya know."

"He escaped from a mental institution. He's dangerous."

"Oh well, thass different. Crazy people are . . . crazy people are wicked strong."

Martin felt the seat move as his attacker settled himself at the wheel, and the car, which was still running, slipped into gear and moved out of the lot.

He blocked the pain in his ribs and in his knees and began to think. He remembered distinctly his training in escaping after capture, taught by Robert Addison, a guest lecturer from the British SOE. "If you are taken, your best chance of escape will be in the vehicle that is transporting you to your final destination. Once you arrive at that destination, be it prison, interrogation center, or place of execution, your chances of escape are drastically reduced. Think of it this way: find a way out of that vehicle, or very probably, die." He presented a myriad of methods to effect that escape, and Martin ran through them in his mind now, while the assassin began to talk.

"Well, that was quite lucky. I didn't think you'd keep the cross in your home, especially after I was there. A deposit box made sense. I followed you to the bank, but I didn't dare hope you would be stupid enough to take it out. I had quite another plan, involving that little girl. Is she your granddaughter? Your goddaughter? Anyway it's clear you are fond of her. But this way is much easier.

I quite like your weapon, sir. It is a classic. Too bad you couldn't hit me with it from five feet, but Martin LeBris is such a pathetic old shadow of what Patrice Quenton was. I have taken back the prize you stole from my family, and now I only have to dispose of you for murdering my *opa*, Horst Grahamar."

He listened to the voice, somewhat muffled by the blanket. One part of his mind registered surprise dimly. *Opa*-grandfather. But who he was or what past nightmare had coughed him up didn't matter. Only Luz and Ana mattered, and this man was in the way of saving them. He was surprised that his glasses still sat on his nose, though somewhat crookedly. Inclining his head toward his hands, he pulled them off, and turned the frame so that he could slide the lens between his teeth. He coughed as he bit down hard, feeling the crunch of glass. Deliberately, while the younger man talked, Martin began to wrest the largest piece from the frame.

"Oh, yes. He was my grandfather, whom you assassinated after the war was over, in front of my mother. What a hell that must have been for her. And they say *I'm* heartless! You see if you had not done that, I would not be here. If you had killed him during the war, I would not be here. Well, I might be here to rob you, but I would not be here to kill you . . . necessarily."

A thin stream of blood ran from Martin's mouth. He held the glass in his teeth, and ran it repeatedly along the duct tape.

"But a Llama pistol, eh? Interesting. I thought the OSS used a Welrod 9mm, or the H1 Standard .22, or a Colt. Yes, now I use a Waffenfabric 7.65 Mauser, Model 1910, very easy to bring into your country by the way, in spite of your so-called Homeland Security. That pistol is the most accurate and effective gun one can find, within the parameters of its cartridge, of course."

Martin let the glass fall from his teeth and twisted his hands out of their bonds. And now he unbuttoned his cuff and began to peel off the tape that held the flat sleeve dagger inside his forearm.

"I think one could make an argument for the Walther PPK, but my preference would always be for the Mauser."

"Just like your grandfather," Martin said.

"Ah, you are listening. Like my grandfather, am I?"

"He was full of shit, too."

The car was slowing slightly, whether for a red light or to turn, Martin didn't know. He would have one shot, and he played out the physical action in his mind, concentrating with every ounce of his mental energy and focusing all of his physical strength. He wiped his hand once on his shirt, and gripped the handle of the flat blade tightly. He took a deep breath and began to ease the blanket away from his head, his eyes focused on the pony tail he could see hanging between the bars of the head rest. And through the haze of days and years, he saw the silhouette of Marius crouched with his machine gun at the mouth of *les traboules*, and again when he'd first seen him in the square, on one knee, firing at the German patrol, a cigarette dangling from his lips. Martin shifted his weight onto his elbow, willing himself slowly upward.

"Well, LeBris, you know I never pay attention to the opinion of a dead man." But while he laughed at his own joke, the dead man rose so suddenly that Karl Hoetger, though he felt his head jerk back violently, had no time to block the blade that plunged into his exposed neck, his blue sunglasses falling from his bulging eyes.

Martin ducked back behind the seat as the car spun once and began to slow, but the dying man in his convulsions kicked the accelerator and the car lurched forward and down an embankment. The old man heard branches cracking and then a few seconds of silence as the car fell. He was thrown forcefully against the back of the seats as it plunged in water. He pulled himself up. The front of the car was lodged in the mud at the shallow edge of the Merrimack River. The engine had stalled, and Martin heard only the hiss of steam as water flowed around the hot engine, and the gurgle of the assassin's blood.

His body ached; his head hammered, and he feared most of all that he would die before he had accomplished what he had to do. He scrambled, almost falling between the seats. In a seeping pool of water on the floor of the passenger's side, he felt the cross, along with his jacket and gun, which he slid into its holster. The door was jammed; he had to lean back against the corpse and kick as hard as he could. It opened with a squawk like some metallic crow. He tore the knife from the neck of the wide-eyed dead man and stepped into the few feet of water at the river's edge, tossing the blade out into deeper water. He threw his jacket over his slim frame, reeled, and fell, sitting in the river under overhanging branches, panting like an old dog. Slowly, weakly, he pulled the cross over his head and stuffed it under his shirt.

A young man arrived and helped him up the embankment. "I've already called the police," he said.

"Can I use your phone to call my wife, sir?"

"Sure." He pulled the phone off his belt and handed it to Martin.

"Can you check on my friend while I call? He's still in the car."

"Yes, sir. I'll check. Take it easy now."

Martin limped out to the road and saw a pickup truck still running. He got in and put it in gear. When the young man returned to tell him the sad news that his friend was dead, he saw

his truck turning in the road and roaring off in the direction of
Lowell.

38

Gerry O'Neil and Ray Cox were inside Room 47 at the Caswell Motel. A Tewksbury cop had come in briefly with them, but he'd offered to go out and keep an eye on the parking lot in case the suspect showed up. Gerry flashed the picture of Hoetger at the cop, a balding veteran, who studied it for a moment and nodded before he left.

"Look at this, Ray." Gerry held up a paperback novel that he'd pulled from an open suitcase on the bed: *Harry Potter und die Heiligtümer des Todes*.

"A Harry Potter novel and a pile of *Wall Street Journals*. Hardly what one would think of as the reading material of a mad hit man," Ray said. He held a digital camera up for Gerry, a Nikon optical zoom, and began to scroll through the saved photos. "Hmmmm. They're kind of cute." There were several photos of a couple of young women drinking Margaritas on a deck by the sea. "Looks like Newburyport."

Ray kept scrolling: sailboats, an old wood carved cigar store Indian that had apparently caught Hoetger's fancy. "He's been having a regular tourist's holiday. Wait! There we are!" Gerry nearly shouted. There were three photos of Martin LeBris walking in Tyler Park, with Ana. Ray wandered into the bathroom, snooping in the medicine cabinet, and said, "I'd better take a leak while I'm here 'cause I may be hanging around for a few more hours until Hoetger gets back, or until you or someone else spells me."

Gerry had specified that they'd be looking for weapons and evidence of electronic surveillance in the warrant, so they would take the camera and Hoetger's laptop. He opened the night table drawer, and under Gideon's Bible, saw an old notebook, bound in brown leather. Its pages were filled with German script. Inside the cover, in an elegant hand, he saw the name: Bruno Lohse, and the date April, 1945. Alain and GIGN had nailed it.

Gerry's phone rang as they walked back to their cars. He handed the confiscated items to Ray and answered it, stopping short as if he had walked into a glass wall, "Where?" He listened for a moment. He took out a pen and jotted a license plate number on his hand. "Thanks."

He closed his phone. "You won't need to stay here, Ray."

"They got him?"

"Somebody got him. I think I know who. He's in his rented car in the river, very dead, with a very big hole in his throat. An old man left the scene in a stolen 2005 black Ford pickup."

"The old bastard killed him with a knife?" He laughed loudly. "Welcome to Lowell, Hoetger."

"Don't ever underestimate that old bastard, Ray."

39

At the red light near the Pawtucket Falls, Martin called the number the Colombian had given him. "*Que quiere?*"

"I have the diamond. Where should I bring it?"

There was a low conversation in Spanish. Martin recognized the next voice as that of the guy who admired the Godfather. "Why you are calling on this phone and not the one I give you?"

"I lost it. A guy tried to rob me. I borrowed this one."

"I don't believe your shit. You tryin' to fuck me *viejo maricon*. You know the deal."

"I got the diamond!" he shouted.

"You got the diamond. You tell me a half hour I give you an hour. Now you call me on some other phone!"

"I got the diamond!"

"You got shit. I take care of you after the others."

"Listen to me!" But the dealer had already hung up.

Martin LeBris was hurting, and he had trouble seeing distance well without his glasses. Squinting, hunched in pain that radiated throughout his body, tore at his back and ribs, throbbed in his neck, and pressed at his skull, he drove the truck on. He pulled in front of the portico of the Pollard Mansion, where Al Lekakis had once left his truck. He forced himself up the stairs, growling at the pain, wincing at each step, never pausing, willing himself onward.

In his apartment, he fumbled in the kitchen drawer for his spare glasses. Things came into focus as he donned them. He pulled an oversized red volume of *Don Quixote* from the shelf and opened it. It was hollow; he picked out the contents and stuffed them into his jacket pocket. Then he got the Colt .45 from the drawer, loaded it, and stuck it in his waistband. He wiped the blood from his temple and headed back to the truck.

Gerry had mentioned that Al's dealer friends hung out at The Tic Toc Club. Five minutes later, he double parked the truck in front of the squat red brick bar. We're going to do this the hard way, Nike man.

Martin flung the door open. "Everyone on the floor! Stretch out your arms!" he shouted, a raised pistol in each hand. He fired a shot into the floor, and the men jumped from barstools and hit the deck. The juke box was wailing some Latin rap; Martin shot it twice with the .45. The music stopped.

"You are one crazy *Viejo*. Holy shit, *hombre*! You need to calm down. You look like hell." The kingpin, with arms raised, was crouched in the corner, near the back of the bar.

"Shut the fuck up!" He fired another shot that made the dealer duck. "And if you call me *Viejo* one more time, I take your head off with the big gun."

"What you want me to call you?"

"You call me sir, and I'll call you asshole. Where are the girls, asshole? I want them. I want them right now."

"They're in the back. The problem is I got a guy back there with a gun, too. And he don't like . . . "

"I don't give a shit what he likes or doesn't like. The difference between me and him and you, and every other asshole in here, is that I really don't mind dying." A voice resounded in his memory. *He wanted to prove his love by dying for me.* He scanned the room and took a step forward. "I've run my race. But if Luz and Ana are hurt I'm taking a whole lot of you with me. I'm takin' *all* of you!"

He shoved the .45 into his belt and from his jacket pulled what looked like two green baseballs. "You know what these are? I'll tell you. These are special incendiary phosphorous hand fragmentation 9 oz. explosive grenades."

"This *hijo de puta* is crazy!" someone shouted. "Do what he says!"

"I got some nasty stuff here. You tell your little pistol-wielding blow boy to bring that innocent woman and her little girl out here now, or this entire place and everyone in it will be on fire in about ten seconds."

The man nodded nervously and shouted something in Spanish. A door opened at the end of the bar, and Luz and Ana emerged. Martin saw that Luz had a swollen lip and her eye was bruised, but he blew a relieved breath. "Get Ana out of here Luz! I'll be coming."

"Come Martin!" the little girl shouted as her mother pulled her out the door. Outside they heard the whoop of a siren.

"Hey, asshole, did you hit her? Did you hit that good woman?" He pulled the cross out of his shirt and held it in front of him as if he were banishing a demon. The tear drop diamond at its heart sent flashes across the far wall. "You don't hurt them — I make you rich. That was easy. But you were too stupid, right?"

"They are not really hurt...sir."

The door from which the women had emerged began to move perceptibly, opening just enough to show a glint of black metal. Martin fired two through the door, and they heard Flaco scream as he was thrown back, and the skitter of his pistol across a tile floor. "*Ave María, papa!*" one of the men on the floor shouted, and began to pray loudly. *Sagrado Corazon en vos confío . . .* Martin turned back to the boss. "I've decided you're not a man I can do business with, and moreover a woman beater and a scourge to the fucking planet. Say your prayers. You're dead."

"Martin!" It was Gerry O'Neil. He stood in the doorway with his weapon raised and aimed at Martin LeBris. "Martin, put the gun down. We'll have this guy, Carlos Luna, on drug and kidnapping charges. He's going to jail."

"Yeah, but he'll be out harassing Luz when I'm dead and gone."

"I swear, I won't, sir!"

"He's a liar. I'm afraid I'm gonna have to kill him, Gerry."

"If you fire, I'll have to shoot you! I have to shoot you if you don't put the gun down!"

"'Yet though he should slay me, will I trust him.' The *Book of Job*, my friend."

"The war is over!" Gerry bellowed. "You're not the fucking jury, Martin LeBris!"

The old man's eyes narrowed as he leveled the gun at Carlos Luna. "I'm his jury today."

"What are you gonna do, O'Neil?" Ray Cox shouted.

Gerry looked along the barrel of his gun at the man he admired so much, a man whom war had adopted in youth and left with such sorrow and such a hard sense of justice. "Don't make me live with killing you, Martin! *Please* don't make me live with that!"

The old man paused. He sighed, and sank to his knees. Slowly, he laid the two pistols on the floor, and the grenades beside them. He shook his head, "I wish you hadn't put it that way." He struggled to rise, but the adrenaline was spent, and only the pain remained, and before Gerry could reach him, he fell.

40

The blonde rubbed the skull and crossbones on Larry's forearm and traced the name, Alice, with her index finger.

"Look at that tattoo! You're awful, what did you say your name was?" Her breasts were spilling out of the plunging neckline of her sequined dress and she was drinking some fruity concoction. Larry Vega was drinking shots of Jack Daniel's and bottles of Heineken at The Prince's Palace in Jacksonville, Florida. "My name is Larry. Larry Bird, just like the greatest fuckin' Celtic ever."

"Larry Bird? Where are you from, Larry?"

"I'm from French Lick, Indiana, but I flew the coop." He bawled out a laugh. "Get it?" The blonde looked puzzled. "Hey, Bartender, set 'em up!" Larry shouted. He tossed back a shot of Jack. He shrugged and stretched his neck, his chin jutting as if he wore a tie that was too tight.

"You kind of move and twitch a lot," the blonde said.

"Yeah, I'm a hyper bastid," Larry said, and he whispered, "an' I got a nice lil' cocaine buzz. Yeah, *The doctor says it'll kill me but he won't say when, cocaine!*"

"Did you say 'set 'em up'?" the bartender asked loudly, leaning toward him.

"What are you fuckin' deaf? Set 'em up!"

"The whole bar?"

"Fuckin' guy needs Miracle Ear! Set 'em up muthafucka! And bring me another Jack and a Heineken."

A few of the patrons leaned back on their stools and shouted a thank you to the skinny patron with the Fu Man Chu like an inverted U over his mouth. Another woman came up and said, "What business you in, honey? Oil?"

The blonde pushed her away and said, "We're havin' a discussion. Screw, Amy!"

"Don't fight girls. I fuckin' hate women fightin' over me. That's not classy. Always try to be classy. Come on. There's enough of old Larry to go around."

The bartender came back and leaned over the bar again. "You sure you can do this, pal? This is a long goddamn bar. You're lookin' at hundreds of dollars."

"Pff! Petty cash. Get these ladies a bottle of champagne. And this is for you!" He leaned over the bar and stuffed a twenty-dollar bill in the barman's shirt pocket while the girls cooed their delight. He slapped him on the shoulder and said, "I'm sorry I called you fuckin' deaf. You know what you are? You're a workin' man! You're the backbone of this country! The salt of the goddam earth, that's what you are!"

He leaned over the bar and kissed the bartender on the cheek with a loud smack.

"Jesus Christ, thanks, buddy. It's your money!"

"Petty cash!"

A bleached blonde with a glass of ginger brandy said loudly, "That guy just kissed the bartender!"

Later, when Larry had paid the two-thousand dollar bill in cash, he suggested to the ladies that they continue the party at his motel room. He slipped them each a C note. "You're a real gentleman!" the blonde said, and the three of them left the bar. With an arm around each of the girls, Larry headed to his car, his voice crooning "Born to be Wild" on the sharp and flat sides of the melody.

"Hey! What the hell!" The two women were on the ground. One high heel still stood where the blonde had been, and the contents of Amy's handbag had spilled across the asphalt of the parking lot. Larry Vega felt a sharp point almost piercing his side as he was shoved into the back seat of his Honda.

"Hey! Don't hurt him! He's a fuckin' gentleman!" the blonde shouted.

"Yeah!" the other cried, but the red tail lights were already fading as the Honda sped into the night.

Larry Vega found himself in the back seat with a bent-nosed guy thumbing an ugly looking serrated blade. The headlights shone on thick undergrowth on both sides of the road; beyond the meager yellow glow of the headlights, all was dark. "I fucked up, Mom," he said, closing his eyes as the tears began to roll down his cheeks. "I'm sorry."

41

Martin LeBris was held without bail at the Middlesex County Jail in Cambridge, pending his appearance before the court. Gerry was allowed to bring the box of books he had requested directly to his cell.

"You don't mind if I don't get up? My knee is still pretty swollen."

"Rest easy, pal." He pulled the volumes out one by one and placed them on the bed beside him: *Tacitus*, vol. 2; *The Compleat Angler; The Consolation of Philosophy; Personal Memoirs of U.S. Grant; Pepys' Diary, vol. 5; Travels With a Donkey; The Iliad*, and *The Crime of Sylvester Bonnard.*

He sat on the other end of the bunk. "Christ almighty, Martin, like I said to Gina, for an octogenarian, you certainly are the focal point of a whole lot of shit storms." The old man smiled weakly. Gerry looked around the cell. The walls were bare, except for a photo of Luz and Ana holding Hannibal, the cat, which was taped to the wall beside his bunk. "Nice photo."

"Yes, they want to come by a lot, but this is not a good environment for a little girl. I told Luz once in a while, but not too much."

"She says you're a folk hero in the Colombian community for going after Luna and his friends. They gave all the hard-working Colombians a bad name. And you saved Luz and her daughter."

"No, Gerry. They saved me."

"Luz is lighting candles for you at the grotto every day and praying to beat the band."

"I can't ask for more than that."

Gerry looked over the books spread between them and continued, "You know I look at that library, your "City of Books" as you call it, and think of you up there reading all those volumes. I'm a reader, too, but you've read so widely, so deeply. What did you learn, Martin?"

There was shouting down the row, and a clacking of something against bars. They heard a guard shout, "Hey Junior, you keep banging on those bars I'm gonna come in there and bang on your head!"

Martin ignored the ruckus. "What did I learn? Well, you know Oscar Wilde said that Pater's *Studies in the Renaissance* was his 'golden book'?" He paused. "Why are you laughing?"

"I'm sorry. I just can't believe that this guy who is talking about Pater and Wilde and 'golden books' is the wild man who was going to blow up the Colombian mafia in a bar a week ago."

"Well, as Shakespeare said, '*In peace there's nothing so becomes a man as modest stillness and humility, but when the blast of war blows in our ears . . .*'

"I understand. So what is your 'golden book' Martin?"

"It's hard to say. There are two right here. *The Iliad*. Before hard battles in the war, I sometimes liked to meditate on Book Twelve, lines 288 to 295."

"Let me write that down." He pulled out his notepad, happy to see the old man once again engaged in thought and conversation.

"The other is this little volume." He picked up a small, green soft-back book. "*The Crime of Sylvestre Bonnard*, Anatole France, 1890. It was Sylvestre Bonnard who first referred to his

Paris apartment as 'The City of Books.' I stole it from him. And if you ask me what I've learned from all my books, old Bonnard said it best." Martin flipped through the pages for a moment. He cleared his throat and began to read:

"What a lot of books!" she yelled. "And have you read them all, Monsieur Bonnard?"

"Alas! I have," I replied, "and that is just the reason that I do not know anything; for there is not a single one of those books which does not contradict some other book; so that by the time one has read them all one does not know what to think about anything. That is just my condition, Madame."

Gerry nodded, his eyes distant and resigned, or maybe regretful. "The vanity of learning. I guess that sums it up." His look gained focus and concern as he looked at the old man. "How are you doing here, Martin?"

"I'm fine. I have my books. And I'm sleeping all night for the first time in . . . well, since before the war. The ghosts have forgiven me." He lowered his voice and added, "And plunging the knife into the throat of that sneering assassin bastard was, God forgive me, but it was therapeutic. I know why you're shaking your head. You're thinking I'm right where I belong, right? Well, maybe I am."

"I didn't say that, Martin. Hell, killing Hoetger was self-defense. And Luz and Ana might have been dead if you hadn't arrived at The Tic Toc Club before they took them for a ride. When they determine that shooting the other guy, Flaco, was self-defense too, you could be out of here. You may get some time for carrying explosives, and you did shoot up the place, but all things considered, there was more good done than harm. Carlos Luna is a very bad guy, but he'll have a hard time regaining any respect . . . sir! His most vicious creature is dead, and he'll probably get fifteen years anyway. No one can figure out what to do with that cross or who owns it. That may take a while. I suspect it will end up in a museum."

"That's all right."

"Who knows, they may even decide that you own it."

Martin shrugged. "Then I have to amend my will. I'm going to leave my books to you and the cross to you and Luz and my sister. If they say I own it."

"I'll be happy with the books anyway, but not too soon, I hope."

"The readiness is all, Gerry. The readiness is all."

The detective stood and put his hand on the shoulder of the old spy. "Damn, Martin, we even like to quote the same lines. I'm half-glad I didn't shoot you."

"Have a good weekend, Gerry. What are you doing?"

"I'm going fishing with my son."

"Sounds good, but I guess I'll stay here."

Gerry's phone went off as he drove back to Lowell. It was Ray Cox. The Tybee Island Police Department had found an abandoned car registered to a woman in Lowell: Agnes Vega. A few hours later some fishermen came upon a body in the mangroves, carved up like a lamb for Easter. Distinctive tattoo of a skull and crossbones over the name 'Alice' on the right forearm. Preliminary investigations had uncovered witnesses who said he was throwing a lot of money around at a strip joint called The Prince's Palace.

"You poor, stupid bastard," Gerry said aloud as he merged onto Route 3 North, and drawing closer to the old mill town he called home, he thought about Larry Vega, a man with no enemy so dangerous as himself. He remembered Dom Trivedi asking incredulously, "He strike you as a throat slasher?"

No, no, damned if he did. But who else hated Al enough to kill, not for drugs or money, but just to see him die. *They say he was at the Savoy earlier with a young broad with dark hair.* All at once, as if he were recalling a scene from a movie, a memory rose in his mind. He sat at the pool with Frank McGuin. *My daughter Ashley is out of her mind! She used to be in the Drama Club. Played Cleopatra in "The Greatest Love Story."* Cleopatra. And Gerry would bet his pension that she had worn a dark wig.

He thought of Frank McGuin, so disillusioned in life and love, and of his tortured children. A death had occurred, but was it a murder, or something else? And where was the line between cop and friend? Who could say that the death of Lekakis had not been justice, of the most elemental kind? Could he send Ashley to jail for this, when he had never let his own more senseless crime be weighed in the scales of justice? Or could it lie buried, as McKidd had said.

If she cries, she cries alone. She's an actress all right. He would talk it over with Gina, but he thought he would let it lie buried with Al Lekakis and Larry Vega and Cheryl, the dead mother that he felt certain the young girl had avenged with such savage love.

He pulled off the Lowell Connector and headed for A&J Cigar House to buy a box of Robustos for a friend.

Martin LeBris did not hear the shouting of the prisoners in his block, or the rhythmic monotonous chanting of some aspiring rapper. It washed over him as a wave washes over the swimmer who dives below it and hears it break far off, above him, in the world of air.

The Land of the Dead is a cold and airless place for a man whose blood still courses warm within him, but Odysseus braved the western expanses of the River Ocean to disembark on that dark and forlorn shore and wander among the thin and wavering shades of those who once had lived. He slaughtered a ram as an offering, and the old ghosts drank the hot blood and spoke to him of their pain and desolation until one arrived who could tell him how to return to his home and those he loved.

Martin had also spent much time among the dead, but the ghosts that haunted him had never been able to tell him how to return to the land of the living. Only now, at long last, did she come and stand before him, not bloodied and broken, but calm and smiling, the woman he had first met in the moonlit space where *Notre Dame des Neiges* presided silently among the mountains of the Massif Central. "I couldn't save you, Odette. I'm sorry."

She drew near him and spoke, and he listened with a full heart because it was not the plea for death that had resounded within him all these years. "I chose my path, Martin, long before I met you. Many died as I did so that France would be free. You did all that you could. You did more than you could, though it was not for your country you risked so much. And even now, so close to the end of your road, you fight, and win."

"Because you are with me."

"Always."

She retreated into the company of Marius and the others who stood in the dim recesses of the cell, and faded from presence to absence. "*Au revoir*, old friends," he said. "I shall join you soon." And like that ancient mariner reboarding his vessel to set a course for sunlit realms, Martin LeBris turned his mind once again to the world where Luz and Ana lived. The account in the other world had been settled.

He lay back on his bunk then, a small lamp directed onto the slim, green volume, and read: *"Yes, Madame, when our globe, no longer inhabited, shall, like the moon, roll a wan corpse through space, the soil which bears the ruins of Sélimonte will still keep the seal of beauty in the midst of universal death; and then, then, at least there will be no frivolous mouth to blaspheme the grandeur of these solitudes."*

AFTERWORD

The Spy in the City of Books is a work that was begun, put on hold, and rewritten several times. There is a strong likelihood that I would have abandoned it in an embryonic stage had not I had the good fortune to meet Lucinda Franks, the Pulitzer Prize winning author of *My Father's Secret War*. It was she who persuaded me that the work had promise, and that if I continued to develop the story and characters, I would find a publisher. Who argues literary matters with a Pulitzer Prize winner? Not me. Her conviction renewed my own energy and commitment to this novel, though in the course of reworking it, I had at times to throw out entire chapters, remove characters and invent new ones.

The initial inspiration for the novel arose from conversations with French people in the region of Ardeche and around Lyon, regarding the French Resistance. Many years later in Lowell, my interest in the subject was reawakened when I met Edwin Poitras, a veteran of the Office of Strategic Services. After the first half hour with him, I realized that I was conversing with the most amazing person I had ever met, or was ever likely to meet. There were some things that he would not tell me; the habit of secrecy is a hard one to break; however, he told me enough to serve as a springboard for this fictional account of Martin LeBris, a former OSS agent who had parachuted into Nazi-occupied France to serve as a liaison between London and the French Forces of the Interior, and to act as a spy and saboteur. Edwin died a few years ago, but it would have been a different book, if it existed at all, without him.

I had spent several months in Lyon, where much of the story is set, but that was many years ago. For specific questions regarding the years of the Occupation in Lyon, I turned to Chantal Jorro, of the Museum of the Resistance in that city. Though we have never met in person, she has always been very kind in sending me all sorts of information and photographs. Speaking of photographs and quick general information, I confess I relied from time to time on Wikipedia. I know the site has its critics, but if you need a picture so that you can describe a German military vehicle or a WWII era gun, it's an invaluable tool. There are many OSS web sites on the internet. I believe I browsed through most of them at some point. My particular method of research was to write notes from all kinds of sites on little pieces of paper and then lose the pieces of paper. It's a tedious method I can tell you. The essential place for those who are interested in further research is the OSS Society web site: (www.osssociety.org) Those interested in clandestine warfare and espionage need only google those terms along with OSS to find a plethora of fascinating books and websites.

There are a few books that I must mention because I found them extremely helpful in gaining an understanding of what was going on in France during the Occupation. The first is the novel *Suite Française*, by Irène Némirovsky, a brilliant Jewish writer, who tragically died in Auschwitz. No work I have read gives a better sense of the chaos and terror that overtook France as Nazi troops moved toward Paris. *Marianne In Chains* by Robert Gildea is a scholarly, but extremely lucid and thorough account or "daily life in the heart of France during the German Occupation." The best general history of the French Resistance I was able to find was *Soldiers of the Night* by David Schoenbrun, "an American intelligence agent and war correspondent in North Africa and France." The character of Odette Prieur was inspired to some degree by Marie-Madeleine Fourcade, the "beautiful spy," whose memoir *Noah's Ark* offers a wonderful first-hand account of the dangers and difficulties of organizing and running a resistance network under Occupation. Not for nothing was she named to the Legion of Honor, and made a member of the Order of the British Empire. Finally, and perhaps somewhat strangely, two books that echo throughout the novel are *The Iliad* and *The Odyssey*, translated by Robert Fitzgerald. Guile and trickery, as well as valor and skill, are the weapons of Homer's Odysseus, as they were of the men and women of the O.S.S.

Among its many rooms full of fascinating artifacts, The Museum of World War II in Natick, Massachusetts, has one room which holds an extremely interesting collection of OSS weapons, radios and memorabilia. A small caveat: the museum is not open to the general public. One needs to contact the curator and get permission and an appointment. I was able to visit the museum several years ago with Jack Flood, a D-Day veteran, and Edwin Poitras. It was a day I won't soon forget. Jack Flood summed up what such a visit must mean to many veterans: "Thanks, Okie, for bringing me here. This is amazing. I'll have nightmares tonight, but it's amazing." Meanwhile, Edwin Poitras looked scornfully at a Sten machine gun, saying, "You couldn't hit the side of a barn with this thing." I cringed as he opened a suitcase radio and began to show me how it worked, certain we would be tossed out of the museum, but no one came running out to stop him. Perhaps they felt he had paid the dues to be able to touch history.

Once, in a post office in Belgium, an old man began to speak to me in Flemish. When I told him that I didn't speak the language, that I was an American, tears clouded his old eyes. He took my hand and said, "I was in a concentration camp . . . almost dead. The Americans come, and I am free forever. Thank you. Thank you." Of course I had nothing to do with his return to life, but men like Jack Flood, Edwin Poitras, veterans everywhere, and the brave men and women of the O.S.S., and of the French Resistance had quite a bit to do with it. They risked everything, and often they sacrificed everything. Honor them, and enjoy this novel, which is a tribute as well as, I hope, a good story.

Acknowledgements: It is always useful to have other eyes searching for typos or inconsistencies, and in this regard I'd like to thank Terrence Downes, Marianne Innis, and Cynthia Adler, who looked at the manuscript and made valuable editing or technical suggestions. Finally, I'd like to thank Detective Raymond Jean of the Lowell Police and Bob Cowan of the Acton Police for their help with questions of police procedure. Any errors are mine.

ABOUT THE AUTHOR

Stephen O'Connor's fiction and essays have appeared in numerous literary journals and magazines. He is the author of a collection of short stories entitled *Smokestack Lightning* (Loom Press, 2010) and the novel *The Witch at Rivermouth* (Merrimack Press, 2015). He was born and raised in Lowell, Massachusetts, a frequent setting for his writing, and attended university in Amherst and Boston, Massachusetts, and Dublin, Ireland. While working and traveling in France, he became fascinated with stories of the French Resistance. The novel *The Spy in the City of Books* arose out of this interest, and out of interviews with a former OSS agent who served in Occupied France as a liaison between London and the French Forces of the Interior. O'Connor lives in Lowell with his wife Olga and their two children.

Made in the USA
Columbia, SC
30 December 2017